It Happened in

Lunenburg

Melanie Robertson-King

King Park Press

Published by King Park Press

It Happened in Lunenburg is a work of fiction. Names,
characters, places and incidents are the product of the author's
imagination or are used fictitiously. Any resemblance to actual
events, locales or persons, living or dead, is purely
coincidental.

ISBN: 978-1-990371-14-1

DEDICATION

For anyone feeling diminished, dismissed, and otherwise
mentally abused.

ACKNOWLEDGMENTS

Thanks to everyone who put up with my daft questions during the research of this novel. Without your help, the book would not have come to fruition.

Huge thanks to my eagle-eyed proofreader, the phenom with the red pen, Leona Berrea.

If I've missed anyone by name, I apologize.

Special thanks to my husband, Don, who continues to support and encourage me, and provides a shoulder to cry on when things don't go well.

He redesigned my website making it mobile-friendly and taken charge on the domestic front giving me time to write.

One

Isabelle Morrison's House, Falkland Street,
Lunenburg, Nova Scotia

July 10, 2019

Amy stepped off the bus, relaxed. The first time she'd had in days. Her house swap contact said her home stood opposite the gas station. She rechecked the address on her phone. An enormous mansion filled the only place fitting that description. This woman wanted to swap for a pokey one-bedroom apartment?

She stared at the massive house, a grand building, with a closed-in porch to one side and a tower bisecting the front. No way. It comprised apartments, right? That made sense. Amy walked to the front door. She tried the latch and found it locked.

Another glance at her phone. A code she had to key in to unlock the door.

Amy had just started to key in the combination when a voice interrupted her. "Oy, you. What are you doing at Isabelle Morrison's house?"

She turned around. A white-haired man stood at the foot of

the outside stairs. "I've done a house swap with her," she said with a hint of frustration.

"Let's just confirm that, shall we?"

As if she hadn't had enough problems back home before embarking on her adventure. Now, she had a nosy neighbour who wouldn't allow her through the door. "I've got the house swap site on my phone and my conversations with her. I'm from Sudbury, Ontario, and we've swapped houses. She said she had severe writer's block and needed a change of scenery."

Had she told him too much? In David's eyes, yes. The information she gave the total stranger would outrage him. But, he wasn't here now. She was.

"All right, lass. You're okay. Isabelle confirmed the house swap. You wouldn't mind showing me some ID? Just to make sure you are who you say you are. Caution is always wise in the current times."

It made sense, but Amy experienced unease showing a stranger her ID. Still, if it meant getting inside, she'd do it.

"Perfect. I live just over the road. Gordon MacLeod. You need anything. Come find me."

"Thank you, Mr. MacLeod." Did she introduce herself? Amy lacked certainty about her next step.

David might be watching from anywhere. She gave in. "I'm Amy Scott, and I've arranged a house swap with the owner of this property."

"Since all is well, I'll head back home."

Amy agreed with his earlier statement about not being sure in the current climate of homelessness and thefts. "Thank you, Mr. MacLeod."

Amy entered the mansion. A wide hallway with a staircase to one side led to a closed door just beyond the stairs. A cut glass shade covered the ceiling light. To her right was a living room. Another stood to her left, featuring a doorway leading to the expansive enclosed porch. She pushed open the door at the end of the corridor and discovered it led to the back of the house and a spacious kitchen. How had she gotten such an enormous place for her small one-bedroom apartment?

Her phone pinged. Per chance, Emma checked in to make

sure of her arrival. It wasn't. Another text from an unknown number.

Big place for one person. Hope you don't get lonely.

The brief text sent a shiver down Amy's spine. Who was doing this to her? She wanted it to stop. It drove her crazy. She found Emma's message thread and tapped one to her, her fingers trembling with fear and frustration.

Made it. It's an enormous mansion and I have the whole place to myself. Will send pictures. And, to put a downer on everything, I received another message from an unknown number.

Amy's fear fell short of the reality. All had been quiet since the text she'd received on the bus not long after leaving Sudbury. She had hoped whoever sent it had grown tired of harassing her, but the silence only heightened her unease, wrapping around her and suffocating her.

Emma replied to her message.

Glad you got there, Ames. You should contact the police.

David had also suggested that. It was the last thing Amy wanted to do, but she'd call them if the messages kept up. All she wanted was for it to stop.

Her phone pinged again. This time it was from David.

I hope you're settling in. You didn't tell me you'd arrived.

How did he discover her whereabouts? Did Emma tell him? No, she wouldn't do that. She didn't like him and only tolerated him, for Amy's sake.

Amy clutched Seamus and darted out the front door. Where did she go? Her knowledge of the town extended only to her residence and the gas station opposite.

Two

Zwicker Wharf, Lunenburg, Nova Scotia

July 10, 2019

Amy wandered, trying to find a comfortable and peaceful place to rest and collect her thoughts. She hadn't told David about the house swap. How did he find out? She found herself down by the water. Boats bobbed on the waves in the harbour. A row of Adirondack chairs lined the boardwalk, facing the water. Tourists or locals occupied the majority, but not all. She found two vacant ones at the end, sat in the outermost one, and placed Seamus in the one next to her.

Seagulls hovered in the air, squawking. One perched on a nearby railing and stared at her, begging for a handout. The bird appeared well-fed, and Amy had nothing, not that she'd feed them, anyway. Most places didn't want you feeding the birds near the water because it caused nuisance birds like these to increase in numbers.

She stared out over the harbour, relaxing since receiving the most recent text from an unknown number. The messages, cryptic, included veiled threats and unsettling implications. Had she blocked the last one that came in? Amy pulled out her phone and checked. She hadn't. She hadn't had the time between when it came in and David messaged her. Amy took a deep breath and blocked the number.

"Is this seat taken?" a polite male voice asked, respecting Amy's space.

Amy turned towards the owner of the voice — a handsome man with dark brown hair and designer stubble, wearing a beige hoodie and jeans. His question disrupted her peace, and she hesitated before responding.

"Ah, no," she said.

He picked up the stuffed dog and glimpsed the tag on the stuffie's collar. "SEA-U-MUS?" he said, pronouncing the name by syllables.

"It's pronounced Shay-mus," she corrected with a roll of her eyes. "Yes, that's not the proper spelling."

"Kyle Ferris, and you are?" he asked, his hair tousled in the wind.

"Amy Scott."

His hand extended, fingers splayed slightly, while hers remained at her side. "Where did you get your friend?" He nodded towards the dog, which he still held in one hand.

"Gift from my father for my first birthday."

Kyle looked at Amy closer, his curiosity piqued. How old was she? He didn't dare ask because he'd put his foot in it sure as anything, but the stuffed dog had to be at least twenty years old, if not more.

"Nice." He handed Seamus to her and sat in the adjacent chair. "So, Amy Scott, what brings you to Lunenburg?"

Did she tell him anything? She had only just met him. He might be as creepy as the person sending her texts from numbers she didn't recognize. Still, he looked harmless. "House swap." The words echoed in her mind, a chilling reminder of her potential danger.

"I've heard of them. Where are you staying?"

That exceeded the boundary. "If you don't mind, I'd rather not say."

"No worries. I get it."

She wanted to tell him he didn't get it, but couldn't muster up the courage to say it. Instead, she bowed her head and cast her eyes towards her lap. Amy fought with her emotions and reasoning. Did she confront David? Not yet. It was better face to face, but when it came down to it, would she have the courage? Not likely. A tear spilled from her eye and ran down her cheek.

"Are you okay?" Kyle asked.

His worry resonated in his voice, a definite contrast to David's indifference. He already differed from David at the outset, not so, but in his altered behaviour towards her now. Her phone pinged.

You think you can hide from me? You can't escape me. I'm aware of your location, and I'm already right behind you.

The words on the screen leapt out at her, each one a threat, a promise of impending danger. Startled by the message's menacing nature, she dropped her phone like a hot potato.

"What's wrong?" Kyle asked, bending over to pick up her mobile.

Amy shook her head.

Kyle scanned the message. No wonder it spooked her. "What's going on, Amy? Who sent you this message? Have you received any others like this?"

"Y-yes," she said, tears cascading down her cheeks. "I-I think it might be my boyfriend, but I can't be sure." Her voice quivered with fear and uncertainty, tugging at Kyle's heartstrings.

"I understand, Amy. You don't have to tell me about it now, but I'm here for you, whenever you're ready." His words were a comfort amid Amy's storm.

A quick scan of the anonymous messages told Kyle that Amy faced danger. Perhaps not physically, but mentally. One look at her said she had reached her limit.

He searched the screens on her device — all normal apps. He looked at the last screen, the App Library, which displayed icons for every installed app. They all lined up with the others on her phone, but an ominous hidden one lurked there. Did someone place something on her phone without her knowledge?

Kyle tapped on that icon. Passcode required flashed up on the screen. "Can you type in your password? There's something

6

on your phone that shouldn't be there."

"My friend, Emma, already checked. She found nothing."

"Let me have a go." He handed the phone back to her.

After entering her password and unlocking her phone, Amy returned it to Kyle. "I don't think you'll find anything," she said.

He ignored her and returned to the hidden library and tapped the icon. A few more taps, and he located it. "Someone has put a tracking app on your phone. I'd bet that person is behind the anonymous text messages." The discovery sent a chill down his spine, and he realized this was the start of a sinister plot.

"What? I only got this phone a few weeks ago. My boyfriend, David, bought it for me to replace the broken one."

Kyle wondered about it. Would her significant other do something like that? The man was a stranger to him, but the woman next to him was terrified of something or someone. He took a deep breath and asked the question that burned in his brain. "Do you think David did it? As in, put a tracking app on your phone?" He feared she would snatch the phone and storm off.

Amy watched Kyle frown in concentration while his fingers moved across her phone's screen. The sight of someone else using her phone, a crucial connection for her, would have deeply upset her, yet it did not. Not today.

A sliver of tension curled in her stomach as her old instincts warned her to stay guarded. She had only met Kyle less than ten minutes ago. He didn't owe her anything. For all she assumed, it was another setup, another trick. After all, David had seemed trustworthy once, too.

She pondered it. Some of the anonymous text messages appeared familiar. Not all, but some. She hadn't told David she was going away. She wanted to, but Emma, her protective best friend, squashed the idea. This trip was to be all about her and no one else.

Kyle's brow furrowed again, his mouth set in determination — not smugness or manipulation. Just focus and care.

Amy reminded herself Kyle was helping her because he wanted to and there were no strings and no games.

Did David send all the messages? Even some he'd sent from

his own number that came up with his name sounded menacing. Would David do that to her? He'd always been so kind and caring. Looked after her, especially after she came home from Melissa's wedding in Percé. It couldn't be him. Or could it?

Her heart thudded in her chest like it didn't believe her brain. Trust didn't come easy for her anymore. It might never again. Amy wrestled with her conscience. David had changed of late. It's possible her thoughts weren't so far off. Kyle was still trying to disable the tracking app someone had installed on her phone when it pinged with an incoming message.

"'You can't escape me,' is what the message says," Kyle said, his voice filled with tension.

"Give me back my phone." She held her hand out for him to return it.

As he handed the phone to her and met her gaze, no pressure showed in his eyes, and no demands. Amy's tensioned eased a fraction. It was a small but real beginning.

She snatched her phone, picked up Seamus and dashed towards her accommodations in Lunenburg. The sensation that someone followed or watched her all the way, clung to her, intensifying her fear. She lacked the capacity to handle this right now.

Three

Isabelle Morrison's House, Falkland Street, Lunenburg, Nova Scotia

July 10, 2019

Amy's hands shook as she struggled with the lockset on the mansion's front door, her vision blurred by unshed tears. Her heart pounded, fear gripped her, making it hard to concentrate on the task.

Once she unlocked the door and stepped inside, she relocked it, experiencing the weight of her isolation. She hurried from room to room, closing blinds and drapes, further isolating herself from the outside world. She sat on the floor behind a sofa, away from the windows, the full force of her solitude settling in. Her phone pinged.

You can run, but you can't hide.

Amy swallowed the lump in her throat, dreading the unknown. Who was tormenting her? Why? Was it a family member of one of her patients at the hospital? Someone who passed away while in her care? The questions only added to her growing sense of dread.

She sucked in a ragged breath, her heart pounding in her chest, as she blocked the last sender. Amy scrolled to Emma's name in her feed, her fingers trembling as she did so.

There was a tracking app on my phone. Hidden. Do you think David put it there? I do, and I hate that.

Amy hit send. She didn't bother to tell Emma how Kyle found the app. There would be plenty of time for that later.

The doorbell rang, spooking her. Who would be at her front door? Temporary front door while she was staying here. Was it someone looking for the owner? Or was it the sicko who had been sending her the messages? Afraid to be seen by the person on the porch, Amy crawled around the corner of the sofa to the window and tugged the curtain back a crack. It was a woman with a dish in her hands.

With trepidation, Amy crept to the front door but put the chain on before opening it a crack. "Yes?" she asked.

"Gordon, my husband, said you only arrived earlier today. I thought you hadn't had time to get any food in, so I brought you a casserole. Put it in the oven at 350 for about an hour and you'll have a good hot meal tonight."

Amy undid the chain and pulled open the door. "Thank you. That's very kind."

"You're fine, dear. Maggie MacLeod." The woman introduced herself.

A lightbulb moment. It was this woman's husband who stopped Amy when she first arrived. This woman appeared harmless enough. Amy opened the door wider. "Come in. I need some company and local knowledge of where to find things."

Mrs. MacLeod stepped over the threshold and into the hallway.

"We'll go through to the kitchen." Amy led the way.

"My, Izzy's house is grand. You might not believe this, but I've never been past the front door until now. Gordon and I spoke to her often. We'd see her once in a while in the pub just around the corner. Run into her different places. Even passed the time in our front gardens."

It became apparent to Amy that if she needed local information, advice, or gossip, the MacLeods were the people to ask.

"I'm sorry, but I haven't learned my way around here yet, so

I can't offer you a tea or coffee," Amy said.

"Don't fuss, dear."

As they sat at the table, Amy's phone pinged.

"Are you all right? You've gone rather ghostly white." Mrs. MacLeod reached over and put her hand on Amy's, who shaken, struggled to keep her composure.

"No. Someone has been sending me messages from numbers I don't recognize. I block them, but they keep coming. One local, a young man, about my age. I met him down at the water, and he found a hidden tracking app on it. I'm unsure if he removed it before I returned here."

"Have you contacted the police?"

"My friend Emma says I should. My boyfriend says he'll deal with it. And the young man at the water said to call the cops."

"And what do you think?"

"I'm not sure what to think. You'll excuse me while I see who this message is from?" Amy turned her back to the woman. Emma's name filled the screen. Relief washed over her, a brief respite from the unease, until she read the reply.

That's not normal, Amy. And you know it.

Emma would say that because she didn't like David. The tension in their relationship was obvious. Amy took another deep breath and texted her friend again.

You've never liked him. Of course you'd think that.

Amy's uncertainty was obvious in her response. She took a moment to collect her thoughts and texted her friend again.

Four

Emma's apartment, Ste Anne Road, Sudbury, Ontario

July 10, 2019

Amy's response didn't surprise Emma. David had gaslit Amy to where she'd believe anything from his mouth. Torn between her desire to protect Amy and her fear of losing her friend, Emma struggled to keep her emotions in check. As much as she wanted to reply and tell Amy to wake up and smell the coffee, Emma didn't. That would only make her friend dig her heels in deeper, and might even ruin their friendship. Emma's phone pinged again. Perhaps Amy apologizing? Emma picked up her phone.

I'm worried about Amy. She's not herself these days, and now she's accusing me of things that just aren't true. You don't like me, so please don't make this worse. She needs stability right now.

Not Amy, but David. Another message appeared before her response to his message, instructing her to get out of Amy's life.

I'm aware Amy has been talking to you. Stay out of it. She needs me, not you.

Emma's fingers itched to type a scathing response to David. She held back, her restraint a testament to her love for Amy. David's manipulation was like a thorn in their friendship, and its pain affected Emma.

Amy needed to see these two messages. Emma copied and pasted the first into a message to her friend, prefaced with 'just received this from David.' Then she repeated the process with the second.

Emma was resolute. She would not let David's manipulation destroy their friendship. When the inevitable fallout came, she would be there for Amy, ready to pick up the pieces and help her heal.

Five

Isabelle Morrison's House, Falkland Street, Lunenburg, Nova Scotia

July 10, 2019

Amy's eyes widened in shock and disbelief as she read the two messages Emma had copied and sent from David. The realization hit her like a ton of bricks. Had she been too blind to see what he'd been doing to her all along? Too naïve? When she first met him, there had been a spark. A connection unlike any she'd had with other men she'd dated. That had to mean something, didn't it? The turmoil of conflicting emotions churned within her, leaving her lost and betrayed.

"Sorry, Mrs. MacLeod, but I'm not good company now. Would you mind leaving?" Amy asked. It was rude of her, but so was paying more attention to her phone.

"Not to worry, dear. Thanks to *social media*, young people have many more things to deal with today than Gordon and I did when we were dating."

Amy walked her to the front door, held her phone, and paid more attention to her screen than anything else.

She had retrieved her messages from David, which only

included those sent after he gave her the new phone, as she pushed the door closed with her hip.

He may have apologized for breaking her phone, but it was too coincidental that her new one came with a tracking app installed. With no idea how Kyle, that was his name, wasn't it, found it, and if he got rid of it, Amy had to find him, and fast. The tension in her relationship with David hung in the air like a storm about to break.

Six

Amy's apartment, Jean Street, Sudbury, Ontario

Earlier ...

June 28, 2019

As Amy opened the bottle of red wine, the doorbell rang. Two glasses sat on the counter awaiting the contents of the bottle.

"I'll get that," Emma said.

"Thanks."

The girls had planned this night for quite a while, and now it had arrived. Wine, pizza, and rom-coms on DVD. When she opened the door, David Carter, Amy's boyfriend, stood in the opening.

"Is she ready?" he asked, extending his arm and rotating it to check the time on his watch.

"Ready for what?"

David pushed by her and strode to the kitchen; Emma hot on his heels.

"Amy, you forgot? We had plans tonight. Typical."

"No, I didn't forget. I've told you for ages that tonight was a girlie night with Emma."

"You did no such thing. Now, are you going to get ready?"

"David, I marked on my calendar that tonight was Emma."

"Your memory isn't what it used to be. Are you sure?"

"Yes." Amy took the calendar off the fridge door and plopped it on the counter before him. "Right here. See? Emma, girls' night in."

"You may have written it on your calendar, but never told me. How do I know you didn't write it there when you saw me coming up the front walk? You always do this — make yourself look right." Palms on the counter, he leaned forward so they were almost nose to nose.

"Don't be ridiculous. Why would I do that? You said nothing about coming over. Emma and I have been planning this for ages. Perhaps it's you with the terrible memory."

Emma folded her arms. "I was here when she wrote it down two weeks ago, David." Emma watched things unfold, ready to intervene. Sure, David was good-looking and had a great job with the city, but there was always something about him she didn't trust. He was smarmy. The type of guy, if he shook your hand, you counted your fingers afterwards.

At least right now, Amy was holding her own against the man.

She had seen no bruises to show physical abuse, but that meant little. David might hurt her in places other people wouldn't see.

He laughed, then glared at Emma. "Of course you'd say that. You feel bad for her. That's the only reason you're even here."

"I think it's time you left, David," Emma said, her voice steady and unwavering. "Amy and I have been looking forward to tonight."

A brief, stunned silence settled over the room.

David stormed to the apartment door. "Enjoy your pity party." When he left, he slammed the door so hard that the building shook. A collective sigh of relief filled the room as the tension dissipated.

Amy turned to Emma. "I-is that true? Do you feel bad for me?"

"I'm sad you put up with that," Emma said, her tone filled

with empathy. She nodded her head towards the door. "I'm your friend because I like you, Amy. Not because I pity you."

Emma hesitated. This was the moment — the fragile crack where if she pushed too hard she'd drive Amy away. She forced herself to tread with care.

Amy swallowed, nodding, but the doubt lingered in her eyes.

Emma wanted to say more. She wanted to lay it all out — how David twists reality, how he makes Amy second-guess herself, how this isn't just a one-off incident. But if she persisted, Amy might shut down.

Amy nodded as the truth settled in. Emma squeezed her arm, offering reassurance. David scared her with his mannerisms and threatening tones. She took a deep breath and sighed. Why did he have to be like that? She had done nothing wrong.

More and more, she and David had argued. It was about the usual things — her spending too much time with Emma and not being attentive enough to his needs. He claimed it was her fault — she was making things up again.

Emma, sensing Amy's distress, picked up the open bottle, poured each a glassful, and handed one to Amy. "Here, you need this," she said, her voice a soothing balm.

Amy gulped about half down at once, then spluttered. "Guess I shouldn't have done that."

Emma set her glass down and embraced her in a warm hug. "After that, are you sure you're up for a rom-com night?"

"Yes," Amy said, her voice showing determination as she turned to retrieve the toppings for their pizza from the fridge. An unopened package of garlic Naan bread sat on a parchment-covered baking sheet on the stovetop. "Let's finish this, then we'll make our supper. We're going to have a good time, Emma."

Emma escorted Amy to the living room, where she helped her onto the couch and sat beside her. Amy's mind was a whirlwind, replaying hers and David's conversation. She was in a state of unease, questioning if her reaction was justified. Emma's reminder of their plans and calendar entry clashed with David's accusation, leaving her unsettled and off balance. She began to discern a disturbing pattern in his actions. Was it always him, never her? How had she let him manipulate her?

Seven

Amy's apartment, Jean Street, Sudbury, Ontario

June 28, 2019

David sat in his car, his knuckles turning white as he gripped the steering wheel. His mind was a whirlwind of frustration over what had transpired in Amy's apartment. He believed he was the victim, the one someone had wronged. Amy's actions seemed unreasonable, and to make matters worse, Emma was influencing her against him. He experienced an urgent need to remind her who she should trust, and it sure as hell wasn't Emma.

He took out his phone and scrolled through their messages, searching for vague or firm proof she had agreed to get together with him tonight.

He typed *This isn't like you*, then backspaced over the entire message.

We had plans. Again, he deleted it.

I'm not sure what's going on with you, but this isn't like you. We had plans. I get Emma is your friend, but I hope that doesn't mean I come last. Tell me when you're ready to talk. After that message, he hit send.

How might she bring up David's gaslighting behaviour

without alienating her friend? It was a mess. She took a deep breath, then asked, "Has he said things like that before? Made you question stuff you consider true?"

"Quite a lot, if I'm honest," Amy said.

"It's not right. Healthy relationships aren't supposed to leave you doubting the people who support you." Emma took a deep breath and held it, waiting for Amy's reaction. "Has he made you feel like this before?" She left it hanging, hoping her friend would see the things Emma could, her hope for Amy's understanding shining through.

"Let's make supper. I'm starving," Amy said.

"I'll open another bottle of wine."

The front curtains were still open. Emma walked to the window to close them. David sat in his car parked across the street. Was he going to sit there and watch them all night? Emma closed them. Showtime was over.

Amy was a bright girl. Why did she not see what David was doing to her? "David is still sitting out front in his car watching you. I closed the curtains." Emma's urgency was clear in her voice.

"He sent me a text." Amy picked up her phone and showed the message to Emma.

She read it in disbelief. "Ames, you see that this isn't right. You and David didn't have plans for tonight. He's just trying to …" Emma stopped speaking, afraid she'd already gone too far.

Amy turned on the oven and opened the Naan bread. The toppings were on the table so they could each put what they wanted on their pizzas.

"What movies did you want to watch tonight? I'll set them up so we can watch while we eat," Emma said. With any luck, there would be something in one of them that would make Amy see David in a character.

"Movies. Honestly, Em, I hadn't given them much thought. I'm not sure what I have on DVD. I pick them up when they're on sale."

Their pizzas were ready, the oven was hot, and the cozy living room was inviting. Amy put their supper in and set the timer. She topped up their glasses from the bottle Emma opened, adding to the warm ambiance, and walked to the living room.

Emma sat on the floor cross-legged, selecting films. "We've got *Notting Hill*, *Four Weddings and a Funeral*, *Bridget Jones's Diary*, *Love Actually*."

"So far, all Hugh Grant movies."

"Yes, but I like him."

"What else?"

"*Legally Blonde*."

Amy absentmindedly walked to the window and pulled the curtain aside. David's car remained parked on the other side of the street. This was new. Did he think she and Emma would throw a wild party and bring men in through the back? "I like that one."

"Okay, so that's one settled. We've got *Bridget Jones: The Edge of Reason*, *One Crazy Summer*, *What a Girl Wants*, and *The Holiday*. Do you want me to keep going, or have you decided on anything other than *Legally Blonde?*"

"Okay, *What a Girl Wants*, and *The Holiday*. That's three. That should get us through the night. I can't wait to start."

The timer beeped, so Amy left the room to take their supper out of the oven.

Fortified with wine and pizza, Emma settled on the sofa and started the first movie.

Amy's boyfriend, David, acted so much like Warner Huntington III from *Legally Blonde* that it was striking, despite it had been ages since Emma had last seen the movie. The similarities were so striking that Emma stifled a giggle. Would her friend pick up on it?

Emma's pizza was so loaded that it was a sight to behold. It had sauce, mozzarella cheese, pepperoni, Genoa salami, sliced tomatoes, mushrooms, red onion, bacon crumbles, black olives, and grated Parmesan on top. It was a pizza lover's dream.

She had just taken a mouthful when Warner did something that screamed David to her. Emma chewed and swallowed her food, then turned to Amy. "Warner, remind you of anyone?"

Emma held her breath, waiting for Amy's reaction. But Amy just turned to her, a blank expression on her face. "No. Why should he?"

"You don't see David in him at all?"

"No."

Why did Emma even suggest that Warner in the movie made her think of David? David was nothing like that.

Warner belittled and dismissed Elle as the movie continued, and Amy shifted in her seat. The parallels were there. She got defensive and said, "David's not that bad." But, after the words escaped her lips, Amy wanted to take them back. David wasn't that bad — he was worse.

She stood and walked to the window and looked outside again. David's car was still there. He hadn't tired of watching her and left yet. The dome light was on, so he must have been doing something that required additional light. But what?

As the movie ended, Amy was relieved. But as she saw David's behaviour mirrored in Warner's character, a sense of fear crept over her.

"What next?" Emma asked as the credits ran.

"*The Holiday*. I like the actors in it, and it's light. Nothing underlying."

By now, both had finished their pizzas and their dishes were in the kitchen. Emma was certain, Amy realized the similarities between David and Warner. She'd watched her shift on the couch a few times when Elle was being ill-used.

With the movie started and their glasses topped up again, they settled in to watch.

"This part is hilarious. Iris and Amanda communicating through the website. In the beginning, neither is letting on to the other what their places are like."

"You should do that, Ames. Do a house swap," Emma said, giggling. The wine was catching up with her.

"Who would want to come to my little apartment?"

"Someone who wants to travel, see another town or city."

"But, it's called house swap. I don't have a house."

This could be the perfect solution for Amy. Get her away for a while. Give her time to think and realize how manipulative and controlling David is. "Worst-case scenario, you hate it, come home early, and I'll make you watch *Love Actually* as punishment," Emma said.

"I don't have a clue how to go about it," Amy said, placing her empty glass on the coffee table.

"First thing in the morning, we'll search online and see what we can find. What have you got to lose?"

David sat outside Amy's apartment, watching and waiting. He was jealous and angry that Amy wanted to spend the night with her friend and watch movies.

He justified his actions by saying he wasn't stalking her — just making sure she was okay. When she came to her senses and realized how irrational she'd been, he'd be there to pick up the pieces. He was certain that would happen.

The inside lights shut off one by one. Even through the closed curtains, he recognized which room and lamp someone had turned off. He started the car and sped off, screeching the tires.

Eight

Amy's Apartment, Jean Street, Sudbury, Ontario

June 29, 2019

Emma's mouth was as dry as the Sahara when she woke up. Since Amy's apartment was only a single bedroom, she'd slept on the sofa. When she crawled out from under the covers, Emma checked outside. David had given up and gone home. That must have been his tires squealing, she heard after she settled on the couch.

Not wanting to disturb Amy's sleep, Emma padded around the apartment barefoot, careful not to make too much noise. They hadn't done the dishes last night, so she filled the sink with hot sudsy water and washed them. She'd cleaned the stovetop, and wiped down the table — two more things that wouldn't need to be done later. Her actions were proof of her thoughtfulness and care for her friend.

With a sense of anticipation, Emma started looking for house swap vacations. She could have a website up by the time Amy got out of bed, and she couldn't wait to see her friend's reaction to the idea.

Emma, always considerate of Amy's preferences, pulled her laptop from her backpack and set it up on the kitchen table. After booting her computer, she Googled house swaps in Canada and waited for the results. She dismissed a site with a hefty membership fee, knowing Amy would never agree to it. Farther down the list of hits, she found a free site, and knowing that free is good most of the time, she decided that would be where they started.

Amy woke to a gleaming kitchen, which, if she recalled, resembled a war zone when she went to bed the night before. The only thing they did was return the pizza ingredients to the fridge. "Did you do all this, Em?" Amy asked, scratching her head.

"Yup. I was awake and didn't want you to have to face the mess when you crawled out of bed."

"Thanks. You're a star," Amy said as she made her way to the bathroom. As she passed the mirror, the reflection frightened her. She had a major case of bedhead. Her hair stuck out in all directions. She'd buttoned up her pyjama top wrong. She then clenched her teeth and opened her lips. No night before fuzz on her teeth, but her tongue was thick and furry.

Once she relieved her bladder and washed her hands, Amy brushed her teeth and rinsed her mouth. She tried to tame her unruly hair, but it had other ideas. At least it wasn't as wild as before. A shower would fix that.

She padded back to the kitchen where Emma was starting a pot of coffee.

"You didn't have to do that, Em. I could have."

"Least I could do. Oh, I found a house swap site we can look at."

Amy's expression changed. They had talked about it the night before. Obviously, her friend had forgotten it.

Emma scrolled through the list. "Looking for a change. Can't afford a holiday. Willing to swap houses."

"Meh," Amy said with a groan.

"You're right, nothing much there."

Emma continued down the list, reading the entries aloud to Amy.

Then, she found this one. "Ooh, this one sounds interesting. Author working to deadline and suffering from severe writer's block. Need a change of scenery."

Amy perked up. "Interesting. Can you send me the link for that one, Em?"

A quick copy and paste and Emma hit send. The email would land in Amy's inbox soon. Now, she hoped her friend would be brave enough to act on it. When they watched *Legally Blonde*, Amy squirmed a few times as she reconciled Warner's behaviour towards Elle, with David's towards her.

The girls checked out more entries at the house swap website, but both kept coming back to the one posted by the author. What sort of place would an author live in? A luxury penthouse? A detached house? A semi-detached? An apartment?

"Look at the time," Emma said after she noticed how late it was. "I have to go. I have a ton of laundry to do before I go back to work. It will take me all day and most of tomorrow to get it caught up. That's if I can get the machines in my building. They're almost always in use."

Emma gathered her belongings, hugged Amy and kissed her on the cheek. "And not a word to David about this," she warned.

"Why not?"

"The whole idea is to get away for a while on your own. Give you some space." And make you realize what that man is doing to you. Emma didn't say that last bit aloud, just swung her backpack onto her shoulder and walked out the door. "Later, Ames."

Emma's apartment building was about a twenty-minute walk from Amy's. She enjoyed walking, even in the bitter cold of a Sudbury area winter. A car came to a stop beside her. There was parking on both sides of the street, so she continued until the driver accosted her on the sidewalk. David Carter. What did he want now?

David stepped out of his car and approached Emma. "You're trying to turn Amy against me. Don't deny it."

"I'm not trying to do anything, David. Amy is my friend and has been for a long time. She's a smart girl and will soon suss you out as being the gaslighting scumbag you are. And when things all fall apart, I'll be there to pick up the pieces and see her through it."

David grabbed Emma's upper arm and squeezed. "You'd like that, wouldn't you?" he said with a sneer. "When I get done, she won't want to have anything to do with you."

"Let go. You're hurting my arm." Emma tried to wrench her way out of his grip, but he held firm and squeezed harder.

"I'm warning you, Emma." David leaned forward so he was nose to nose with her. "Don't you dare try a thing. You'll regret it. Trust me." He loosened his hold on her arm and shoved her back. "You're nothing but a two-bit tart, and Amy will soon find out the truth about you."

Amy found herself in a dilemma. Emma's apparent dislike for David was a constant reminder, but the movie they watched last night had peeled away a layer of his facade. The thought of a house swap crossed her mind, but the idea of hiding things from David made her uneasy. The question lingered in her mind— should she risk telling him about her plans to go away for a while?

David's charm and kindness drew Amy to him in the first place, not to mention his good looks. His looks, sure, made his self-centredness forgivable. He had a stable job at the city's finance department, and something about him was attractive. His charm was like a spell, but his unpredictability was like a thunderstorm, striking when least expected.

What would Mel do in her place? Her younger sister didn't have luck with men, either. She'd caught her fiancé in bed with his boss's wife. Karma bit him big time, though, when the train hit him at a level crossing on his way to work. She wouldn't wish that on anyone. Mel seemed to have landed on her feet with Gareth, even though he had PTSD. They were a cute couple, and he loved her.

Her twin Michael had a few sour relationships before he met Jennifer. She must have loved him since she travelled halfway around the world to surprise him.

Amy's siblings seemed to be drawn to those who had experienced hardship. Serenity, Roger's partner, had a tough upbringing. Chris's fiancée, Lori, had suffered from sexual abuse. Jennifer had lost her parents and brother in a tragic accident, which she survived as a young teenager. Despite these

challenges, they had all found love and happiness.
What dark secrets in his past did David have?

Nine

Emma's apartment, Ste Anne Road, Sudbury, Ontario

June 29, 2019

Emma still vibrated from her encounter with David when she arrived home. Her arm hurt where he had squeezed it. Had he ever done anything like that to Amy? Despite the unpleasant encounter, she grabbed her phone, rushed to the bathroom and removed her outer layer of clothing. With her arm held in the air, the bruises from his hand were visible in the mirror's reflection. She opened the camera app, positioned the phone and took pictures.

Emma figured David was at Amy's now, grovelling and manipulating. Still, she had to let her friend know what kind of man he was, so she selected the picture and attached it to a message.

Met David on the street. He did this to me. Said I'm trying to turn you against him. Thought you needed to see.

It might be all for naught because David, being the charmer he was, could deny it all and convince Amy that Emma was lying. That Emma was trying to break them up because she wanted him for herself.

The whole thing was a colossal mess. If Amy didn't soon

come to her senses, she'd have a nervous breakdown. But if that happened, she would be easier to manipulate and gaslight.

The doorbell rang, and Amy headed to the door. She opened it straight away. David stood in the corridor.

"How many times have I told you to put on the chain lock? Anybody could be out here ready to force their way into your apartment."

"Sorry, I forgot."

"Don't in the future. I'm only looking out for you. Speaking of that, I saw Emma on my way here. She's trying to come between us. Spread lies about me. Don't believe a word she says."

Emma wasn't like that, was she? Amy and she had been best friends since nursing school. Why would she change? Just then, Amy's phone pinged. A picture of a bruised arm filled the screen.

Thought you'd like to see what your loving boyfriend did to me.

David wasn't capable of that. He'd done nothing like that to Amy. Why would Emma say that?

"Who was the message from?" David asked, his voice menacing.

"Em-Emma."

David snatched the phone from her hand. "See, what did I tell you? She's trying to turn you against me." He hurled the phone at the wall, where it shattered on impact. "That will keep you out of each other's pockets."

For a moment, Amy was stunned. David had done nothing violent like that before. The broken phone cost her well over $1000. She hadn't finished paying for it yet and doubted if she could get it replaced. Tears pricked the backs of her eyes.

Amy's eyes were red and glassy with unshed tears, and her helplessness was evident. "Have you any idea how much that phone cost me?" she asked, her voice low. "I'll never be able to afford a new one."

"If it keeps you and Emma away from each other, what difference does it make?" David smirked.

In his mind, he held all the cards now. He had Amy under his thumb, where he could manipulate her to his will.

Her tears began to flow, which irritated David. "Quit your snivelling. If it helps, I'll buy you a new phone." He'd install a tracking app on it before he gave it to her. That way, he could see where she was and who with 24/7. That would be perfect.

Amy had to interact with people on her job. She had no choice. There was no fear as long as the app showed she was at the hospital. He was interested in checking where she was and who with away from the job.

Ten

Health Sciences North, Ramsey Lake Road, Sudbury, Ontario

July 2, 2019

Amy returned to the nurses' station after helping Mrs. Smith, an independent woman with a fractured hip, settle into a chair. The woman had already refused rehab after her release many times. "I'm not a nursing home case," she snapped. Amy understood her stubbornness and even respected it.

She didn't notice anyone waiting in the corridor until a wall of blooms blocked her path. Someone thrust the massive, overpowering bouquet into her hands. Only when Amy stepped back to steady herself did the face behind it come into view.

David.

He smiled, as if they hadn't argued the last time they were together. As if he hadn't hurled her phone at the wall. "I'm sorry about the other day," David said, like an actor reading a line he'd rehearsed a hundred times.

Amy blinked at the bouquet. A single red rose stood in the middle surrounded by white lilies, pink carnations, baby's breath, yellow chrysanthemums and greenery. The perfume was heavy and cloying, making her stomach turn.

"Someone's a lucky girl," the head nurse said as she walked by the nurses' station.

Amy's throat tightened and her hands gripped the bouquet too hard, causing the stems to bite into her palms.

"You okay? You've gone a little pale," David said, leaning towards her so she had to step back.

"I'm fine," she lied.

"I remembered you liked lilies. They're so elegant — just like you." His tone was soft, but his eyes pinned her like a butterfly to a spreading board.

She didn't answer. She couldn't. The lilies reminded her of her father's funeral and how the funeral home reeked of them. She hadn't realized it until now.

David reached into his coat pocket and pulled out a small, wrapped box. "Here," he said, pressing it into her free hand. "You don't have to worry about the old one anymore."

Amy looked down. The weight of a new iPhone in its sleek packaging pulled at her fingers. Guilt, obligation, and unease churned inside her. She hadn't asked for a new phone. He hadn't asked what model she wanted. He had chosen for her.

One of the other nurses rescued her. "Let me get a vase for those."

"Thanks," Amy said, her voice a whisper, grateful for the excuse to look away.

She set the bouquet down and focussed her gaze on the counter instead of David. His gesture appeared overly dramatic, obvious, and precisely orchestrated.

"I just want us to be okay again," he said, his voice low now, almost tender. "My frustration came from my caring for you."

Amy swallowed hard and nodded, because it was easier to say nothing.

The call light for Mrs. Smith's room lit up, a tiny salvation.

"Sorry, David, I have to go." She left the flowers and the phone on the counter and strode down the hall to the patient's room. At the doorway, she paused and took a deep breath before stepping inside.

Emma approached the nurses' station from a different corridor. When she saw David, she ducked into a room and watched him. She couldn't contain her fury. He was manipulating Amy again, sure as anything. Why else the grand gesture with the oversized bouquet of flowers and the present? Did he think he was some romantic hero?

Emma had sensed David's malevolence the first time Amy introduced her to him. Emma's fear for Amy was obvious. After his weekend display of menacing behaviour — parking outside her apartment all night and leaving bruises — her fear was undeniable.

She reached into her pocket and pulled out her phone. Amy's body language made Emma pause. Her friend looked so small and unsure. For Amy's sake, she wanted to believe David, but after what he did, could she? Did she text Amy? What if David saw? Better yet, what if Amy didn't read it right away? The internal conflict was tearing Emma apart.

David accompanied Amy to the patient's room, kissed her on the cheek, and then carried on down the corridor to the elevators. He said something to her but she was too far away to hear. What was he saying? The mystery only added to the tension.

Emma remained where she was until Amy returned to the nurses' station before making her way there. She had overheard most of the conversation between them. "So what's with the flowers and a new phone? And not just any old phone, but the latest iPhone?"

"Mine got broken the other day," Amy said, mumbling.

An insulated water jug stood in for a vase. She stuffed the bouquet in, wrappings and all, and turned it so the lilies faced the wall.

"How did yours get broken?"

"What does it matter? David bought me a new one," Amy said, her voice a shade too bright. Why did she find it necessary to defend him?

"Aren't you going to open it? Do you have the same number? If it's different, I need to update it in my contacts."

Amy stiffened. "Please, Emma, back off."

The words snapped louder than she intended. Emma flinched, then lifted her hands in surrender.

"Sorry," Emma said, backing away with grace. "Just trying to help."

Guilt surged in Amy's chest like the incoming tide. She picked up the gift-wrapped box and removed the fancy wrappings. The phone gleamed in rose gold beneath the plastic cover, nestled in a clear case with a pre-installed screen protector. She powered it on. The lock screen slid open with her usual passcode. Contacts. Photos. Apps. Even her Home Screen wallpaper. Everything was there.

Too seamless. She had synced nothing. Hadn't backed up anything. The realization sat heavy in her chest.

Still, Amy tapped out a message to Emma.

Sorry, Em. Didn't mean to snap. Hopefully, you get this. Let me know.

She hit send and waited, her fingers trembling. Relief washed over her when the status showed delivered.

But it didn't dull the creeping unease. Everything was already … here. Just as she'd left it. How had he done that?

Emma was in a different wing when the message came through. She pulled her phone from her pocket and breathed a sigh of relief when she saw it was from Amy and that everything seemed okay.

Almost lunchtime. Let's do the chip wagon down the street.

She had to talk to Amy. Find out how her phone got broken and did it happen before or after Emma had sent her the pictures of her bruises.

They only had thirty minutes for lunch, so Emma hoped the line up for fries wouldn't be too long when they arrived.

Meet you at the main entrance.

They had everything set. If the girls were lucky, they'd find a bench with a view of the lake where they could eat. Getting Amy away from the hospital and on her own so they could talk was paramount.

Emma waited for Amy to arrive for over five minutes. Soon, her friend came down the corridor towards her.

"You never answered my texts after I sent you the picture. I sent quite a few. I lost track of the number."

"I didn't get them," said Amy.

The dots began to connect. "Ah, so David broke your phone. He saw the picture and the message I'd sent with it."

Amy nodded.

"Ames, I'm worried about you. I don't want to see you get hurt. You're afraid of David, aren't you?"

"N-no."

Amy couldn't meet Emma's eyes. Her head remained bowed. How she hesitated when she said 'no' and avoided looking Emma in the eye couldn't have made it any clearer. She was sure Amy was terrified of the man. However, getting her to admit it was urgent.

Amy struggled to understand David's behaviour the other day. His anger was obvious, and she couldn't shake off the impression that Emma might have provoked him. The thought of him hitting her, even for the first time, sent shivers down her spine.

They ordered their fries, the tantalizing smell making their mouths water. But they didn't have enough time to find a place to sit and eat, so they munched on their way back to the hospital. The sun was shining, and they could see benches and picnic tables outside, a perfect spot for a leisurely meal.

Amy's phone pinged. "Can you hold this for me, Em? I need to get this." She passed her lunch off to her friend and dug out her phone. It came from a number she didn't recognize.

Miss me?

Who was this? A wrong number? David's name always came up with his number. Or was it him trying to be funny? Her hands began to shake, her mind racing with possibilities.

"You okay? You're white as a ghost."

Amy turned her phone so her friend could read the message.

"Meant for someone else, I would think. Just delete it. It wouldn't be the first time a message got sent to the wrong recipient."

"You're right." Amy swiped from right to left across the screen and eliminated the message. That was the only one. All her other messages were gone, including the photo of Emma's bruised arm and the house-swap link.

Did David know this would happen? Was he trying to isolate

her from Emma? The thought lingered, casting a shadow of doubt over her trust.

"I've lost all our messages. They didn't come through."

Emma pulled out her phone and opened the text messaging app. She went to the thread between her and Amy and saw so many one-word or question mark messages from the past few days. She couldn't delete them, though, because doing that would erase their entire conversation back to the first message.

She turned her phone to Amy. "Look at the number of times I tried to reach you after I sent you the picture. It was like you disappeared."

Amy nodded.

"I know you don't want to hear this, Ames, but I think David destroyed your old phone on purpose. He was angry when I sent you the pictures of my arm that he bruised when he squeezed it. That explains why you didn't respond to my text."

"I can't believe David did that. It's not like him."

"But gaslighting, controlling and isolating you is. I wish you could see it. I think you started to when we watched *Legally Blonde* the other night. This grand gesture with the new phone, it wouldn't surprise me if he put a tracking app on it."

Amy stared at her. "He told me you'd do something like this. You're twisting me up about him." She then took off running back towards the hospital.

Emma had overstepped the mark, and she regretted it. But no more than she would if she sat back, did nothing, and David hurt her friend. She threw her fries on the ground, to the delight of the squawking seagulls, and ran after her friend. If David were aware of this exchange, he'd be rubbing his hands together and smiling gleefully.

Eleven

Health Sciences North, Ramsey Lake Road, Sudbury, Ontario

July 2, 2019

Amy's phone pinged. She ignored it at first, but in the end she couldn't resist. Was Emma sending her a message apologizing for what she said on their way back from the chip wagon? She pulled it out of her pocket, not from Emma. It came from the same number as the one she received earlier.

I bet you're thinking about me.

Who was it sending her these messages? It wouldn't be David because everything from him came up under his name.

Amy couldn't go to Emma because of how she left things with her. Perhaps her sister, Melissa, could offer some guidance? The only way to find out was to ask.

Hi Mel. Got a couple of odd text messages from a number I don't recognize. 1st one said 'miss me?' And the 2nd said 'I bet you're thinking about me.' What should I do?

Her lunch break was over, so she returned to the hospital and up to her floor. She hadn't seen Emma yet, which was just as well with what she said about David. He wouldn't do something like that to her. He loved her, didn't he? When was the last time he said that to her? She dropped onto the chair at the nurses' station to finish entering the paperwork into the computer she had started before lunch. The closest he ever came to saying it was when he said 'You know I love you.' Did she? Some of his grand gestures said he did. Like the flowers and the new phone.

Melissa returned her message about five minutes later.

Sounds like you have an admirer.

Maybe that simple. Perhaps she had an admirer. But how did he get her cellphone number? Anyone she'd given her number to might have passed it on when asked. Amy's perspective on the matter didn't improve. But she trusted David. He was the one person she could count on, so she decided to message him.

I received a few weird text messages today from an unfamiliar number. Emma thought the first one was a wrong number, but I received another one after that.

Amy slipped her phone back into the pocket of her scrubs. She didn't expect to get an answer from David right away, but within seconds of her taking her hands off the device, it pinged.

Of course, Emma'd say that. She's been trying to turn you against me. Wouldn't surprise me if it wasn't her who sent them.

On the heels of that message, another came in from David.

That's creepy, babe. You okay?

David's first reply caught Amy off guard. She'd never thought Emma, her best friend since nursing school, would stoop to something so low. She still didn't believe it was Emma behind the two texts. The second response from him was more what she expected. At least in that one, he showed concern. She replied.

I will be.

Amy returned to entering the patient records into the computer. It was a tedious task, one she disliked. She'd rather be out on the ward, comforting the people in need, than stuck behind a desk. Her phone, a sleek rose gold device, was on the desk, face down. When it pinged this time, it vibrated.

Someone is trying to get under your skin. Watching you? Do you think it might be an ex?

This whole thing was so bizarre that it was laughable, except it scared Amy. She did not know who this person was or why they tormented her. Her heart raced as she read and contemplated the message, and she was on edge when another message came in.

Let me help. I know people who can trace numbers. You shouldn't have to deal with this alone. Send me the number, and I'll pass it on.

It was heartening for Amy to see David step up to help her with this. Knowing he had her back, a sense of relief washed over her, so she sent him the number the messages came from.

705-555-5678 Thank you.

Until Amy received this new phone from David, she never had mysterious text messages come to her from unknown numbers, or number withheld. It didn't sit right with her, but she wasn't tech-savvy enough to know how to figure it out. David did, and she was sure he'd help her.

Pick you up after work and drive you home. You don't need to be alone with some stalker out there.

Great, that was all Amy needed. Why would David even mention stalker?

Amy heaved a sigh when her shift ended. The jug with David's flowers sat on the desk next to where she worked. She left them there so that the nurses on the night shift could enjoy them, too.

She gathered her belongings and plodded to the elevator, her steps heavy with exhaustion. As she reached the main entrance, David's waiting figure met her.

"Where are your flowers?" he asked.

"Left them for the staff on the night shift to enjoy."

"I bought them for you, not them."

"Fine, I'll bring them home tomorrow."

"I had a brilliant idea on the way over here. Why don't you change *your* phone number? I can take it and get you a new one tomorrow," he said as she eased into the passenger seat.

That was the last thing Amy wanted to do. Her family, the hospital, the utility company, Internet and TV all had that number. "No, there are too many people and places to notify. I'll leave it as is. If I get any more messages, I'll block the number."

David turned to her, shaking his head. "Fine. Do whatever

you want, but don't cry to me when it gets worse."

His response caught Amy off guard. She had expected him to understand her decision to block the number and not be angry.

After he stopped outside her apartment, he leaned over and kissed her. "What time is your shift tomorrow?" David asked.

"Same as today, why?"

"Do you want a ride to and from? I don't mind."

"I'll get the bus in the morning because it's so early, but you can pick me up afterwards."

"Okay. Goodnight, Amy."

As she watched him drive away, she couldn't help but wonder what had caused his sudden shift in mood. Had he had a bad day at work? One moment, he was full of ideas and offering her a ride, the next, he was upset with her.

Twelve

July 2, 2019

Amy had no sooner stepped inside her apartment and closed the door when her phone pinged.

Blocking me won't do any good.

Who was sending her these messages? If they were doing it to scare her, they had succeeded. Was it Emma having a laugh? It didn't seem like something she would do, but things had been weird between them since lunchtime. But the first one came in when they were together. Perhaps someone was having a laugh at her expense. But who? Amy's mind was a whirlwind of questions, and she couldn't find a single answer. She sighed and sent a text message to Emma.

Will you knock it off with the messages? Please!

Did she say more? Yes. Amy tapped out another.

You're scaring me.

Amy sat on the floor with her back against the door. Had she even locked it when she entered? These texts left her so rattled that she couldn't remember what she had and hadn't done. She pulled her knees to her chest, wrapped her arms around them, and buried her head.

About a minute later, a reply came back.

It's not me. I swear. I'm coming over.

Now, what did she do? Was she ready to face Emma? Tears welled in her eyes, and a surge of emotions made her vulnerable and exposed. She was mad at herself for crying, for showing weakness in the face of this unknown threat.

Why did Amy think she was sending the text messages, Emma wondered. David. He was the person behind it.

She shoved her phone into her purse, grabbed her keys, and raced to Amy's apartment. Emma was out of breath when she arrived, but her determination to help Amy was unwavering.

Emma knocked on the door. "Ames, it's me, Emma. Let me in." She turned the knob. Although unlocked, Emma couldn't open it. "Amy, are you leaning against the door? Move, please, so I can get in."

She pushed on the door again, and this time it opened. Amy never wore much makeup, but what she wore had smeared. Tears filled her friend's eyes, and some had run down her cheeks, streaking her mascara.

"Em-Emma, I'm so scared," Amy said, her voice trembling with fear.

Emma pulled her into a hug, her comforting gesture wrapping around Amy like a warm blanket. "It's okay. I'm here now. You're going to be okay."

"I knew it wasn't you," she said, sobbing. "You wouldn't do that to me."

"Let's go sit on the couch. You can show me these messages. Then we'll figure out what to do." Emma helped her to the couch and sat beside her.

Amy opened the text message app and the string from the unknown number. "Here. That's all of them. Well, except for the first. The one that said 'miss me?'. I deleted it." The remaining messages contained threats and disturbing references to Amy's personal life.

"These are creepy. Oh, Ames, I don't know what to say. Did you try a reverse number lookup?"

"No. David told me he had friends who could trace numbers, so I gave it to him."

"No doubt some shady characters," Emma pulled her phone

out, opened a browser and brought up the reverse phone lookup site. It came from the same area code, but that meant little because it covered a massive area. "It just says not enough information, just that it's a landline."

"I'm still no further ahead," Amy said.

"Well, you're not staying here. Grab everything you need for a couple of days. You're coming to my place."

"I can't do that."

"And why not?"

Amy bowed her head.

Her gesture said it all. David, her boyfriend, who'd been more aggressive and controlling of late.

"I think you need to contact the police. Whoever is sending you these calls will not stop."

"I-I can't."

"Why not?"

Amy, wearing a blank expression, looked at Emma.

"Fine, I will."

"It will just make things worse. I'll just block the number."

Amy took her phone back from Emma and, following the instructions on her friend's screen, blocked the number from which the text messages came. "That should work. If it doesn't, I'll just keep blocking the numbers."

"If that's what you want. I still think the police should be involved."

Amy shook her head. "No police."

"Will you at least come to my place for a few days? I don't like the idea of you being here alone with some nut job texting you all the time."

"I'll be fine."

With Emma's reactions to the text messages and how quickly she got to the apartment, Amy realized her friend had nothing to do with them. Emma wasn't trying to come between Amy and David either. Amy understood that. She knew better than to have doubted her friend.

Her phone pinged. She picked it up and read the message.

Blocking me won't stop me. I know where you live, Amy. I'm coming for you.

Amy stifled a scream. She struggled to contain her fear as she read the message. Her heart pounded so hard in her chest, she swore it would burst out of her body.

Emma's protective instincts kicked in. She was determined to keep Amy safe. "That's it. You're coming to my place, and we will call the police."

Amy didn't want to leave her home, but realized Emma was right. She packed a couple of days' worth of work clothes, other things, and toiletries into an overnight bag. Emma put her arm around her shoulders, took the bag, and they left.

Thirteen

Emma's apartment, Ste Anne Road, Sudbury, Ontario

July 2, 2019

Emma ushered Amy inside her apartment and straight to the spare room. "This is yours as long as you need it," she said, sensing the urgency in Amy's eyes.

"Don't call the police, please. I'm sure this is just some crank having a laugh. Unfortunately, it's at my expense. I'll keep blocking the numbers."

"But you'll still see the message first." After a brief pause, Emma continued, "What if you change your number?"

"David suggested that. But, work, my family, landlord, utilities, and such all have this one. It's too much hassle to change it and notify everyone."

She might have known David would factor into the equation at some point. Emma had seen through his gaslighting and controlling behaviour. What if he was sending these messages? No, that was a stretch even for him.

"Since you refuse to change your number or contact the police, a temporary house swap might be an excellent solution to help you relax and get away."

"I can't. I've got work."

"With the state you're in now, you could get a leave of absence. You need to go somewhere, Ames. Somewhere away from Sudbury."

"How can I afford to go anywhere? Going to my sister's wedding ate up almost all my savings."

"There are no other costs involved. You stay in their place, they stay in yours."

"Still, it's a lot of money."

It would take a lot of convincing to get Amy onboard with it, but if she didn't get away, she'd have a breakdown. Somehow, Emma had to convince her it was the best thing to do. Amy's well-being was at stake, and Emma couldn't let her friend suffer.

Amy paced around Emma's apartment, her mind whirling with conflicting thoughts. She shouldn't be here, she reasoned; she should be at home in case David comes by. She needed him in this crisis. Yet, it was sweet of Emma to rush to her side and offer her a place so she wouldn't be alone.

Emma had her laptop on the coffee table and was typing something. Amy didn't want to disturb her, but wandering around like a caged animal did. She sat in the rocking chair on the other side of the room.

This apartment was a stark contrast to hers; it was larger, more tastefully decorated, and had nicer furniture. The two worked at the same place and for the same time, so they made the same wage. What was the difference?

"Come here, Ames. I've found you the perfect place. It's in Lunenburg, Nova Scotia. The owner wants a quick turnaround. That would be perfect. I mean, the sooner you get away, the better," Emma said, her voice filled with a genuine desire to help.

Amy sat next to Emma. "No pictures?"

"Not yet. Not until closer to the end."

"Have you done this before?"

"Looked into it."

Photos of the picturesque village filled the screen — the boardwalk, the quaint houses, and the restaurants.

"So what do I do?"

"Type in that field and tell the person you're interested. After that, how much you share is between the two of you."

Amy slid over to the front of the computer and typed, *I love the pictures of your village. I'm interested in doing a house swap.* Not too much, not too little. Now, she waited for a response.

Emma brought Amy a glass of cold water with a wedge of lemon and sat beside her. "Are you still waiting for a response?"

"Yes. Not sure this is the right thing for me, though."

"Don't give up on it yet." Emma rubbed Amy's back. "You need a break, and the East Coast is the perfect place to get one."

Amy nodded then sipped her water. Emma watched her friend's body language. She was tense and unsure of herself, all down to David. Emma was positive, but she had overstepped things when trying to get Amy to realize it, regarding that man.

Emma was sure he had put a tracking app on Amy's phone, but to get in to look for it, she had to get it. If it wasn't visible on the phone, Amy would never think to search for it; she was so besotted with David. How could she get the phone away from her friend long enough to search for anything untoward?

The house swap app on Emma's laptop pinged. Amy read the message with a mix of excitement and trepidation. She needed a break — even she had to admit that — but going to the East Coast?

What do you want to find out?

"Now what do I do, Em?" Amy asked.

"Tell her you need to get away. Her location sounds perfect."

Amy typed in the message and waited.

I'm flexible. I'm an author with writer's block at the worst possible time. My manuscript is due at my publisher's in a month. I've just started it.

"Go for it, Ames. This person needs a break as badly as you do," Emma said, her confidence in Amy's decision clear.

I'm in Northern Ontario. Is that too far?

She waited.

No, that sounds perfect.

I only have a one-bedroom apartment. Will that be all right with you?

Another pause.

I don't need a lot of space. As long as I have an Internet connection, I'm good.

"She's willing. The size of my apartment hasn't put her off."

"Wonderful! Ask her how soon."

When do you want to swap houses?

Next week, if that's not too soon for you.

Amy's initial excitement was obvious as she looked at Emma. "How can I do that? I need to arrange the time off first." But as the practicalities set in, it waned.

"I'll go with you. We'll get you a medical leave starting today. Make a doctor's appointment for some time this week. I've got your back, Ames," Emma said, her supportive nature shining through.

Fourteen

July 3, 2019

Emma was determined to accompany Amy to the doctor's meeting, driven by her deep concern for Amy's well-being. She could provide valuable information that Amy might be hesitant to share. However, Amy dismissed the idea, leaving Emma in the waiting room, and her worry for her friend grew more intense.

Within fifteen minutes, the usual allotted time for a visit, Amy exited her doctor's office with a note in her hand. "I've got it, Em, I can take the time off."

"Wonderful. Now, to take it to the hospital and get your sick leave started."

Amy stopped. Emma turned around. "You okay. Not having second thoughts?"

"No. Just wondering what David will think of all this."

Emma was on the verge of telling Amy that David's opinion didn't matter, but she bit her tongue. The last time she spoke her mind about him, it led to a rift between her and Amy. The tension in their friendship, thanks to that man, was apparent.

"I'm sure he'll understand," she said, thinking the opposite. Amy taking a leave from work would show weakness, and knowing how David acted, he'd use that to his advantage.

Amy's phone pinged and she pulled it from her jacket pocket.

Saw you enter the doctor's office. Taking care of yourself? Good.

Amy gasped when she read the message and turned the phone to Emma. The message was from an unknown number, adding a layer of mystery to the situation.

Emma scanned the area. She didn't see anyone in a car who might have been sending messages to Amy. She snatched the phone from Amy's hands and began a search of the apps on the home screen. Nothing odd there. More than ever, Emma was sure there was a tracking app on Amy's phone, but she wasn't tech-savvy enough to find it.

Fifteen

Health Sciences North, Ramsey Lake Road, Sudbury, Ontario

July 3, 2019

After Amy met with her immediate supervisor on the floor, she headed to Human Resources with her sick note. The anonymous messages, like venomous arrows, injected her with fear and worry, making her sick. Despite her desperate need to escape Sudbury, this wasn't a ploy to get time off.

As with the other texts from numbers she didn't recognize, she blocked this number, too. But the stalker was relentless, like a shadow that refused to be cast away. Once she blocked the number, another message arrived from a different one.

She selected David from her text conversations.

Another message from a number I don't recognize. It's like a pair of unseen eyes always watching me.

That chilling thought sent shivers down her spine.

Amy leaned against the wall and took a deep breath after she sent the message.

Now you know why I told you to change your number. You didn't listen to me, but that's okay, I'll handle this. I won't let anything happen to you.

David was right. She should change her phone number. It would be a lot less hassle than blocking numbers.

Thank you. I'll think about it.

Thinking and acting were at opposite ends of the spectrum. Giving her mother and siblings a new number was easy until the questions started. These days, when you changed providers, you took your phone number with you. Her family would want to understand the reason behind the change. If she told them, they'd worry about her.

After this last message, Emma searched for a tracking app but couldn't find one.

David and Emma's dislike of one another burdened Amy. He said her friend didn't know what she was doing. That was too much. She'd keep this conversation to herself for now. It, and others, were on her phone, as were all the ones between Emma and her, as well as her siblings and mother. For now, she'd act like nothing else had happened.

"I'm officially on sick leave," she told Emma when she left the HR office.

Emma pulled her into a comforting hug. "You need this. You need to do the house swap. Let's return to my place, and you can complete the details."

Emma doesn't know what she's doing. Of course, she found nothing. There isn't anything to find. She's just trying to make you paranoid.

Amy stared at her phone. David's message was anything but comforting.

Sixteen

Emma's apartment, Ste Anne Road, Sudbury, Ontario

July 3, 2019

With the house swap website back up, Amy sat in front of Emma's laptop and typed.

I have the time off work. Now I just need to arrange transport to Lunenburg. Is there anything I should know?

"This is really happening, isn't it, Em," Amy said, her voice filled with anticipation, excitement, and nervousness.

"It sure is." Emma put her arm around Amy's shoulder. "If anyone deserved a getaway, it's you. While we wait, let's check transportation links for you."

Emma took over the laptop and soon found the route from Sudbury to Lunenburg. "Hey, this is a breeze. The bus from here goes to Toronto, then the train to Halifax, with a change in Montreal. Then the bus from Halifax to Lunenburg. It's all straightforward."

"And how much are the fares?"

"I haven't checked them. This was just a map view. I need to go to the VIA Rail site for the train."

"Sorry. Worried about money and all. Like I said, the trip to

55

Mel's wedding almost wiped me out."

"No worries. I can help with the money. Pay me back when you can."

A tear escaped Amy's eye and ran down her cheek. "No tears. Okay, trains run from Toronto to Montreal daily," Emma said. "Pretty sure the bus to Toronto is daily as well. The first train from Montreal to Halifax is the eighth."

"Sound simple enough."

"For now, I'd just book one way. That way, you can come home when you're ready. You're not on a fixed schedule."

"Oh, Em, what would I do without you? You've been fantastic. Even if I have been a cow, you're the best friend ever!"

Seventeen

Emma's apartment, Ste Anne Road, Sudbury, Ontario

July 3, 2019

Something dampened Amy's enthusiasm. "How will you get me to the bus station? You don't have a car?"

"You let me worry about that." Emma turned and winked at her.

What was her friend up to? The sudden plan to get her out of the city and go to Nova Scotia was more than necessary, filled Amy with intrigue and curiosity.

"Should I tell David what I'm doing?" The question hung in the air, adding to the suspense and anticipation.

"No." Emma's answer was harsh.

The directness of Emma's response took Amy aback. She understood David's feelings towards Emma, his protective nature, and hers for him. A few things twigged in her mind, but nothing significant. David had always been wary of Emma, and Emma dismissed David.

He didn't need to know every detail of her life, although it seemed like it most of the time. For now, she'd keep it to herself. She might say something on departure day. Even though he'd never come out and said he loved her, Amy knew he did. Why else would he be so protective of her? She often wondered if she loved him back, or if it was just the comfort of his presence in her life.

A chime sounded. The same one as the incoming messages from the house-swap app.

That's wonderful. My house is on Falkland Street, almost directly across from the gas station. And that's where the bus arrives and departs from, so you won't have a long walk.

The house swap sounded better by the minute. Amy's excitement grew as she looked forward to leaving Sudbury on her own again. The memory of going solo to Melissa's wedding in Percé in 2018, because David was working and couldn't get time off, added to her anticipation. He had texted her several times when she was away, a clear sign he cared and missed her, didn't he?

Eighteen

Amy's apartment, Jean Street, Sudbury

July 7, 2019

Returning to her apartment, a wave of vulnerability overcame Amy. The sender of the text messages had invaded her personal space, knowing where she lived, her recent visit to the doctor, and every move she made. The thought of this unknown person, likely a man because of the intensity of his interest, lurking in the shadows sent shivers down her spine.

She dragged her large suitcase out of the closet. Amy would store it under the bus to Toronto. From there stowed in the train's luggage rack. She'd have to check it in Montreal, though; her small cabin lacked space.

Emma had arranged her one-way train fare and paid for it, in part with her VIA points and the rest on her credit card. There wasn't a lot of time to pack before she had to leave for the bus station. Summer clothes, but a couple of hoodies and pairs of jeans. Anything dressy? She opted for business casual and threw a few pairs of dress pants and nice jackets in the case, too. Toiletries. Amy preferred using her own. There would be some at the house, but she preferred the brands she used. Computer, power supply and two days' worth of clothing in her small bag. Her phone and tablet in her purse.

She glanced out the front window, and a dark, shiny car pulled up. Emma got out of the back. Had she hired a limo to take Amy to the bus station? That was too much. But then again, Emma had always been the extravagant one in their friendship, the one who liked to make grand gestures. Amy couldn't help but smile at the thought.

Amy zipped up her bags and opened the apartment door. Emma helped her take the luggage to the car. After she had ensured she locked the apartment, Amy handed her keys to her friend, who would see that the person swapping living accommodations with her had them.

Her phone pinged as she put her small case in the trunk. Amy pulled it out. Another text from a number she didn't recognize.

I see you're going away. I hope it's some place nice.

Amy's sense of helplessness grew as she read the new message. Tears streamed down her cheeks. "I can't do this, Emma," she said, sobbing, her voice breaking. She turned her phone to show her friend the disturbing message.

"Yes, you can. You need to do this."

"But what if this person continues to text me when I'm in Lu …"

Emma cut her off. "Don't say it. If this sicko hears where you're going, you'll never have a minute's peace."

In Emma's mind, David was bad news, but he'd never stoop so low as to harass Amy with anonymous text messages, would he? He might. Then swoop in and play the dutiful boyfriend. For now, she'd keep this thought to herself. If it wasn't David behind them, and she accused him, it would drive a wedge between her and Amy.

They climbed into the back of the limo, the leather seats cool against their skin. "Ontario Northland Bus Station, please," Emma said, her voice trembling. She turned to Amy, her eyes filled with concern. "Who is the person, and why is he doing it?"

"Should I respond?"

"No. Don't engage the person. Just block the number and move on." Emma's voice was firm, her hand reassuring on Amy's knee. "You're going to be just fine. I won't let anything happen to you."

"Wait. I can't go yet."

"Why not?"

"Seamus. I always take him with me. Give me my keys. I can't leave without him." Amy worried for her beloved stuffed dog.

Amy exited the car and darted back to the building. Once in her apartment, she headed straight to the bedroom where her stuffed Scottie dog sat on her pillows. "I almost left you behind, boy."

She picked him up and turned to leave. Was that? Did she just see David? Why would he be outside? Better yet — hiding. Amy shook her head. It couldn't have been him. She returned to the limo with her dog.

"Okay, we can go now."

The driver pulled away from the curb. Amy turned and stared towards the building. Again, she caught a fleeting glimpse of David, or someone who looked an awful lot like him. The sight sent a shiver down her spine, and she took a couple of deep breaths trying to calm herself, but they did the exact opposite. She couldn't push down her panic, the fear that was like a knot in her stomach.

"You okay, Ames?" Emma asked.

Amy nodded, her fear palpable in the air. She was too afraid to say anything because she feared breaking down. As it was, she was barely holding it together. Fifteen minutes later, the limo stopped in front of the bus terminal.

"Should I text David and let him know I'm going away?"

"No," Emma snapped, her voice firm with conviction. "Sorry, Ames, didn't mean it to come out like that. You're going away because you need to get away from Sudbury, your job, David, and even me. But even more importantly, these anonymous messages."

Nineteen

Ontario Northland Terminal, Kingsway, Sudbury, Ontario

July 7, 2019

Emma leaned back into the limo and dismissed the driver. "Come on, let's go in. I'll wait with you until your bus arrives." She took Amy's large bag in one hand and wrapped her other arm through Amy's.

Inside, Amy relaxed. The bus depot was a cacophony of sounds, with the hum of conversations and the occasional announcement over the loudspeaker. The smell of coffee from a nearby kiosk wafted through the air. She was in a bus depot, and other people were waiting for their bus to arrive. She headed towards them when she spotted a row of seats backed against the wall. If there was a solid barrier, no one could sneak up behind her, and the entrance was in her direct line of sight.

Amy double-checked her phone. Her tickets were all in her email so the conductor could scan them. This wasn't a huge deal. She'd gone to Percé last summer by train and bus. She could do this, too. Amy Scott wasn't as weak and helpless as David made her out to be. Then the doubt crept into her mind, a knot forming in her stomach, and her hands starting to tremble. She hadn't been with David long when she made the trip to Melissa's wedding.

"Ames, you okay? This trip is for you. No one else." Emma's comforting words were like a warm blanket on a chilly night. She squeezed Amy's hand, a silent promise of her unwavering support.

Amy nodded and glanced towards the door.

Emma checked her watch and the arrivals board at the station. The bus was ten minutes late. The tension in the air was evident, and the delay added to the unease.

Amy's eyes were restless, scanning the room for any sign of danger. The ticket office, the entrance, the windows, knowing she was being watched.

"Are you okay? You seem nervous."

"A bit."

"You're safe here, Ames. I won't let anything happen to you," Emma said, her voice tinged with concern.

"I understand, but I don't understand. I can't describe it," Amy admitted, her trust in Emma clear.

Emma scanned the bus depot. There wasn't anyone in the room who shouldn't have been there. Everyone was a passenger seated with their luggage or an employee. There was no one loitering.

The police should have been involved from the start, but Amy didn't want to take things that far. Emma should have been more forceful and made her go to the police. Amy had blocked the numbers, but that didn't delete the messages from the phone. They were still there. What if the stalking escalated beyond sinister texts? Could her friend be in danger? The best thing for Amy was to get out of the city.

The bus pulled in, and the arriving passengers disembarked and collected their luggage from under the bus. Emma walked Amy outside and stowed her big bag in the compartment. She hugged her friend at the door and helped her get her smaller tote, purse, and Seamus on board.

Amy held Emma in a tight embrace, her heart heavy with the impending separation. As she climbed the steps, she turned back.

Unshed tears filled Emma's eyes, mirroring Amy's own emotions. A tear escaped Amy's eye, a silent echo of their shared sorrow, and traced a path down her cheek.

"Have a wonderful time, Ames," Emma called, waving her hand.

Amy found a window seat on that side of the bus so she could wave back. But all she did was press her palm against the glass.

Emma waved and blew kisses to her from the parking lot.

Soon, everyone was on the bus, and they pulled away. The driver had barely turned onto Kingsway when Amy's phone pinged. Must have been Emma telling her to enjoy herself. Amy pulled out her phone.

Leaving so soon? I'll miss you.

Twenty

Between Sudbury and Toronto

July 7, 2019

Who was tormenting her? The tears began to flow. She didn't stem the tide, but tried to keep the sobbing quiet. Her shoulders shook with each sob. Amy rested her forehead against the back of the seat in front of her and wept.

Someone pressed something into her hand. She turned. It was the older woman from the other side of the aisle, perhaps about the same age as her mother, short and chunky with grey hair. The woman, her eyes filled with understanding, had found a tissue for her.

"Sometimes, sweetheart, you just have to let it out."

Amy nodded and mouthed thank you.

"If you want to talk, I'm across the aisle."

Amy nodded again, then drew in a ragged breath. Breaking down like this in front of everyone was the last thing she wanted to do. She stared out the window, clutching a tissue. The older woman's offer of a listening ear gave her a glimmer of hope. The bus's motion and the weight of everything settled in.

Twenty-One

Outside Amy's apartment, Jean Street, Sudbury, Ontario

July 7, 2019

Where was Amy going? It wasn't at all like her to not tell him. She almost caught him when he was outside her apartment. David had hidden before any actual damage was done. If she saw him, it was such a brief moment that she'd doubt herself.

His last message was a work of art, culminating in his manipulative efforts. It was the best of all the anonymous messages he had sent. He chuckled, knowing Amy would be too terrified to seek help and too bewildered to trust her instincts. His satisfaction was apparent, and the tension in the air thickened.

Impatience gnawed at him, contradicting his giddiness at his manipulation's success. He needed to regain control over Amy and complete his plan. He glanced at the burner phone, resisting its allure. No, the next message had to come from him, from his number, the one Amy recognized. He composed a message and hit send, the situation's urgency palpable.

There. That should unbalance her. He was determined to keep her off balance, to keep her guessing. It was all part of his plan.

Twenty-Two

Between Toronto and Montreal

July 7, 2019

Amy's phone pinged again. She hesitated to look at the screen, her heart pounding in her chest, fearing it might be another one of the sinister messages. It wasn't. It was David.

I know you're scared. I'm just trying to protect you. I know what's best for you. No one else can keep you safe like I can. I'm the only one who can help you now. Don't block me again.

An icy chill ran down her spine. David. Was he behind the anonymous messages? She had never blocked his number. Why would he even say such a thing? He had no reason. He was always there for her. He was her rock. The confusion was overwhelming.

David's last text message had unsettled her. Was that his intention? If so, why? At least she'd made it to Toronto and was now on the train to Montreal. Well out of his clutches — she hoped. But hope was a fragile thing, especially in her situation. If everything went according to plan, she'd arrive in Montreal and only have a short layover before boarding the Ocean train to Halifax. From there, it was the bus to Lunenburg.

Twenty-Three

Amy's apartment, Jean Street, Sudbury, Ontario

July 11, 2019

Someone pounded on the apartment door. Isabelle released the deadbolt and pulled the door open. "Who are you?" she asked.

"I'm David Carter, Amy's boyfriend."

Her stomach twisted into a knot at his harried appearance. His eyes were bloodshot like he hadn't slept in days. He clenched his jaw and Izzy's eyes darted around the hallway. She released the chain and opened the door so he could enter.

"I'm looking for her. It's vital I find her. She hasn't been answering her phone," he said, his voice filled with panic. "They rushed Amy's mother to the hospital last night. She had a heart attack and is in critical care. I've tried everything I can think of to reach her, but she's gone off-grid. Her friend, Emma, wouldn't talk to me. You're the only other person who can help," David said, "The hospital won't confirm anything until family shows up."

Isabelle blinked, processing the flood of information. "Amy mentioned nothing," she said. "Are you sure?"

"Yes, I'm sure." He raked his hand through his hair. "We might lose her mother. Please, I wouldn't be here if it weren't serious. Just tell me where she's gone. A general area — town, street, whatever, I can take it from there.

She hesitated. Something seemed amiss, but what if it *was* true? What if Amy's mother was clinging to life in a hospital bed, and no one could reach her?

David stepped closer and lowered his voice. "If something happens to her and Amy isn't there ... I don't know how she'll live with herself. And if you could help ... and didn't ... well, I wouldn't want that on my conscience."

That did it. The guilt hit her like a punch. Isabelle nodded. "In that case, she's in my house on Falklands Drive in Lunenburg, Nova Scotia."

"Thank you. That's more than enough."

As he turned and walked away, something in her stomach twisted.

After David left, Isabelle sat at the kitchen table, her untouched cup of tea cooling beside her. She had tried to shake the panic that whispered to her she'd done something unconscionable.

At first, she told herself she'd done the right thing. Amy would be grateful. But, the longer she sat with that thought, the less it comforted her.

Isabelle opened Facebook. She had looked up Amy after they had set up the house swap. Amy's profile was mostly private, but her friend, Emma's, wasn't. She was the one who David said wouldn't talk to him. There had to be a reason. She scrolled through Emma's timeline. Her latest post turned Isabelle's blood to ice.

Some people will say anything to get what they want. Be careful who you trust. #NotYourInformationtoShare #ProtectYourFriends

Isabelle's stomach dropped. Someone aimed that post right at her.

She continued scrolling with trembling fingers. No sign of Amy. No update about her mother. No emergency. She'd been tricked.

He'd lied and she handed everything to him on a plate.

"Oh, no," she said, opening her browser to the house swap

site and left a message for Amy. Afterwards, she buried her face in her hands and did her best not to cry.

Twenty-Four

Isabelle Morrison's House, Falkland Street, Lunenburg, Nova Scotia

July 11, 2019

Amy grabbed her jacket and dashed out of the house. She almost forgot to pull the door closed in her haste to leave. She headed straight for the docks, where she had spent time yesterday with a young man who had helped her. She hoped he would be around to assist her again.

Her phone pinged, and terror rushed through her veins. What kind of message was she going to get now? Not wanting to see bad news, she pulled it from her pocket. It was a message from the house swap app.

A young man was here. He said your mother had a heart attack and is in critical care. They won't confirm anything until family arrives. I'm afraid I told him where you were. I am so sorry. I hope your mother recovers completely.

That was the last thing Amy needed. It was bad enough that David texted her from his own phone, and the more she thought about it, he was behind the anonymous messages. And that didn't take into consideration the tracking app on her phone. He'd be on his way here, a betrayal that cut deep into her trust.

It's okay. You weren't to know, Amy replied to the message. In their exchanges, she never thought David would stoop so low. But to ensure everything was all right with her mother, she texted Melissa.

Hey Mel, don't want to scare you but is Mum all right? The woman I'm house swapping with messaged me Mum went to the hospital.

Finding Kyle was more important now than before. Amy, her heart pounding and her breath ragged, took off on the run again. By the time she reached the harbour, she was out of breath, and her legs had turned to jelly.

Every time her phone pinged, she panicked. She didn't want to check it, but thought it might be her sister with news.

House swapping? You'll have to tell me all about it. Mum's fine. At home, having coffee with the neighbour.

That lying scumbag! He fooled Isabelle into telling him where she was. At least she knew her mother was fine, and a wave of relief washed over her.

Twenty-Five

Zwicker Wharf, Lunenburg, Nova Scotia

July 11, 2019

Amy sank into one of the Adirondack chairs and stared at the boats bobbing on the waves. A soft metallic clang filled the air as the sailboat swayed on the moving water. The sound should have soothed Amy with its rhythmic lull, but her pulse refused to slow. She tightened her grip on her phone, rereading the message from Isabelle. The tracking app was bad enough, but David lied to get her exact location. The peaceful harbour with its salty breeze and the cry of gulls circling was a cruel contrast for the anxiety twisting within her.

It was all Amy could do to stem the tears that threatened to flow. A mix of anger, fear, and helplessness, swirled within her, threatening to overwhelm her.

"Hey, I didn't expect to see you here again so soon," Kyle said as he eased into a chair beside Amy.

She didn't smile. Her knuckles were white around her phone. "The tracking app. Did you delete it?" Her voice wavered — urgency wrapped in panic.

"I didn't get the chance. You wanted your phone back and

you took off from here like someone had lit a fire under you." He kept his tone light, but his gut tightened. Something was wrong.

She thrust her phone towards him. "Can you finish removing it, please? It might be too late now, but I'll still be happier knowing it's gone."

"Of course." He took the phone, brushing her fingers in the handoff. "Are you okay? You look scared to death. Want to talk about it?"

"No." But then, almost as if the dam had burst, she said, "I did a house swap with Isabelle Morrison. My boyfriend — David — I'm almost certain put the tracking app on my phone, went to my place and got her to tell him where I was. He had a fair idea thanks to tracking me." Her voice dropped. "He's going to come here. I know he will."

Kyle's jaw tightened. "And you don't want to see him, right?"

She nodded once. He reached out and placed his hand over hers — warm and steady.

Amy flinched, then stilled. For a second, she let it be. "My friend, Emma warned me. David has been gaslighting me for months — if not longer. I was just too stupid to see it."

She pulled her hand out from under Kyle's, but not as fast this time.

Kyle didn't push. "You weren't stupid. You trusted someone who didn't deserve it. That says something about him, not you."

Kyle returned his attention to her phone, tapping through menus. She sat stiff beside him, silent except for the occasional shaky breath. When he finished, he glanced over. "Here. All done," he said, returning the phone to her. "I deleted the app and wiped the history. It's gone."

Amy took her smartphone from his hand, her fingers brushing his again. "Thanks." She stared at the screen. "Easy for you to say. You weren't the one being played like an idiot."

He wanted to reach for her again, but didn't. Instead, spoke gently. "The one who manipulated, not the one who trusted, is at fault."

She turned away, but not all the way. He stayed beside her, quietly present.

Amy hadn't bolted and that was something.

It was only a matter of time before David's ominous presence loomed over Lunenburg like a storm cloud, turning the peace she'd found into a memory. The thought of his control creeping back into her life made her stomach churn.

Kyle, seated beside her was the opposite of everything David had been. Kind, present, gentle. Or, he was good at pretending.

Her fingers relaxed around her phone. "Thanks for getting that off my phone. It's one less thing I have to worry about."

"I still think you should go to the police about those messages," Kyle said, looking her in the eye. "The ones from unknown numbers."

"They won't care, not unless he shows up and does something." She hated how bitter that sounded, and worse that it was probably true.

Kyle didn't argue. "Some of those messages crossed a line, Amy. They weren't just creepy — they were threatening. It could escalate."

Amy stared out over the harbour and the boats rocking on their moorings. It was quiet here until a gull let out a shrill cry overhead, shattering the calm.

"David always knows the exact pressure point to push. What to say. What lie will sound genuine enough to keep me off balance." Amy's voice trembled as she spoke, the fear and frustration clear in her words. "He could make me question what I saw, what I sensed, and even what I knew was real."

Kyle didn't move closer, but his quiet strength remained beside her. Not pushing, not judging, just there "He's not getting near you again. Not while I'm here," he declared, his eyes reflecting a fierce determination.

Amy nodded."I know." Amy said, her voice tinged with uncertainty. She wanted it to be true. She almost believed it. Her voice faltered. "I want to believe that."

She pulled her jacket tighter around her body, trying to block out the chill, but it wasn't the wind that made her shiver. "David doesn't like to lose. I didn't break up with him by coming here. I betrayed him by coming and not telling him about it. And he doesn't let things go."

The realization landed with quiet force. "He twisted things so I'd doubt myself. Made me think like I was the one in the wrong. But now, I see it, and I see him."

Her voice grew steadier. "He's not done. He's coming. I can feel it."

She stood, then paused. This was where she shut down. Made a joke and kept her distance. Instead, she turned back and looked Kyle in the eye. "Thank you for helping me. For listening, and not pushing when I couldn't give more."

After a brief pause, a small and almost sheepish smile formed on her face. "Still, it *is* nice having a personal tech guy at my beck and call."

Kyle chuckled. "Happy to be of service."

This time, she didn't rush away.

Kyle observed Amy's departure, her shoulders rigid under her jacket. She had expressed her gratitude, referring to him as her 'personal tech support,' yet the worry lines around her eyes remained, a silent plea for understanding.

He lingered on the wharf, the gulls circling above him. The sun had descended, casting the boats into shadow, but his mind was elsewhere. All he could see was the unspoken fear that Amy struggled to conceal.

Kyle hated that someone had made her insecure. David. The mere thought of him made Kyle's blood boil. He had never met the man, but he'd heard enough to realize he was manipulative and controlling. The kind who used his charm like a crowbar to pry people open and take what he wanted.

Kyle rubbed his hand over the back of his neck, a gesture of his resolve. He wasn't a violent person, never had been, but if that guy dared to show his face near Amy again, he would be ready.

He'd check with Amy later to see if she wanted company or space. She was good at putting up walls when threatened, and he was learning to recognize the signs.

Twenty-Six

Isabelle Morrison's House, Falkland Street,
Lunenburg, Nova Scotia

July 11, 2019

Amy shut the front door behind her, clicked on the deadbolt, and attached the chain. She would not make it any easier for David. She walked through the house, checking the windows and ensuring she had secured the other doors. One in the kitchen led to the backyard, and another into the closed-in porch. Still, she couldn't relax, her fear of David's presence undeniable. She removed her phone from her pocket and tapped a message to Emma.

Met someone. His name is Kyle. Polar opposite to David. Kind, smart, funny. He found a tracking app on my phone and deleted it. Relief washed over me when it disappeared.

Amy shared the good news with Emma first. They had been friends since nursing school, and Emma was always there for her in times of need. She wasn't sure how to tell her the rest, but Emma needed to know.

David lied to Izzy, my house swap partner. Told her they rushed my mother to the hospital and he needed to get hold of me. She knew nothing different, so told him where I was. Mel confirmed mum was all right. He's coming to Lunenburg. I know he his and I'm terrified.

Amy had eaten nothing since breakfast and was starving. She took out the casserole Mrs. MacLeod had brought for her, dished another portion, and heated it in the microwave. Unfortunately, her stomach was so knotted with fear that she could only manage a few bites. Her anxiety was overwhelming.

She poured herself a glass of water, tidied the kitchen, and climbed the stairs to the bedroom.

Glass of water placed on the bedside table, phone next to it, Amy took advantage of the ensuite and ran herself a hot bath. With any luck, it would ease the tension that filled her body. Hopefully, Emma would have seen the messages she sent and a reply would be waiting for her.

The water was lukewarm when she climbed out of the tub. A heavy, red velour robe hung on the back of the door, so Amy pulled it on, wrapped it around her, and padded back to the bedroom.

She picked her phone up from the table. She had two new messages. When Amy unlocked her phone and saw Unknown Number displayed, her blood ran cold. David. It had to be. Her finger hovered over the screen while she debated with herself whether to open it. She didn't want to. But she couldn't ignore it either. She tapped the screen.

Kyle here. Got your number when I removed the app. Hope you don't mind. Just making sure you're okay. If you need anything, say the word.

Her breath escaped in a whoosh as the tension eased. Amy reread the message twice to ensure what she saw was real. She was angry that he did that without letting her know, but, relieved that the message was from him and that he cared enough to take that step.

Thanks for checking in. I'm okay-ish. Your message means more than you know.

As soon as Amy hit send, she opened the one from Emma.

Are you serious? He lied to Izzy? That's not okay. Don't let him near you again. My shift ends at midnight but text me if anything else happens. Glad you met a nice guy.

Amy held her phone to her chest and walked to the window. Her reflection stared back at her — tired eyes, pale face, tension in her shoulders. Did she text Kyle and ask him to come over? Or was she too stubborn? Wanted to face this alone. She didn't want him to see her this way again. It was bad enough he did earlier.

Twenty-Seven

Isabelle Morrison's House, Falklands Street, Lunenburg, Nova Scotia

July 13, 2019

David exited his car, his steps heavy with exhaustion and determination. He had driven straight through from Sudbury, with only a few power naps in rest areas, and he was in no mood for Amy's games. He pounded on the front door, his voice echoing through the mail slot. "Amy, open up. I know you're in there," he called out, his annoyance increasing by the second.

"Isabelle isn't home, young man. Can I help you?"

David turned towards the voice. An older, grey-haired gentleman stood on the walkway. His calm demeanour was a stark contrast to David's irritation.

"I know Isabelle isn't home," David said, his frustration bubbling to the surface, "She's in my girlfriend's apartment in Sudbury. It's Amy, my girlfriend, I'm looking for."

"Saw her go out earlier, but she hasn't returned yet. She might be at the wharf. There's a spot there with chairs overlooking the water," the older man said, his helpfulness relieving David's tense situation.

"And just how do I get there?"

"Go back to the corner just beyond the gas station. Turn right, then take another right at Linden Avenue. After that, follow your ears and nose. The salty smell and squawking seagulls will tell you when you're getting close."

David thumped back down the steps and climbed back into his car.

"Oh, and you're welcome," he called after him.

From the moment he saw him, Gordon hadn't liked the guy's look. His suit was so sharp it could cut through the air, and his smile, a mere facade that never reached his eyes, sent shivers down Gordon's spine. The man never even introduced himself. He just said he was looking for Amy and referred to her as his girlfriend.

Something about the encounter didn't sit right. The guy's gaze shifted towards the road, as if he thought he was being watched. Gordon's unease was clear, his instincts screaming at him to be cautious. He stood back and watched David storm off, a prickle of unease climbing his spine. Perhaps it was nothing, and he'd read something that wasn't there. Had he done the right thing or not? He sauntered back across the road to his house, the unease lingering like a shadow.

Twenty-Eight

Gordon and Maggie MacLeod's house, Falkland Street, Lunenburg, Nova Scotia

July 13, 2019

As he stepped back into his house and closed the door behind him, he couldn't shake the suspicion that he'd just handed a fox the directions to the henhouse.

He walked to the window and peered through the curtains as David's car disappeared around the corner.

"What's wrong, Gordon?" Maggie, his wife of forty years, asked him when he returned.

"Young Amy's fellow was banging the door down at Izzy's. I told him he'd likely find Amy down by the wharf."

"You seem worried. Is everything all right?"

"Something about him I don't like. Don't trust. God help me if I've done the wrong thing," he muttered. Gordon busied himself around the house while Maggie worked in the garden. He couldn't shake the creeping unease that had settled on him during his brief encounter with the young man, the suspense intensifying with each passing moment. He made himself a mug of tea and sat with it and his newspaper, but it didn't hold his attention. Young Amy didn't seem to be the type to be in trouble, but there had been a flicker of something in her eyes when she first arrived. And now this man shows up like he had a right to know where she was.

He set his tea down, walked outside, and stood on the porch, his hands resting on the cool, weathered railing. Across the street, the shadows started to lengthen, casting the neighbourhood in an eerie light. He scanned the sidewalk, the sound of his breath the only thing breaking the silence, as if he might spot that slick car circling the block again.

That man would double back if Amy wasn't at the wharf. And, if he did, Gordon was ready to stand in the way of trouble, his sense of responsibility towards Amy driving him forward.

Twenty-Nine

Zwicker Wharf, Lunenburg, Nova Scotia

July 13, 2019

Even when crowded, Amy loved coming to the wharf. She sat on the same Adirondack chair as she did the day she first met Kyle. The sun-warmed wood warmed her back, and she tried to draw comfort from the familiar surroundings. Any other time, the slap of the water against the pilings, the sharp squawks from gulls, smelling salt, fish and old rope would have calmed her. But today, the peace didn't sink in.

Her eyes drifted over the boats bobbing on the water, their masts swaying. People passed behind her, laughter and conversations drifting on the breeze, but the anxiety hummed beneath her skin.

She wrapped her arms around herself and kept her gaze fixed on the fishing boat moored nearby, willing her thoughts to quiet, but they didn't. They wouldn't, not with David knowing she was here. Not with the memory of Izzy's well-meaning but misguided slip of the tongue echoing in her mind.

David would show up. Amy knew he would.

Her stomach clenched. She didn't know how or when, but it was only a matter of time. Out here in the open, she was vulnerable and exposed. Amy closed her eyes and took a breath but it did nothing to settle her. She'd come here to find space — to find herself, but the water's rhythm, once soothing, had become like a clock counting down, each tick a reminder of her vulnerability.

She opened her eyes and rubbed her arms. The wind had picked up, and strands of hair blew across her face. As she was about to stand to leave, her phone vibrated in her pocket.

Her breath caught, and she froze.

When she pulled it out of her pocket and glanced at the screen, her stomach dropped as an unfamiliar number filled the display. Her thumb hovered over the screen. Had David gotten another phone or another number? Amy's instincts screamed to ignore it. Something stopped her. A tiny glimmer of something softer, quieter. Hope perhaps? She opened the message.

Hey, it's Kyle. Just checking in to see if you're okay.

Amy exhaled and let the phone rest in her lap, staring over the water again. Her vision had blurred. She was still tense and afraid, but not alone. The message had brought a glimmer of hope, a shift in her emotional state.

She typed a quick reply.

Thanks for asking. I'm at the wharf. Trying to be okay, but not succeeding.

His reply came quickly.

Want some company?

Amy stared at his words longer than necessary before she answered.

Yes, please.

Knowing Kyle would be with her soon eased her troubled mind. She added his number and name to her contacts so she wouldn't be terrified whenever his number without his name filled her display.

Kyle pocketed his phone and grabbed his hoodie, pulling it on as he left his apartment. Amy needed him, and he was resolute in his commitment not to let her down. Most of the day, he'd had an unsettled twitch in his gut that meant something was brewing. Seeing her message only confirmed it.

As he rounded the corner, the wharf came into view. He saw

her sitting alone in that same Adirondack chair she was in when he first met her. But today, her posture was different, too still. This wasn't the same woman he'd met here before. She sat hunched over, as if bracing for something.

He slowed as he got nearer, not wanting to spook her.

"Amy."

She looked up, eyes wide, until she registered him, and her shoulders sagged.

"Hey," she said.

Kyle sat in the chair beside her, making sure he wasn't too close, giving her the space to breathe.

"I wasn't sure you'd want company," he said after a pause. "Glad you did."

"I wasn't sure either, but ... I do." She wrapped her arms tighter around herself. "It isn't peaceful here anymore. It used to be."

He looked out over the water, the soundtrack of creaking ropes and the cries of seagulls playing in the background. "Yeah, I get that. This town — this wharf — it can carry ghosts."

"I think one followed me here."

Kyle's jaw clenched, but he didn't push. She'd tell him when she was ready. He sat with her for now, letting the quiet fall between them. "You're not alone. Whatever's happening, you're not facing it on your own. Not here."

Her eyes met his, full of unspoken things.

"I don't want him to ruin this place for me," she said, her voice a whisper.

"He won't," Kyle said with a conviction that surprised him. "Not if I can help it."

Amy hadn't realized how much she craved Kyle's company until he was beside her. His arrival was unassuming, yet it brought a sense of stability and calm, a familiar comfort that always anchored her in times of uncertainty. He didn't bombard her with questions or demands. He simply existed, and that was what she needed.

She gazed out at the tranquil water, but its serenity no longer had the power to pacify her. She resented this. Resented that David's influence reached even this far, disrupting the peace that the sea breeze used to bring.

"I keep trying to tell myself it's okay. That I'm safe here. But there's still a part of me waiting for the other shoe to drop."

"You don't have to pretend anything with me," Kyle said.

She met his gaze. His expression was one of understanding, not criticism. It caught her off guard, tightening her throat. "Thank you."

"For what?"

"Showing up. Not asking too many questions. Just … being here. I can't tell you how much that means to me."

Kyle smiled. "We all need people who do that."

Amy nodded, and after a pause, she said, "I don't want to sit here anymore. Can we go somewhere? Anywhere."

"How about the pub?"

She hesitated for a moment, then nodded. "Yes, the pub."

They stood together, and Amy shoved her hands into her jacket pockets. As they started walking towards Montague Street, her shoulders began to loosen. Relief washed over her, and she could almost believe everything was going to be okay.

Almost.

Thirty

The Knot Pub, Dufferin Street, Lunenburg, Nova Scotia

July 13, 2019

Kyle held the door open and let Amy go ahead of him into the quaint pub and restaurant. "This is my local. If you drink too much, you're only across the road from where you're staying," he said, with a smile, allowing the warmth of the place to envelop them.

He knew the interior like the back of his hand, which floorboards creaked, which didn't. The best seats. Best foods on the menu. It was as if the pub was a part of himself, a place where he belonged.

However, Amy hadn't crossed the threshold since she'd arrived in Lunenburg. At least her actions told Kyle that. She took in the artwork on the walls, the tables, the round booth in the far corner, and the bar.

Two stools were available at the bar, so he ushered her to them and helped her onto one. He took the one beside her.

"This is quite the place."

"The whole town is a treasure trove of quaint buildings like this. Well, not the Esso across the way, it's new. The rest of the town, however, hasn't changed in centuries. Perhaps some interior renovations have occurred in some buildings, but their exteriors remain unchanged. Were you aware it's a UNESCO World Heritage Site?" Now, he sounded like a tour guide with his ramblings, but the town's history was too fascinating to ignore.

"I didn't." Amy turned to him and smiled.

The door opened, and David stormed in with a face like thunder. Amy shrank back. Kyle looked over his shoulder.

"That the person you've tried to get away from?"

Amy nodded.

"I'll deal with him, if you like."

"No, this is something I have to do. If I don't, David will keep on gaslighting me."

"I'm here if you need me."

Kyle had ordered them fish and chips, and until David entered the building, Amy looked forward to the meal. She tried to ignore David, but he made it difficult. The next thing she knew, he wrapped his hand around her wrist.

"Come on, Amy, you're coming with me."

"I don't think so, David."

The pressure on her wrist increased.

"Let go of my arm." He didn't. If anything, he gripped it even tighter. "I said let go of my Goddamn arm." Amy wrenched her way out of his grip and stood before him. Her heart raced. It thumped so hard, she thought it would burst through her chest. So far, she hadn't backed down.

"What's gotten into you, Amy?"

"As if you don't know. You broke my phone on purpose so you could replace it with one you hid a tracking app on so you could keep tabs on me 24/7. Emma was right not to trust you. You've been gaslighting me for over a year, David Carter, but not anymore. Amy Scott will not kowtow to you any longer."

"It's him." David nodded towards Kyle. "You two seemed chummy when I came in. He's put you up to this."

"Kyle has done nothing of the sort. He's been supportive. He found and disabled the tracking app you put on my phone, which made me realize what a lowlife you are."

Kyle moved to her elbow. "You're fine. I can do this," Amy said.

She turned her verbal assault back to David. "All those phone calls from numbers I didn't recognize? They were from you. I didn't realize it at first, but when you sent the one that ended with *don't block me*, I knew for sure."

By now, everyone in the restaurant had stopped what they were doing and watched Amy tearing a strip off David.

"I'm tired of being dismissed, diminished, told I overreact, and you twisting everything I say and do to make you look good. We're done!" She removed her water glass from the bar and threw the contents at David. "Now, get out of my life!"

"Enough is enough," the man behind the bar said. "You need to calm down or I'll have to bar you."

"She's okay. Once he's out of here, normal service will resume."

Furious, David grabbed napkins, dried his face, and dropped the soggy mess on the floor. Afterwards, he stomped out the door.

The entire room burst into applause. The blood rushed to Amy's face. She had never been the centre of attention like this before and wasn't sure she wanted to be now.

Kyle wrapped Amy into a warm embrace. She did what she had to, and he was proud of her. She had stood up to the gaslighting bastard.

Complete strangers, moved by Amy's bravery, approached and congratulated her. Some offered warm hugs, others extended handshakes. Even the bartender, who had witnessed the entire confrontation, wasn't upset when it was all said and done.

Kyle knew he had to be vigilant to ensure David didn't linger in Lunenburg and cause Amy further trouble. He was determined to have a quiet word with the MacLeods, who lived across the street from the author's mansion, which Amy called home.

Before their meal arrived, he led her to a corner table where they weren't under the constant eye of the rest of the punters.

"I'm proud of you. You let David have it. You didn't hold back, Amy. That took immense courage," Kyle said, praising her and planting a gentle kiss on her forehead.

"I'm still shaking." Amy held her hand out.

"Adrenaline rush. It will pass."

"Scared stupid more like."

The bartender brought their meals to them."I thought I might have to bar you until I got the gist of what was happening. If you fancy staying around, I'll hire you as my bouncer."

Amy's lips curved into a smile, a rare sight since their impromptu meeting on the wharf. She was beautiful before, but now, after standing up to David, she seemed to radiate a newfound strength and beauty.

"Did I do all that? Say those things," Amy asked, still in disbelief at her courage to stand up to David. Her voice trembled with a mix of shock and pride.

"You sure did. I think the best part was when you threw your water in David's face," Kyle said, his tone filled with admiration for Amy's boldness.

"I can't believe I saw through his BS. I wish I had known sooner. I can be such a dunce sometimes."

"Don't beat yourself up over it. I saw some messages on your phone, don't forget. Not that I was being nosy. His methods were slick."

Amy turned her gaze to the plate of food before her and cut off a chunk of her fish. The freshness overwhelmed her. Unlike the fish and chip shops back home, someone must have caught this fish today. It was good there, but this blew them out of the water. The fries were golden and crispy, and the tartar sauce was homemade, not in those packets.

Amy ate every crumb on her plate, her appetite growing with each bite. When she and Kyle first came in, she was unsure what to expect and wasn't hungry. But as she savoured the flavours, she realized she had been more than she admitted. Her hunger extended beyond food.

After Kyle paid the bill, the two stood on the sidewalk facing the house she called home for the duration of the house swap. It was a mansion complete with a tower, surrounded by a low lintel-topped stone wall, and a garden bursting with colourful flowers. The front porch was cozy, perfect for lazy afternoons with a book and a cup of tea.

"Come back with me, please? I don't want to be alone right now."

Kyle thought all of his Christmases came at once with the invitation to go back to Amy's with her. Still, anything that happened would be up to her, not him. He'd be her punching bag, sounding board, whatever she needed.

They turned right when they left the Knot Pub and carried on up that side of the street. "If you go that way, there's a walking trail. I've never done it. Didn't fancy doing it by myself. Would you like to before you go home?"

Amy turned to him, her eyes still moist with tears. It was heartbreaking to see her like this, knowing that that creep had manipulated their relationship.

"Did you see the look on his face? He thought I'd let him waltz in and take over again."

Kyle nodded. Did he reply or let it fall unanswered? If he didn't give her the correct answer, things between them could end up pear-shaped. "You don't owe him anything, Amy. Not your time, not your explanation, nothing."

"I know, but we were together for a while. It's going to take me some time to process everything."

"You're on the right track. You've stood up to David's gaslighting, something I'm willing to bet he never expected."

Amy sighed. Best to let her come to terms with things in her time. He could still point out a few places of interest.

"This impressive place is the Lunenburg Inn," Kyle said, pointing to a grand Victorian building. "From what I've heard from tourists, their breakfasts are amazing."

"Looks nice."

Concerned for Amy's well-being, Kyle tried to gauge her comfort level. He didn't want to appear too overbearing, especially since he had been silent since they left the pub. He matched his pace to hers, not wanting to leave her behind. "Are you doing okay?"

No answer. Kyle and Amy continued in companionable silence until they crossed to the other side of the street to go down Archibald. "I just asked if you were okay," Kyle said.

"Not quite."

He reached towards her hand, and his fingers brushed against hers. She didn't pull back, so he took her hand.

Thirty-One

Isabelle Morrison's house, Falkland Street, Lunenburg, Nova Scotia

July 13 2019

The long walk after their pub meal helped Amy's frame of mind. A calmness had settled over her like a warm, fuzzy blanket.

The porch was serene, with two wicker tub chairs and a matching table set against the open side. Amy settled into the seat closest to the door, the evening's tranquillity wrapping around her. The space was snug, with little room between the furniture and the railing, forcing Kyle to sidle past her.

"I thought standing up to him would strengthen me, but I'm not so sure now," she said.

Kyle's hand reached across the table, enveloping Amy's in a warm, reassuring grip. "It's going to take time. You've proven you're strong, but you must have had some positive moments with him in all the negativity." His words were a comforting balm to Amy's troubled mind.

Amy sighed. Positive moments? Few. Perhaps in the early stages of her relationship with David. The only negative since she'd met Kyle by the water when she first arrived was David arriving unannounced.

The setting sun bathed the town in a breathtaking orange glow. As it dipped out of sight, the sky near the horizon turned a mesmerizing mauve and darker purple.

"There's the first star, Amy. Why don't you make a wish on it?"

"Isn't that kind of hokey?"

"Not a bit. Come on. If you do, so will I."

"All right," Amy said, closing her eyes and making her wish.

Kyle gazed over the street, his heart heavy with how David mistreated Amy. His past relationship had flaws, but he never subjected his partner to such manipulation. This David, he concluded, was on a power trip, and Amy was his unfortunate target. Kyle's heart bled for Amy, unable to fathom how anyone could inflict such cruelty on her.

He had vowed to stand by Amy, no matter the duration. He stole glances at her, searching for ways to ease her pain. For now, his mere presence seemed to bring her comfort. He was ready to take more drastic measures, even if it meant involving the MacLeods from across the street. The news of the pub incident had already spread through the town, but Kyle was determined to support Amy.

He glanced in her direction again. She had drawn her knees up to her chest, her toes gripping the edge of the seat. Her sandals sat on the porch where she'd slipped out of them. He couldn't tell if she looked at something specific or was in a deep meditative trance.

"Penny for them?" he asked.

"Hmm, they're not worth that much."

"They're worth more."

"I was thinking about Isabelle. How she's settling into my apartment. I miss my job," Amy said, her voice tinged with longing for her past life.

"What is it that Amy Scott does?" He leaned towards her.

"Nurse. I'm an RN and work at the new hospital in Sudbury. I miss the patients and looking after them. So what is it that Kyle does for a living?"

"Well, I work in Quality Control for High Liner Foods

during the week," he said, leaving it open for her to ask more.

"During the week, does that mean you have a second job?"

"I work for a company that does walking tours."

"You're a tour guide?"

"Yes, and a mighty fine one, if I say so myself. You'll have to come with me on one. I'll get you mate's rates."

"Shouldn't you have been at work the day we met?" Amy asked. She had lost track of time since she arrived. The simple fact of being out of David's reach had relaxed her so much.

"Holidays. I often pull a few tours during the week when I can."

Amy nodded. That made sense. What kind of tour guide would he make? The only way to find out would be to take him up on his offer. She yawned.

"Keeping you up?" Kyle asked.

"No. Just not used to this sea air."

"It is nice. I don't notice it so much anymore, having lived here all my life," Kyle said, his contentment clear in his voice.

"You never had the urge to leave? Go somewhere larger?" Kyle's life choices piqued Amy's curiosity.

"My father was a commercial fisherman. Wanted me to follow in his footsteps. Went out on his boat with him once. The seas were rough, and I got sick."

Amy giggled then asked, "Did you go away to school? Uni?"

"No, I didn't. I stayed here. Started working at the High Liner plant once I finished high school. Back then, I was on one of the processing lines. Over time, I worked my way up to my current position."

Kyle looked away. So far, he hadn't had to tell Amy about the accident that took his father's life and changed his world forever. The accident, a tragic fishing disaster, had left him with a deep sense of loss and guilt. He'd just as soon not do it now. Everyone who lived in Lunenburg at the time of the tragedy knew what happened.

"You're going to be all right?"

"I think so."

"I'm going to have a word with Gordon and Maggie, so you'll have someone else looking out for you. Not convinced David has left the village."

"I'll lock the door when I go in. Thanks for treating me to a meal. It was delicious."

Amy lowered her legs and slipped her feet into her sandals.

This was his cue to leave. She was strong, and he admired her for it. Still, he'd sleep better knowing the MacLeods across the street, his friends, would also look out for her.

Amy opened the screen door and punched in the combination for the lock. When she had it unlocked, she turned to Kyle again. "Thanks for everything. For being there. Believing in me."

"You're a strong woman, Amy. Stronger than you think." He leaned down and placed a gentle kiss on her lips. "Tomorrow, I'll come get you early and then you can go on my walking tour."

Kyle jogged down the steps, turned around and waved. Amy remained in the doorway. Before he reached the sidewalk, he heard the door close behind him.

Later that evening, after Kyle had stopped to talk to the MacLeods, Amy pulled out her phone. She had gained a peace she hadn't had in ages. The locals had been so good to her, treating her well and standing by her, especially one person. And when she stood up to David, something she never thought she would do, the whole pub rallied behind her. She shared her experience in the pub with Emma, sharing the warmth and solidarity of the community with her friend. She pulled out her phone and typed a message.

You'll never guess who just turned up here in Lunenburg. David. You'd be proud of me, Em. I stood my ground against him, something I've never been able to do. But I did it. I've grown so much, and I'm proud of the person I'm becoming.

Her mind flitted back to the confrontation in the pub. The low lighting, the smell of beer and sweat, the way David's sneer twisted his face. She liked the strength she displayed standing up to the creep. Even the other customers cheered for her when it was over. Kyle had wanted to intervene, but she refused his help. It was something she had to do herself. And she did.

Thirty-Two

Gordon and Maggie MacLeod's house, Falkland Street, Lunenburg, Nova Scotia

July 13, 2019

Kyle walked up the front steps at the MacLeod home. He'd known the couple all his life, and used to be close with their son, John, until he moved to British Columbia for work. The two stayed in touch, but it wasn't the same as when they lived here in the sleepy town of Lunenburg. Although today, that wasn't so much the case.

It wasn't because he thought the MacLeods would refuse his request, but it brought everything home — it made things real. As Kyle raised his hand, Gordon appeared. "Hi, Mr. MacLeod. I wonder if I might have a quick word with you and your wife."

"Of course, come on in," Gordon said, ushering Kyle to the kitchen. "You don't stop by often anymore. What can we do for you?"

Gordon's tone was friendly, but a flicker of concern had crept into his eyes.

The man pulled a kitchen chair out from under the table and beckoned Kyle to sit. He took a deep breath. Was he overstepping? After what happened at the pub, he didn't think so.

And the MacLeods were this area's unofficial neighbourhood watch couple.

"Well, it's about Amy."

"What about her? Is she sick?"

"Not really, but I'm worried about her. When I left her, I told her I was coming here to have a quiet word with you folks."

"Go on."

Was Kyle right to share Amy's personal history? Probably not, but if it meant someone else keeping watch meant keeping her safe, then it was worth it. "Her partner/boyfriend, whatever you want to call him, found out where she was. He learned about the house swap when he visited her apartment in Sudbury. And to make a long story short, he lied to Izzy, saying they rushed Amy's mother to the hospital and he needed to find her."

"And that would be the young man who arrived here earlier today. Flash car, suit."

"He's not a nice guy. He mistreated Amy in the past. He's been gaslighting her for ages. I don't want her to be blindsided by him and his behaviour again." His voice hadn't betrayed him, but he clenched his hands. Kyle stopped and took a deep breath. Had that come out like a rant? He hadn't planned to sound panicked — just honest.

Gordon mulled over everything Kyle had told him. Amy seemed like a nice girl based on what he had seen and what Maggie had shared. His wife brought Amy a meal soon after her arrival, then left. Amy seemed distracted, apologized for not being good company, and repeatedly checked her phone.

And now, he had told David where to find Amy. If he had known then what he found out now, he would never have suggested David try the wharf.

"Did he find her?" Gordon asked.

"Yes, but not until we'd gone to the pub for something to eat. You would have been proud of her, Mr. MacLeod, she stood up to him. I wanted to step in, but she didn't need me. She did it all on her own. I'd like it if you and your wife would keep an eye out for her. Make sure he doesn't come back."

That was it, Gordon decided. He'd sent David straight to Amy. Knowing he'd unwittingly helped, the guilt settled in his chest, a constant reminder of his unwitting involvement. But, he was even more determined to keep her safe. He had listened to Kyle and started planning in his mind.

Small-town living meant everyone knew everyone else's business. Most times, it was a burden, but sometimes, like now, it was a blessing. If Gordon had anything to do with it, this David character wouldn't so much as glimpse Amy again. The community was a shield, and Gordon was ready to wield it.

Footsteps on the stairs preceded Maggie's arrival in the kitchen, where her husband and son's friend sat at the table. She pulled out a chair with a sigh of contentment. "It's nice to see you, Kyle."

"Good to see you, too."

"Kyle was asking if we would keep Amy in our sights. I knew she was afraid of something or someone when I saw her the first time, but I didn't want to pry," Gordon said. "And now, I understand that first impression was right."

"What do you mean, dear?" Maggie asked, rising to fill the kettle.

Maggie said nothing more, letting the memories of her quick visit with Amy fill the space between them. She had taken a casserole, nothing fancy, but something warm. Even then, the tension radiating from the young woman was tangible. Apologetic, distracted … haunted. She hadn't asked questions. She hadn't needed to. It wasn't the first time a woman arrived in town to escape something or someone. She didn't need all the details to connect the dots.

"You'll stay for a cup of tea, Kyle?"

"No thanks, Mrs. MacLeod. I've taken up enough of your time already," he said, standing. "I'm glad you'll keep an eye out. Amy is vulnerable now and doesn't need David to add to her stress."

Maggie walked him to the front door. In Lunenburg, folks looked after their own, and Amy was one of them as long as she stayed across the street in Izzy's house. The villagers would look out for her.

"That's Kyle away," she said when she returned to the kitchen.

Gordon nodded.

The teapot, cozy snug around it, steam curling from the spout, sat in the middle of the table. Her husband had tended to it while she walked Kyle to the front door.

The protective tone in Kyle's voice stuck with her. It reminded her of Gordon when their children were small. The worry that only came from instinct. Maggie had learned long ago to trust instinct. Kyle's anxiety stems from David's troubles. In the morning, she'd take a spare set of house keys to Izzy's so if Amy needed a quiet, safe place to get away from David, she'd have one.

Thirty-Three

Isabelle Morrison's House, Falkland Street, Lunenburg, Nova Scotia

July 13, 2019

Amy sat on the edge of the bed in Izzy's front bedroom, staring out the window into the deepening twilight. A breeze lifted the curtain just enough to flutter it like a ghost, soft and uncertain. Below, the porch light from the MacLeods' house glowed warm and familiar.

She drew her knees up, resting her chin there.

Kyle had assured her he would talk to them, just a quick word, he'd promised. And while she trusted him, more than she should after so short a time, the idea of someone else knowing made her stomach tighten. Not because the MacLeods weren't kind, but because that made it real.

No longer just a terrible memory or a buried part of her life in Sudbury, where she had experienced David's gaslighting.

Now, it was here. In Lunenburg. Breathing the same sea air, which was now tainted with unpleasant memories.

Her phone vibrated on the nightstand. She froze. It wasn't Emma. She wouldn't text this late.

The screen lit up, and though Amy didn't turn her head, she

saw the telltale length of the preview flash and vanish. David. It had to be.

She didn't reach for it. Didn't need to see the words for the familiar unease to tighten her spine. She had already spent too many hours analyzing David's messages, questioning their intent and looking for hidden traps beneath a surface of concern.

Not tonight.

Amy crossed to the window, folding her arms across her chest. The MacLeods' kitchen light flicked on. A soft shadow moved past, Maggie, she assumed, making tea. That thought gave her an odd sense of comfort. Maggie reminded her of her grandmother who'd taught her to bake and not take nonsense from anyone.

If Kyle had gone there asking them to keep an eye out, she knew he'd done it with her best interest at heart. He was like that, gentle but unafraid to stand firm.

She let her fingers rest on the windowsill.

Tomorrow she'd go for a walk up through the old town. The thought of fresh air, quiet, and crooked houses calmed something in her.

One step at a time. That's all Amy could manage.

And for tonight, she didn't have to be strong. She could just be still.

Thirty-Four

Isabelle Morrison's House, Falkland Street, Lunenburg, Nova Scotia

July 14, 2019

The soft morning light filtered through the curtains in the bedroom window. Amy blinked, letting her eyes become used to it. Her phone pinged with a notification. She reached out to pick it up from the bedside table, fumbling with it and almost dropping it.

When she grasped it, Amy touched the screen, and Emma's name appeared. She opened the text app.

Just got your message. Holy, Amy! I am SO proud of you. You stood your ground. That man doesn't deserve a second of your time or energy. I hope you're basking in that strength right now because, wow, you did that.

A second message came in on the heels of the first.

Text me when you're up. I want to hear everything. Also, I hope Kyle cheered. Or swooned. Or both.

Amy's lips tugged into a grin. The memory of her standing up to David was still fresh. She held the phone to her chest for a second and breathed in the soft scent of sun-dried sheets. She tapped a quick reply.

Thank you. It felt good, liberating even. I'll fill you in after breakfast. Kyle swooned. Quietly, but I saw it.

As Amy suspected the night before, the other message came in from David. He'd only send her more if she ignored it and persisted until she replied. She didn't need the hassle. She had hoped that after she stood up to him, he'd return to Sudbury with his tail between his legs. Go home, lick his wounds, and stay out of her life.

With a steadying breath, she opened the thread. The message was shorter than she expected.

Amy, I didn't come all this way to fight. I think we should talk. We were good once, weren't we? I know things got off track, but I still care about you. Let's not throw it all away.

She read it twice. Not because she believed it, but because it still had that familiar undertone. The guilt-wrapped kindness. The invitation to step back into a role she no longer wanted to play.

Once, a message like that would have cracked her resolve.

Not today.

Amy hit the 'info' button in the top corner of the screen, scrolled down, and tapped *Block this Caller*. Her thumb hovered over the ultimate confirmation.

She pressed it.

And just like that, David's number was blocked. No fireworks, no confetti. Just quiet silence. But inside, a heavy burden lifted.

Amy swung her legs out of bed and stretched, the tension unwinding from her shoulders. Downstairs, she imagined the kettle in Izzy's kitchen starting to hum.

Today, she'd make breakfast. Text Emma. Spend time with Kyle. She didn't need David's permission for any of it.

Amy was rinsing her cereal bowl when the knock came at the door.

Not loud. Just a polite *tap-tap*, followed by the soft creak of the screen door opening and closing again. Amy, unsettled, dried her hands on the dish towel and peeked through the side window. Maggie MacLeod stood on the porch, a familiar basket in one hand and a small ring of keys in the other.

Amy opened the door. "Morning, Maggie."

"Morning, dear." Maggie's warm smile, a beacon of comfort, deepened the soft lines around her eyes. "Thought you might be up. I brought these." She held up the keys. "Spare set for our place. In case you ever need a quick getaway, or just a cup of tea without an audience."

Amy blinked. "Thank you. That's ... so kind."

"Lunenburg looks after its own," Maggie said, her words a blanket of security. "And while you're staying in Izzy's house, that includes you."

Amy swallowed the lump in her throat. "I'm not planning to run, but it's good to know I've got somewhere to go if things get weird."

Maggie nodded. "Kyle filled us in. Not all the details, but enough. Gordon and I, well, we just want you to realize you're safe here. That man shows up again, and he'll have half the street watching him like a hawk."

A small laugh slipped out of Amy, unexpected and a little shaky. "Remind me not to get on the wrong side of your neighbourhood watch."

"Smart girl," Maggie said, eyes twinkling. "Now. There are blueberry muffins in the basket. Warm them up a bit, and they'll taste fresh out of the oven."

Amy took the keys and the basket, her fingers brushing against Maggie's. "Thanks. For everything."

"Anytime, love." Maggie turned to go, then paused. "Oh, and Kyle mentioned you're off on the walking tour later?"

Amy nodded.

"He said to tell you he'd come by before it starts. Something about a surprise. Sounded like mischief to me," Maggie said with a mischievous twinkle in her eye, her humour lightening the mood.

With a wink, Maggie was off, the screen door clacking shut behind her.

Amy stood there for a moment, holding the still-warm basket, keys dangling in her fingers, her heart just a little lighter than it had been.

Kyle stepped onto Izzy's porch, the morning sun glinting off the brass mailbox as he rapped his knuckles against the door. It opened almost immediately, like she'd been waiting just behind it.

Amy smiled, tucking a loose strand of hair behind her ear. "Morning."

"Hey." He shoved his hands in his pockets to resist the urge to smooth down his hair. "Ready for the tour?"

"As I'll ever be. I still don't know what to expect."

Kyle grinned. "That's half the fun."

She stepped out and pulled the door shut behind her, slipping the strap of her small crossbody bag over her shoulder. He noticed the edge of a muffin peeking out of a napkin tucked into the side pouch.

"Did Maggie already pay you a visit?" he asked.

"She brought muffins and spare keys. It seemed like a hug in basket form."

He chuckled. "That sounds like her. You must've made a good impression."

They started walking toward his place, the sidewalk warm under their feet the ocean's scent curled through the breeze.

"I'm guessing you live nearby?" she asked.

"Yup. Apartment over a bakery on Lincoln Street. Close enough to smell bread at 3 a.m., which is a blessing or a curse depending on how hungry you are."

Amy laughed then said, "Dangerous."

They walked in a comfortable silence, the only sound being the rhythmic tapping of their footsteps on the warm sidewalk. "So, any hints about what this tour involves?"

He smirked. "Let's just say I have to make a quick wardrobe change before we head out."

"Wardrobe change?" she echoed.

"You'll see," he said, eyes forward but a mischievous smile playing on his lips, adding to the playful mystery of the moment.

She gave him a mock-suspicious look. "That sounds ominous."

"I prefer mysterious. Builds suspense."

Amy shook her head, but he caught the smile she tried to hide. The tension etched into her shoulders when she first arrived in Lunenburg was lifting. And if walking her to his place and making her laugh, even a little, helped chip away at it, he'd consider it a win.

They turned the corner, his building now in sight.

"Welcome to the launch pad," he said, gesturing to the stairs leading up to the upstairs living quarters. "You'll wait in the living room. No peeking while I change."

She raised an eyebrow. "Now I *am* curious."

"You should be," he said. "Just ... try not to laugh too hard."

Amy's smile widened. "No promises."

Thirty-Five

Kyle's apartment, Lincoln Street, Lunenburg, Nova Scotia

July 14, 2019

Amy gasped as she entered the cozy space and into Kyle's apartment. Kyle held the door, allowing her to enter first, then rushed across the room and picked up a few errant pieces of clothing on the hardwood floor. A skylight over the wall of windows let in even more light, making it bright and cheery. One wall had shelves of nautical books and an old coast map. Her eyes landed on a wooden panel with the name *Seaworthy* painted on it.

"What's that?" she asked, her voice soft as she crossed the room to look closer. Although chipped in places and worn at the edges, the bold letters of the name still stood out against the bright red paint.

Kyle, who had disappeared, returned and glanced over at it. A flicker of emotion crossed his face before he turned back to her. "That came off my dad's boat," he said, his voice quiet but steady. "It was his pride and joy. She sank in a storm about fifteen years ago, and, well …" His words trailed off.

Amy took a step closer, her hand reaching out to trace the

name with her fingertips. "I'm sorry, Kyle," she said, her voice softening. "That must've been so hard."

Kyle shrugged, though his eyes clouded for a moment. "It was. It's hard not to think about all the what-ifs. The boat was more than just a means to make a living. It was … him, y'know? Every time I see that panel, it reminds me of him and what he did. And everything that went wrong after." Despite the weight of his words, there was a resilience in his voice that was inspiring.

"My mother had to go out to work after that. The insurance company refused to pay out. She never said why and thought I was too young to understand, but I think the policy had lapsed, so there was no insurance on the boat. My older brother was on the boat that day. Lost him, too. Mom died two years ago. Ovarian cancer got her."

Amy met his gaze, her heart heavy. "You've been through so much," she said, her voice thick with emotion. She empathized with his situation, drawing him closer to her in that moment.

Kyle nodded. Neither of them spoke.

"Thanks for sharing that with me," she said, breaking the silence. "I appreciate it's difficult."

Kyle turned to her. "It's all right. Part of who I am. And speaking of that, I have to get dressed and ready for the tour. Make yourself at home."

Once again, Kyle disappeared into another room. Amy looked around the combined living room and kitchen. A stack of dirty dishes sat in the sink. She looked around for a dish rack and placed it on the counter. Before Kyle returned, she had washed, rinsed, and left the dishes to air dry in the rack.

"Well, what do you think?" he asked.

Amy turned around and burst into laughter.

Kyle stood in the doorway, decked out in costume. Her hands flew to her mouth, trying and failing to stifle the sound. "I don't know what to say," she said, her laughter bubbling up at the sight of him.

He struck a dramatic pose, chest out, with one hand on his hip. The other held a brass spyglass for show. His outfit was peak theatrical flair — a loose, billowy shirt tucked into knee-length breeches, a brown vest cinched over top, and a red sash knotted around his waist. Buckled shoes completed the look, and an askew tricorn hat perched on his head somehow made it all even better.

Amy bent forward with laughter. She couldn't help herself. "Well, you look like a pirate. Do you talk like one, too?"

"Argh, me hearties. Shiver me timbers, if it isn't a pretty lassie."

That did it. Amy laughed so hard she had to grab the back of a nearby chair to stay upright.

"We'd better make tracks if I'm going to get there on time." Kyle guided Amy towards the door.

"I'm sure the tourists love it." She paused. "Where does the tour start?"

"Lunenburg Academy. About a ten-minute walk from here." Kyle ushered Amy into the corridor and locked the apartment behind them. He wasn't sure what kind of reaction he would receive from Amy, but her laughing wasn't it. Still, she seemed happier and more relaxed than the previous evening after her partner turned up at The Knot Pub.

Recounting the story of his parents and older brother brought the night of the storm back into his conscience. He had buried it deep, in what he thought was a secure place. But now, the flood of memories was overwhelming. Each time it resurfaced, it took longer to push it back into the depths of his mind.

"What made you decide to dress like a pirate for your walking tours?"

"Not a pirate, but a privateer. John Ordronaux was a privateer back during the War of 1812. They claim I'm a descendant, but I've never been able to trace it. All I've discovered was he was born in France and died in Colombia."

"It explains your flair for drama. The costume. The poses." A snicker escaped again. "Sorry. I'll try to be serious. Are you still trying to prove your connection to the man?"

"Gave up. It's more of a family legend but works well when I give tours."

"Have you ever done one of those genealogical DNA tests? Would that help prove anything?"

"Not interested."

Thirty-Six

Essential Lunenburg Walking Tour, Lunenburg, Nova Scotia

July 14, 2019

Amy stopped asking questions about Kyle and his connection to the privateer before he thought she was being nosy. "My grandfather used to come out with some strange things. Michael and I were little when he died, but I remember his saying, 'you're just a Tom Longboat.' I never understood what he meant when he said that to one of us. I thought he was saying he was a relative. My older brothers likely knew, but they weren't about to tell us. When I got older, I looked up Tom Longboat at the library. He was a long-distance runner, and, not that this is politically correct, he was a North American Indian. No way, he's related to me."

"Brothers? How many kids are in your family?"

"Christopher is the oldest, then Roger, then Michael — my twin — and Melissa is the youngest. Besides your brother, who died with your father, do you have any other siblings?"

"No," Kyle said.

It must have been hard for him to lose his only sibling in the same accident as his father. She had only lost one, and that was long before Amy was even born. And then, she and her sister and brothers didn't find out until after their father's funeral. He had forbidden their mother to talk about her, ever. Punishment for the baby being stillborn?

"We're here. You think you'll be able to remain serious for the tour?"

A smile tugged at the corners of Amy's mouth. "I'll try." She couldn't guarantee it would work, but she'd at least give it a go.

Between ten and fifteen people milled about in front of the academy building.

Kyle stepped up to the stairs. "You're all here for the tour?" he called out. "Great! If you could come a little closer? That's it. Don't worry, I don't bite. My name is Kyle, and I'm your guide for this walking tour of Lunenburg. And the one giggling over there, that's Amy Scott. Expect her to burst out laughing during our walk through the town. She's been doing it since she saw me dressed in my privateer costume." Kyle's introduction was humorous, and ended with a flourish, when he swept off his tricorn hat and gave an exaggerated bow.

"Do we get costumes, too?" A man near the back of the group asked.

Amy couldn't help it; she burst into laughter again, surprising even herself.

Kyle's tour of the town took Amy through streets she would never have found on her own. He paused in front of a bright blue house on one narrow lane. "Now, if you look up at that distinctive overhang," Kyle said, gesturing, "you'll see what's known as the Lunenburg Bump — a signature feature of our local architecture. These were common in the homes of merchants and sea captains. It gave them a clear view of the harbour, perfect for watching their ships. Also, the fishermen's wives waited up here for the safe return of their men." Kyle's breath hitched. "Of course, some say it was less about spotting ships and more about ensuring their crew didn't sneak off to the taverns."

"You mean the eighteenth-century version of a tracking

app," Amy said, drawing giggles from the others.

"That's right. We're not the first generation to keep tabs on people. That's the version I prefer, anyway. But if you ask an architect, they'll tell you it was just about getting more light inside. Boring."

Confident, knowledgeable, funny. Amy could even get past the crazy costume, a flamboyant 18th-century ensemble complete with a tricorn hat and a long coat that billowed dramatically in the wind. They moved on, winding through streets lined with churches, houses, shops, and restaurants. The tour ended at the water, where the group drifted off. A few tourists approached Kyle to thank him, and to Amy's surprise, several slipped him tips. She didn't know if it was a paid or volunteer gig, but he was excellent.

Amy walked up to him when the last group members had wandered off. "You had them eating out of your hand," she said. "I knew nothing about Lunenburg when I first arrived, but now I do. The houses are beautiful. I think the 'bump' might be my new favourite thing. I've seen nothing like it before today."

"Careful." Kyle lifted off his tricorn and fanned himself. "Flattery will get you everywhere."

Amy rolled her eyes, but the grin was already forming. Before she could respond, one straggler from the tour doubled back towards them — an older gentleman with sunglasses and a wide-brimmed hat.

"I just want to say, young man, you missed your calling," the tourist said with utter seriousness. "You could be in movies. You've got the look, the hat, and the flair. Ever thought of Hollywood?"

Kyle blinked. "Only every time I walk by a window and catch my reflection."

The man nodded, then turned to Amy. "And you, young lady, don't let this one get away. He's got charisma."

Amy opened her mouth, speechless, and watched as the man tipped his hat and wandered off, convinced he'd just set them up for life.

She looked at Kyle, and he looked back, trying to keep a straight face. It lasted all of three seconds.

Amy burst out laughing, clutching her side. "I can't — I

don't even know what to say. That was … incredible."

Kyle grinned. "Told you this costume had powers."

"Now that my tour is over," Kyle said. The last echoes of the crowd's energy drained from his limbs, "is there anything you'd like to do or see on our own?"

Amy stood a few feet ahead, her back to him, facing out over the water. The breeze, carrying the sea's salty tang, lifted a strand of her hair, and Kyle watched her. The way she held her arms around herself, the subtle shift in her weight, like she wasn't ready to move on just yet, was a sight to behold.

She turned towards him with a shrug. "It's a small town, what else is there to see? I think we've walked down every street imaginable."

"Not quite," he said, his voice filled with anticipation. "You haven't seen my street without me dressed as a privateer."

That earned a faint smile, not a laugh, but close. Encouraging.

"Why don't we go back to mine, and I'll get out of my privateer get-up. I promise I'm less embarrassing in regular clothes." He grinned at her, his eyes sparkling with mischief.

Her smile widened, a warm expression that hinted at her growing fondness. "I'm not sure I believe that."

"Guess you'll have to find out," he said, a mischievous glint in his eye.

They started walking back up the hill, the streets quieter now that the tour groups had dispersed. The town was tranquil without the buzz of visitors, like it had exhaled. Kyle also liked this version of Lunenburg — quieter, more personal, just them.

As they neared his apartment on Lincoln Street, Amy slowed, her gaze caught by the window display next door. It was a little artisan shop filled with hand-painted ceramics and coastal artwork.

Kyle paused beside her. "You can stay here and look. Go in. I'll meet you back here. Won't be long."

Amy glanced at him. "Are you sure?"

"Yeah." He gestured towards his front door with a grin. "I need to ditch Captain Bucklehat anyway."

That got a soft snort. "That's not his name."

"It is now."

She rolled her eyes and turned towards the shop. Kyle watched her enter before heading to his place, a smile tugging at his mouth. He'd retire his privateer costume for the day, but how Amy looked at him now, maybe he wasn't just comic relief, that stuck with him more than anything else.

Amy nodded as Kyle continued to his apartment. An antique shop bell sounded above her when she pushed open the door and stepped inside. The aromatic scent of citrus and wood greeted her. The shop was a treasure trove — a mix of locally made jewellery, coastal-themed home accessories, whimsical T-shirts, and handmade goods. Everything appeared vibrant and intentional. It was a place that invited slow growth.

Drawn to the display of scented candles, Amy picked up one in an open jar and sniffed it. It smelled of driftwood and sun-warmed sand, like walking along a quiet beach. She smiled to herself and reached for another.

Nearby, a small stand of incense caught her attention. She wasn't a fan — most brands were too overpowering, but this one intrigued her. The label read *Orange Grove + Herb Garden*, and the scent was warm and earthy with a soft citrus note that made her mouth water. Twenty bamboo sticks came bundled inside the package. She could give Emma one even if she didn't use them all. She tucked two into her basket, along with the beach-scented candle.

It was too early to even think of Christmas, but the shop exuded a cozy, gift-worthy vibe surrounding Amy. She could spend far more here than she intended, and part of her didn't mind.

The door chimed again as she paid for her purchases, and Kyle walked in. The shop attendant smiled at him in a way that made Amy wonder how many people he knew by name in this town.

"You have me for the rest of today and all day tomorrow," he said, stepping beside her. "What would you like to do?"

"You're the local," Amy said, slipping her change into her wallet. "What else is there to do? Honestly, before the morning walking tour, I didn't know what was there in Lunenburg. Izzy

— she prefers that to Isabelle — said little about the town. Not even about her mansion."

"You mean Izzy Morrison, the author?" the shop worker said, looking surprised.

"Yes. I'm on a house swap with her. She's at my place in Ontario," Amy said, keeping it vague. The size of her home province gave her confidence to tell the woman that much.

"She is, shall we say, eccentric," the woman said with a polite laugh.

Kyle nodded. "That's fair."

Amy still hadn't met Izzy, but her enormous house's decor leaned in that direction.

"May I suggest the Haunted Lunenburg walk?" the woman offered. "You've led that one before, haven't you, Kyle?"

"Covering for a regular guide. Could be fun. We just finished the Essential Lunenburg Tour. What do you say, Amy?" he asked. "I mean, if you're not too tired from walking." The prospect of the Haunted Lunenburg walk, with its promise of mystery and history, was too intriguing to resist.

Amy shook her head. "I'm a nurse, so I'm used to being on my feet for long periods. Sure. Let's do it. But before we do anything else, I want to take this stuff back to the house so I'm not dragging it around all day."

"Fair enough. Captain Bucklehat needs a break, too."

She groaned and said, "Stop calling him that."

"Never," Kyle said, smiling with a mischievous glint in his eye, their banter adding a lightness to the air.

Thirty-Seven

Haunted Lunenburg Walk, King Street, Lunenburg, Nova Scotia

July 14, 2019

Amy pulled her zip-front hoodie around her. She and Kyle were the first to arrive at the King Street starting point for the Haunted Walk. "Did you say you led this tour before?" she asked.

"Yes. I covered for the regular guide who was sick. Only did it the once, though."

"Get spooked by a ghost?"

"No."

"Is Lunenburg haunted, like for real?" She fidgeted with excitement, or was it nerves? "I know growing up in Ottawa, there was talk about several haunted places there. I did no tours, though."

"You'll be fine." Kyle put his hands on her upper arms. "You're with me. What could go wrong?"

Amy suppressed a giggle. Where Kyle was concerned, plenty could go wrong. Still, it was nice of him to spend time with her. Except for the MacLeods, he was the only other person she knew in the town.

Their guide arrived soon after, and after that, the others who had booked the tour did, too. Lanterns were lit, and the tour began. It was eight thirty and wasn't quite dark yet, but it would be soon. This last bit of light disappeared quickly.

"It won't surprise you to hear that this building is haunted. If you look up into the windows in the 'bump', sometimes you'll see the image of a woman gazing out as if looking for someone to come back. Legend says she's the ghost of a woman who lost her lover at sea. Now she's waiting for his return from the beyond," the guide said, adding a chilling detail to the story.

Amy looked up, as did the others on the tour. Unfortunately, whoever the ghosts were, they weren't in the mood to manifest this night.

The next stop on the tour was the Bascawen Inn. "The lovely, quaint hotel is home to a nasty ghost. The poltergeist activity ranges from playful to downright murderous. I'm sure you've all read the book, *The Shining*, or seen the movie based on it. This place reminds me of the hotel in it."

Amy listened intently, her eyes wide with anticipation.

Someone asked about the ghostly activity, but the guide was reluctant to say more. Her eyes darted around as if she were afraid of being overheard. "If you follow me, we'll walk towards Lunenburg Town Hall."

The group stopped just short of the building near the bandstand next door. "This quiet, quaint town wasn't always this way. We had an overabundance of axe murderers here in Lunenburg, and one poor soul met his end here."

"*So I Married an Axe Murderer*," someone said, drawing laughter from everyone.

"You could say that, but it wasn't comedic. Apparently, the murderers got it into their heads that it was the quickest way to dispatch someone," said their guide.

The night air became damp when darkness set in, bringing Amy out in goosebumps. Or was it the talk of axe murders that chilled her?

Kyle leaned closer to Amy. "Lunenburg, come for the scenery, stay because you've been … axed." He paused, then said, "Guess that's why they didn't put 'axe murderers' on the town welcome signs."

The tour guide led them to the next stop. As they walked, the gravel along the edge of the narrow street crunched under their feet.

"This is St. John's Anglican Church. Unfortunately, arsonists set fire to this church in 2001. The townspeople rebuilt it using timber recovered from the fire. During the restoration, they discovered a pattern of stars in the dome over the altar. Something didn't look right in their layout, but investigations showed they were in the right position for Jesus's birth."

That drew a few oohs and aahs from the attendees. "Another thing is that when they open the crypt to add another coffin, those already there are in disarray, as if they had shifted on their own. Even after re-stacking the coffins, the crypt showed the same disarray upon the next opening. Ghostly disturbances? Shifting ground because of underground springs? You be the judge."

A shiver ran up Amy's back. She rubbed her upper arms to warm herself. She turned to Kyle. He was examining the ceiling.

They made their way to Hillcrest Cemetery, but stopped outside the Lunenburg Academy, where the walking tour she had taken earlier started. "People know this area as Gallows Hill. A few ghosts also haunt The Academy, built in 1895. The students referred to the basement as the 'dungeon' because, according to them, there was an evil presence about the place. Boys egged one another on to go down there alone, but girls wouldn't go on their own. They always went in twos. One day, while a carpenter worked in the building, the hairs on the back of his neck stood on end." A dramatic pause for effect. "He saw the ghost of a man strung up by the neck before it faded."

Their guide led them to the nearby cemetery. "Generations have passed down many stories about this 300-plus-year-old place. But, the grave I most want to tell you about is this way."

Until they reached the cemetery, people had walked in a spread-out line. Here, they walked either single-file or, with Amy and Kyle, side by side. Amy kept her eyes on the ground to ensure she didn't trip over a headstone. The evening dew had settled on the grass, making it damp and cold. Perhaps wearing shorts and sandals wasn't the best at night.

They stopped when they reached a stone surrounded by a wrought-iron fence.

"This is the grave of Sophia McLaughlin, who died at fourteen in 1879. Now, you might not find it all that unusual that a young girl died back then. Vaccinations didn't exist. Antibiotics were unheard of. But Sophia died of a broken heart."

Something furry rubbed against Amy's bare leg, making her jump and yelp.

"You okay, Amy?" Kyle asked.

"Something touched my leg."

"You so wrapped up in the tour that you're imagining things?"

Amy swatted his arm.

The guide continued her story. "A woman who owned a dressmaking shop on Lincoln Street apprenticed Sophia. Her employer often left her son and Sophia alone in the shop while she did her other chores. After counting the money, the till was $10.00 short one day. Back then, that was a huge amount of money. The woman accused Sophia of stealing it, which she denied. It didn't end there. The employer went around the town and told everyone the girl was a thief. These actions devastated Sophia and ruined her family's reputation."

"Did they ever find out who stole the money?" someone asked.

Amy sidled closer to Kyle and took hold of his arm.

"Just checking ... you're not getting spooked by *ghostly* fur, are you?"

"Laugh it up, pirate boy. Just you wait until something brushes against your leg," Amy said with a hint of snark in her voice.

The guide continued. "Sophia became very ill. Townspeople often saw her lying on her sister's grave, reading her Bible and crying. Even her mother accepted the version of events and that her daughter was a thief. In time, her condition worsened, and her family confined her to her room, where she died. The cause of death was 'paralysis of the heart, brought on by extreme agitation and peculiar circumstances.' On her deathbed, Sophia wrote to the woman, still denying the theft. In that letter, she quoted several passages from the Bible. After her death, the employer's son confessed to stealing the money."

Before they left the cemetery, Amy reached out and touched the heart suspended on a chain from the wrought-iron fence surrounding young Sophia's grave. It was ice cold and clammy. She yanked her hand back as if something from the other side had touched her.

Kyle had heard many ghost stories over the years growing up in Lunenburg. Even the one about Sophia. But when Amy jumped and yelped, it spooked him. He saw nothing in the lantern light. Not that they were bright. It was probably a cat. Plenty of them were around town, and even more mice in the cemetery. A raccoon, maybe? Or a fox? Still, unless spooked or sick, they wouldn't barge through a group of people. Or would they?

He stole a glance at Amy. She was brushing her hand on the leg of her shorts, as if trying to rid herself of something sticky or clinging. Her sudden change in demeanour was evident. She looked pale, and the bravado she had shown moments ago was now replaced with uncertainty.

The rest of the Haunted Lunenburg walk was with no further incidents, furry or otherwise. It was just after ten o'clock when the tour ended. All the walking he'd worked up a thirst. A pint at The Knot Pub, or one of the other bars in the town, would be most welcome. "Do you want to go for a drink and something to eat? We didn't eat much between the tours."

"Sure. Same place as before? That way, it's not too far for me to walk home."

Kyle nodded. He'd walk her home anyway, even though the house was just across the street from the bar. They walked in companionable silence. He debated putting his arm around her, but she might think that was too personal. After all, they'd only met a few days ago. He reached for her hand. It was freezing. "Are you cold?"

Amy shook her head.

"You're awfully quiet. Are you okay?"

"Thinking about that poor girl who died. If that boy had confessed straight away, she wouldn't have."

"We don't know that for sure," he said. "Losing her sister

must have been devastating. There might have been more going on. Something no one could see."

Thirty-Eight

The Knot Pub, Dufferin Street, Lunenburg, Nova Scotia

July 14, 2019

Kyle held the door for Amy, a gesture she acknowledged with a nod. "You paid yesterday, so it's my treat tonight," she said as she strode past him.

He had never let a woman pay for his meals before, and the idea didn't sit well with him. It was a role reversal that unsettled him. "I don't mind, you know. You're supposed to be here on holiday."

Amy turned and stared him in the eyes. Her expression said it all — over her dead body. The Haunted Lunenburg walk, with its spine-chilling tales, had been enough. He wasn't interested in hearing more ghost stories. "All right then."

They found the same table available as the day before. It was later in the evening, so Kyle wanted nothing heavy to eat. Amy might share the same sentiment. A big meal this late could disrupt the night in various ways.

In the end, they both chose the Roast Beef on a Bun and got a side of sweet potato fries to share. The aroma of the roast beef made Kyle's stomach growl, and Amy's eyes lit up at the sight of the sweet potato fries.

Amy's taste buds went into overdrive with the first bite of her sandwich. It perfectly combined cheese, mayonnaise, garlic butter and tomato. The whole thing was so thick that she couldn't get her mouth around it, so she cut hers in two. Still, it wasn't easy, but she only had to handle half at a time.

"I'm looking forward to exploring the walking trail near here. Are you available to do it with me tomorrow?" Amy asked, her eyes sparkling with anticipation.

"I can be."

"Don't take time off work on my account."

"Holidays. I don't have any walking tours scheduled, so we need to decide which one you want to take. We could visit Mahone Bay, or take the Back Harbour Trail back to town. This trail goes along the other side of the peninsula. We could finish up with a stop at the Ironworks Distillery. No, can't do that. They aren't open on Mondays. So much for that idea."

"I don't mind not being able to do that. Hopefully, we can go when the place is open before I go home."

"You just got here. Don't talk about leaving." Kyle said, reaching across the table and placing his hand on Amy's, a gesture of his comforting presence.

"I don't want to leave, but I understand Izzy wants to return to her house when she finishes her novel. I don't think she'd be too happy if I were to stay on at her place when she gets home." Amy expressed her empathy for Izzy.

"When you return to Izzy's tonight, check if she has any reusable water bottles. You'll want to fill one to take with you, unless, it's raining, which means we have to postpone for another day. If she doesn't, send me a text. I have a couple of spares."

Kyle sounded like a mother hen as he instructed Amy to bring water for the walk. He always carried a bottle when he led a walking tour because he got thirsty from talking. He noticed she didn't have one when they did the tour earlier. And the haunted walk started at dusk and finished after dark. Now, they were in the pub enjoying a late meal.

If he were smart, he could find out tonight. He could walk

Amy back to the house, and she could check before he walked down the street to his apartment.

He pulled out his phone, brought up the trail map, and turned the device so Amy could see. "It looks like it's quite the distance, but it's only about three kilometres. So forty minutes to an hour to walk. And when we reach the end, we can go down to Sawpit Wharf Park and sit by the water for a bit."

Amy took his phone from him to inspect the trail. She was used to being on her feet for long periods. The trail followed the old rail line, with trees lining both sides, their leaves rustling in the gentle breeze, and, likely, bugs, specifically mosquitoes, buzzing in the air.

She handed Kyle's phone back to him. There hadn't been an abundance of insects during the ghost walk, so maybe Lunenburg wasn't to their liking. She had packed lightweight long pants and would wear them with socks and her track shoes. She'd be fine.

"So, what critters are we likely to see in our travels?" she asked, her curiosity piqued.

"Frogs and toads. Perhaps the occasional garter snake sunbathing."

Amy shuddered. Not that she didn't like snakes, but the thought of them always made her uneasy. It was at the last minute you saw them, and they startled you. "Besides that."

"Snowshoe hares, white-tailed deer, maybe raccoons, and if we're right next to the water, you might get lucky and see a muskrat."

Having a local with area knowledge like Kyle appealed to Amy. If she was unsure about something, she could always rely on him. He hadn't led her astray yet.

Thirty-Nine

Back Harbour Trail, Lunenburg, Nova Scotia

July 15, 2019

Before they parted company the previous night, Kyle had walked Amy back to the mansion and waited while she checked for a reusable bottle. She found one in the back of one of the kitchen cupboards, filled it, and put it in the fridge overnight.

The last thing she did before she left the house was grab it and put it into a pocket on the side of her backpack.

She and Kyle met on the corner by the pub and headed for their walk.

"This used to be the train station. People from farther away drive this far, walk the trail, sometimes bring their dogs, then come back afterwards," Kyle said, pointing to the building.

"I love the style." Amy paused and took a picture with her phone.

A soft breeze rustled the leaves in the trees. They hadn't walked far when she heard the familiar call of a chickadee, and a wave of homesickness washed over her. There were plenty of them in Sudbury near her apartment and around Ramsay Lake, where she walked often.

"You okay?" Kyle asked. "You went quiet on me."

"Fine. Just hearing the chickadee reminded me of home."

Amy stepped forward and began walking.

Kyle grabbed her arm and stopped her. "Look up there, just to the side of the trail," he said in a low voice.

"What?"

"Up there. Don't make a sound or you'll frighten it away."

"I don't see anything."

"Up there in the patch of sunlight on the grass to the right of the path. You don't see a snowshoe hare?" Kyle extended his arm and said, "Follow my arm."

"I see a rabbit."

It wasn't a rabbit, but at least she'd seen it. They approached slowly, but it hopped off into the underbrush.

A short time later, they met a man walking his dog. The black Lab wagged its tail so hard its entire body shook.

"Friendly, is he?" Amy asked.

"Yes. Very. No matter how often we walk the trail, when she meets people, she wants them to pay attention to her."

"Oh, sorry. She," Amy corrected herself.

Kyle and Amy fussed over the dog, their hearts warmed by its friendly nature, before continuing their walk.

"Once we get past Kissing Bridge Road, we'll be close to the Back Harbour. We might get lucky and see an osprey or two and maybe some herons," Kyle said, his voice filled with anticipation.

They hadn't gone far after crossing the road when the shimmering water appeared on their left, reflecting the bright rays of the morning sun.

"There used to be a picnic table up the trail a bit. We can stop there if you like," Kyle said.

Amy didn't sit when they reached the location where the bench was. She stood at the edge of the mown grass. "Too bad the highway is there."

Kyle joined her. "There are more places like this where we can stop. At least there used to be." He pulled his water bottle out of his backpack, took a swig, and put it back in place.

At the next clearing, a couple of people occupied a park bench. Amy thought they were about her parents' ages — her mother's anyway. Unfortunately, a bush had grown up between the bench and the road, obscuring the view of the water.

"I can't get over how quiet it is. Traffic noise, sirens, and other sounds always exist around Ramsay Lake. I can hear the birds and nothing else, maybe the occasional vehicle on the road. And that's with the houses so near the trail."

The air was still, and there was no breeze. Amy took her phone from her back pocket and photographed the harbour at this clearing, where nothing obstructed her view of the water.

Chickadees and goldfinches flitted back and forth from the trees lining the trail. Amy drew a deep breath, her senses immersed in the natural beauty surrounding her. The air was fresh with a salty tang, a characteristic of Lunenburg, but here, away from the town, it was purer, untainted by the fumes of the city.

"We're almost at Sawpit Road. When we get there, we'll go down to the park at the wharf. You'll get excellent, unobstructed views of the water. When we get there, we can spend as much or as little time as you want."

Amy nodded. She only half heard Kyle because she was so engrossed in the peace and beauty of their location.

Kyle guided Amy across the main road and down to the small park. It was a tranquil oasis, a stark contrast to the bustling town. It wasn't as busy as he expected it to be for a July day. But then, it was a Monday and locals had returned to work unless they were on vacation, as he was.

"The water is so still, it's like a sheet of glass," Amy said, her voice filled with awe at the serene sight.

That could work for or against him. He glanced around. "There's a heron on the boat ramp," Kyle said, pointing it out to Amy. The bird's graceful form against the still water was a sight.

She pulled out her phone and snapped pictures of it. "Guess it's afraid to get its feet wet. I could stay here and look out over the water forever."

"Let's sit on one of these benches, and you can enjoy the view for a while," Kyle suggested, leading Amy towards a bench. "I find this spot much more peaceful than the bustling wharf in town. It's a bit of a walk, especially for those on a bus tour, but the peacefulness here is worth it."

"Percé was crazy busy like here when I went to my sister's wedding last summer. And most were seniors, so I get them not wanting to walk too far. In Lunenburg, you have the busyness of the wharf or the tranquillity here."

"Never been to Percé. Heard of it. Seen pictures of the rock."

"I'd recommend visiting Percé in the off-season. It's less crowded, but remember many places close once the tourists leave," Amy advised, turning to face Kyle and resting her elbow on the bench's back.

A group of children arrived on bicycles interrupting the tranquil scene. Their chatter and shrieks spooked the heron, causing it to take flight with a graceful sweep of its wings. Amy, quick on the draw, snapped a few photos with her phone, capturing the heron's elegant flight. Her phone took decent pictures, but she had always wanted a proper camera to do justice to such moments.

One child produced a soccer ball, and the sound of their game filled the once tranquil air. The sudden racket made it impossible to hear anything other than their excited shouts and the thud of the ball.

Without warning, Kyle's arm shot out, a protective gesture that startled Amy. His quick reflexes saved her from a painful collision with the soccer ball. "You okay?" he asked, his concern clear in his voice.

"Yeah. I didn't see it coming. Glad you did. Since we no longer have peace and quiet, we might as well head back into the town."

Kyle pondered a tranquil destination for their outing, when a unique idea struck him. He kept it a secret, adding an element of surprise for Amy when they arrived.

Once the traffic cleared, they crossed the main highway and continued down Sawpit Road. The fresh pine scent from the surrounding trees filled the air. Trees lined the narrow road, their leaves rustling in the gentle breeze. It widened a bit as houses popped up on both sides. They also had to climb a long hill and then a short hill back down to the end of the road.

They crossed Pelham Street to use the sidewalk, but a crowd gathered in the green space beside it, and some stood on the path. Kyle scanned the water to see why the crowd had gathered. Besides those on shore, several small boats dotted the water. Then he saw it: Bluenose II sailing towards the wharf.

"Look out there, Amy. There's the Bluenose II," he said, pointing to the ship.

"The one that's on our dime?" Amy asked, referring to the vessel featured on the Canadian dime, a symbol of national pride and maritime history.

"That's the one."

Amy pulled her phone out, photographed, and shot a short video of the vessel.

Kyle waited by her side until she was ready to move on. He saw it daily when docked at the wharf, but this was the first time Amy had seen it. "The locals all know when it's leaving or returning, and flock to the area to watch her."

"She's beautiful. I can see why they would want to watch," Amy said, her eyes sparkling with admiration.

Something in her voice made him wonder if she regretted her stay was temporary. Or quite the opposite, she couldn't wait to leave the small town.

Homes on one side of the street were right up against the sidewalk. On the other side, there was room for a car to park in front of each house. A few that didn't have as much space had small flower gardens between the houses and the on-street parking.

When they reached the Knaut-Rhuland House, the sidewalk began on that side. "C'mon," he said. "I think you'll be in for a treat."

Forty

Knaut-Rhuland House, Pelham Street, Lunenburg, Nova Scotia

July 15, 2019

"1793? Has this been standing that long?" Amy said, her voice filled with wonder at the weight of history. The town, with its old-world charm, now appeared even older. "Can we go in?" she asked, eager to enter the past.

The door groaned when Kyle opened it, ushering Amy into a world of history. The wide floorboards creaked beneath their feet, each step a whisper from the past. The air was cool, carrying the distinct scent of beeswax polish, faded linen, and the intangible essence of time.

An interpreter, dressed in period costume, handed Amy a brochure and gave them a brief history of the property. "Benjamin Knaut built this house in 1793. Preservation efforts have kept the house in its original state as much as possible, offering a unique glimpse into the past. Explore at your leisure," the woman said.

The interior of the house surprised Amy. Tall ceilings, windows that let in natural light, and ornate light fixtures adorned the ceilings. The floor in the dining room was wide planks painted blue. An area rug covered the section under the table and chairs. The only thing not original to the house was the electric baseboard heater. A tall dresser stood kitty-corner in the room. Next to it was a table with a wooden silverware chest on its surface.

Ropes attached to doorways prevented access to some rooms, so you could only view them from the corridor. The furniture in all the rooms was similar.

Kyle drifted ahead to the back of the house. When Amy reached the staircase, she put her hand on the worn banister. A hush descended over her like a warm, wool sweater. She paused there for a few minutes before following Kyle into the home's kitchen. Heavy pots hung beside an age-blackened hearth that still held the ghost of ash.

A butter churn stood in the corner like a silent guard from another world. Amy ran her fingers over the surface of a pine table worn smooth in the centre.

He stopped before the enormous kitchen fireplace with an iron kettle suspended over the ashes. "Imagine having to boil your water for everything," he said, shaking his head. "You'd have lost patience in less than an hour."

Amy smirked. "Bold of you to assume I'd be the impatient one."

He opened a cupboard door and peered inside. "Think I'd last a week living like this?"

"I'd give you three days, and that's only if the Wi-Fi held out."

He grinned, but she could tell he was only half-listening now, distracted by something else. Amy turned away from him and paused beside a small cradle in a shadowed corner. The quilt inside was hand-stitched and straightforward. She imagined a mother here once, tending to bread in the oven while her baby slept and the wind howled outside.

Upstairs in the bedroom, the floorboards groaned with every step, echoing the weight of the years. Amy paused at a writing desk beneath the window. A faded journal sat open in a glass case, the ink browned but still legible. Her eyes caught on a single line, the words whispering a promise from the past.

He promised to return before the frost, and I believe he will. Though the days grow short, my hope has not.

She stood still, focussed on that one line, her fingers resting on the edge of the case. Kyle stood next to her now, quiet. She glanced at him and found his gaze wasn't on the journal but on her.

"What is it?" Kyle asked.

Amy nodded but didn't speak, not trusting her voice just yet. She let the weight of the words settle in her chest. Hope, carved out in ink, long before she was born. Did he keep his promise and return before the frost? The words, heavy with anticipation, echoed in the silence. "Nothing. Just … imagining what it would be like, waiting like that."

She lingered by the door on their way out, taking one last look back.

Later, as they stepped out into the brightness and warmth of the late afternoon, she turned to him. "Makes you wonder what they'd think of all this — tourists wandering through their lives."

Kyle gave her a small smile that made her steadier than she was. "I think they'd be glad that someone's still paying attention."

"Could be. Or they would consider us invading their privacy," she said, her voice conveying reverence for those lives.

"Anything else you'd like to do today?" Kyle asked.

"Honestly, I'd rather head back to Izzy's and crash."

That wasn't the response Kyle wanted. He was hoping to spend more time with Amy. He put his arm around her and pulled her in for a hug. Before he let her go, he kissed her cheek.

Amy's emotions were in turmoil, and a tear escaped her eye. Kyle brushed it away, his heart aching for her. The stop at the museum had a more profound effect on her than he expected. Still, he respected her wishes and let her go. "Tomorrow?"

"Sure," she said, turning and walking up Pelham Street towards Izzy's house.

Kyle watched her walk away, his mind swirling with uncertainty. What was it about the Knaut-Rhuland House Museum that rattled her? She had gotten thoughtful in the kitchen, and the letter in the display case in the bedroom upstairs pushed her over the edge. Should he have let her go alone? At least walked with her? The street was busy enough now with foot traffic, he couldn't see her. He turned onto King Street and walked the block to Lincoln before heading in the same direction as Amy, just on a different course.

Forty-One

Isabelle Morrison's House, Falkland Street, Lunenburg, Nova Scotia

July 15, 2019

The door clicked shut behind her, and silence wrapped around her for the first time that day. Amy kicked off her shoes and padded barefoot to the kitchen, the air's briny tang and old wood clinging to her like a second skin.

The depth of Amy's emotional response to the historical objects surprised her. The cradle, churn, floorboards, and panelling stirred something profound within her.

With the kettle clicked on, she needed time to think. Let the threads of the day settle in her chest. She remembered the fridge magnet someone had given her mother. It said, 'Where there is tea, there is hope.'

Everything about Lunenburg had a way of seeping in. Not just the town, its history, and the people she met, but Kyle. His quiet steadiness. His laughter that caught her off guard. He watched her, not only when she smiled but also during the quiet moments in between. She believed herself unobserved during these times, lost in thought or searching for the right words. In those moments, his gaze was a comforting presence, a silent reassurance that she was not alone.

Amy cupped the steaming mug between her hands and leaned against the counter. The late afternoon light, a warm golden hue that seemed to wrap the room in a gentle embrace, caught the curtains. This wasn't just an escape anymore; she wasn't the same person who stepped off the bus a few short days ago.

Kyle took her to the museum, not out of obligation, but out of a genuine desire for her to understand something important to him. He wanted to share a piece of his world with her. This was a stark contrast to David, who would have made a joke, brushed it off, or acted like it was a waste of time.

But Kyle noticed the way her eyes lingered on details. He saw her curiosity and quiet wonder, and rather than dismiss it, he leaned into it and encouraged it.

Amy sank into an armchair near the front window, the steaming mug cradled in her hands. Outside, a breeze fluttered the peonies along the walkway. Inside, the house was still.

From the start, Amy had sensed that Kyle was different. Now, she saw the depth of that difference. He didn't just make her understand he noticed her. Respected her. He wanted her for who she was, not for who someone else wanted her to be.

For the first time in a long time, Amy realized she wasn't afraid of what came next.

When Amy returned from putting her empty mug in the sink, she started to close the curtains but froze. David had parked his car on the street out front. She was sure of it. He used to park that same dark sedan like that in front of her Sudbury apartment when he would show up uninvited. Icy dread slithered down her back and chilled her to the bone.

He hadn't left town after all.

Now what did she do? Panic clawed at her throat, making it difficult to breathe. She grabbed her phone from the end table, her mind racing as she rushed through the house, checking to ensure all the doors and windows were closed and bolted. All secure, but was it enough? Was it him out there, or did her imagination make her see something that wasn't?

No way was she letting him into this house. This was her

sanctuary. Her space. The thought of him walking through her door again, and intruding into this fragile peace she'd worked so hard to find, made her stomach churn. No way on earth she'd give that up.

Keys. The ones Maggie brought over for her. Where did she put them? Amy's mind fumbled as she dashed to the kitchen and scanned the counter. Not there. She checked the hallway, then the living room. Still nothing. Her pulse thundered in her ears, the sense of being trapped growing. She was desperate, her mind racing with fear and uncertainty.

She couldn't just leave. No, she wouldn't. David would see her and follow her. How could things go from perfect to a complete disaster so fast? Then it hit her.

Kyle.

She couldn't phone Maggie or Gordon as she didn't know their phone number, but Kyle would help. He'd get them to her.

Amy darted up the stairs to her bedroom, her bare feet not making a sound as she moved. She slammed the door behind her and locked it before heading to the ensuite. Her hands shook so much that she couldn't type. But somehow, she managed through the haze of panic.

David parked outside. Please help.

The urgency in her message was clear, her fear and desperation pouring out.

With no hesitation, she hit send. The seconds that passed seemed like hours. She gripped the edge of the sink, staring at her phone, willing it to buzz to bring some kind of reassurance. She had to believe Kyle would get the message—or at least that help would arrive before David got any closer.

Now wait for the cavalry to arrive or the other shoe to fall.

Forty-Two

Gordon and Maggie MacLeod's House, Falkland Street, Lunenburg, Nova Scotia

July 15, 2019

Maggie had just put the kettle on when the phone in their kitchen rang. She reached for it. "Hello."

"Amy's in trouble," Kyle said without preamble, his voice urgent. "David's back. Parked out front of her house. She's scared and needs help."

Her breath caught, her heart pounding in her chest. David. Only two days ago, Kyle sat in their kitchen, asking for help keeping Amy safe. That name came with an icy chill.

"Amy's safe, though? She's inside with the house locked?" Maggie asked. She didn't wait for Kyle's response. "Okay, tell her Gordon and I are on our way."

She hung up, already moving with her mind whirring into action. The kettle whistled, Maggie turned off the burner, and grabbed her jacket. Her thoughts were on Amy. She wouldn't let her get caught up in whatever game David had in his mind.

Gordon was in the living room reading the newspaper. He looked up when she stormed in, and his eyes narrowed, showing he knew something was wrong.

"It's Amy," Maggie said. "David is outside her house. We need to go. NOW."

Gordon's head snapped up. His eyes darkened, and he stood, his hand on his jacket. Maggie didn't need him to say anything; she grabbed her purse and led the way out the front door.

As they stepped onto the front porch, Maggie saw the light of Amy's house, a single window glowing against the evening dusk. The air was cool, carrying the fresh cut grass smell. They'd be there in a matter of seconds.

"Act naturally," Gordon said. "Like we're going over for a visit. We don't want this David character to know we're onto him."

Natural. Calm. Those two words were lacking from Maggie's current vocabulary.

Gordon had been sitting by the window, his eyes scanning the surroundings for anything out of place. He'd tried to focus on the newspaper, but the words blurred together. The faint hum of the kettle in the kitchen broke his concentration, a sudden interruption. Maggie called him from the kitchen, asking if he wanted tea. That shifted his attention for a second. That brief distraction was all it took.

How could he have been so careless? How could he have let his guard down for even a minute? He had promised Kyle that he'd keep Amy safe. The night was still, but his mind raced. He should have seen the car. Should have spotted it when it first pulled up. But he hadn't, and realizing his mistake was tearing him apart. He'd let his guard down at the wrong moment. One that could make all the difference.

His phone buzzed in his pocket. Kyle's name flashed on the screen. He accepted the call. "Yes, Kyle."

"I'm on my way. Almost to Nova Insurance. Be with you in a couple."

Gordon's guilt threatened to swallow him whole. He had let Amy down. Let Kyle down, Maggie, and most of all, himself.

"Kyle's coming with us. He's almost here," he said, pausing by the car that had panicked Amy. It looked like the exact flashy vehicle. No one was in it. Was David hiding nearby? Prowling on Izzy's property? Before things got out of hand, maybe it was time to call the RCMP.

Forty-Three

Isabelle Morrison's House, Falkland Street, Lunenburg, Nova Scotia

July 15, 2019

Startled when her phone vibrated, Amy jumped. Was it David being his hateful self again? She didn't want to look at it, just in case. Was it Kyle? She hoped so. With trembling hands, she picked up her phone. It *was* Kyle. She breathed a shaky sigh.

At your front door with Maggie and Gordon. Can you let us in?

Her gaze flicked back to the window. The same car still sat in front of Izzy's house. She didn't want to leave the safety of the bedroom, but then, a glimmer of hope. Her friends, her support, and her cavalry had arrived. Relief washed over her, easing the tension in her body.

She moved downstairs, her heartbeat fluttering. Before she pulled the door open, she slid the chain lock in place and opened it only as wide as the length would allow. Once she confirmed it was them, she released the chain and let them into the house.

Gordon entered with his phone pressed to his ear, talking to someone. Maggie followed close behind, her expression etched with concern.

Amy didn't hesitate. She threw her arms around Kyle's neck and clung to him, finding comfort in his embrace. Her composure unravelled, and she began to sob. "I-I was s-so sc-scared."

"It's all right. We're here now."

Maggie touched Amy's shoulder. "I'll make us some tea."

Kyle guided her into the living room and sat her on the couch. He joined her, keeping her hand in his.

"You're certain that's the car?" Gordon asked. "I noticed no one was in it when we came over."

"I-I'm positive." Amy pulled a tissue from the box on the side table and dabbed her eyes. "Then he's *outside* prowling around the house, lying in wait?" That thought terrified her more than she already was. "I hoped he'd left Lunenburg when I stood up to him in the pub."

"I've called the RCMP. They're sending someone over. We'll get to the bottom of it." Gordon's reassuring voice promised a solution, offering a glimmer of hope amidst the tension.

At that moment, Maggie returned, carrying a tray laden with a teapot, cups, saucers, cream, and sugar, and placed it on the coffee table. Her calm presence was a quiet anchor in the storm of emotion.

Kyle's grip on Amy's hand remained firm, his unwavering protectiveness shone through. The tremors still coursing through her were like echoes of a distant storm, stirring a deep-seated knot of protectiveness and anger within him. Seeing her so shaken by the mysterious car, whether it was David's, was unacceptable. Not on his watch.

Maggie, the calm and collected one in the group, poured tea as if it could soothe the tension in the room. She was like a mother to them all, always there to provide comfort in times of need. She passed a cup to Amy, who took it with both hands like a lifeline, a silent plea for reassurance.

Kyle leaned forward and, in a low voice, said, "You did the right thing. Locking the doors. Calling for help. Even when scared, you stayed smart."

Amy's nod was barely perceptible, her gaze fixed on the cup in her hands. Her tightly wound fingers around it showed her lingering fear.

He wanted to hug her, tell her she was safe, and promise to stay. But she was still full of adrenaline and he didn't think she could handle more physical contact.

Gordon drifted to the front window and monitored the street. Kyle followed his gaze to the sleek, black car — the flashy thing David would drive.

"Headlights haven't flicked once," Gordon said. "It's just sitting there."

Kyle stood. He needed to move. "I'll step outside. Keep tabs on the car from the porch until the RCMP arrive."

"No," Amy said, harshly. "What if he's out there? What if he's waiting for someone to come out?"

Kyle knelt in front of her and rested his hand on her knee. "Then he's already missed his chance. I'm not going far. Just to the porch. I want to see if anyone comes back to that car."

Amy hesitated and gave a slight nod. "Just be careful."

"I promise," Kyle's voice was steady, his eyes locked with Amy's, his promise a beacon of reassurance in the tense atmosphere.

As he strode to the door, Maggie touched his arm. "Don't do anything rash. Let the authorities handle it."

"I will." Kyle wasn't sure his definition of rash matched hers. He struggled between his protective instincts and the need to follow the law. But at this moment, his need to protect Amy overrode everything else.

The cool night air hit him as he stepped onto the porch. The street was too quiet. He crossed his arms and stared at the car, daring whoever might be watching to come out and face him.

Let them try something. Just let them.

The sound of a car engine grew louder as it approached. A marked RCMP cruiser turned onto Falkland Street and pulled in behind the suspicious car, bathing the vehicle in bright white until the driver shut the car off.

Kyle stepped down from the porch as an officer climbed out. The man looked forty-ish, had a solid build, and a calm demeanour. He approached the vehicle with his flashlight in hand. Kyle kept his distance but never took his eyes off the man.

The officer circled the vehicle, his flashlight sweeping across the interior. He then bent to peer through the windows, his scrutiny unwavering. After a long moment, he straightened and walked towards Kyle, his thorough investigation clear in his every step.

"Evening. You the one who called this in?"

Kyle nodded. "Well, Gordon MacLeod made the call. I'm the one who got him first. It's my friend who's inside. She recognized that car. Belongs to someone she's afraid of."

The officer glanced back towards the street. "Car's locked. No one inside. Cold engine. My guess is it's been sitting a while."

"He must have taken off on foot," Kyle said, his jaw tightening.

"Possible. Or may not even be his. Got a plate number. I'll run it."

"Out of province?" Kyle asked, opening the door for the officer and leading him inside, where Maggie stood waiting with Amy and Gordon. Amy sat curled up on the couch, clutching her mug of tea so tight that her knuckles had gone white.

The officer introduced himself as Constable Danvers. "I understand there's some concern over a vehicle parked out front. Mind if I ask a few questions?"

Danvers sat in the chair next to the sofa to meet Amy's gaze. "Can you tell me about him? Why you think he might be here?"

As Amy began her explanation, Kyle stood behind her. He didn't interrupt, didn't speak unless asked, but he had every muscle in his body coiled, ready, and alert.

The constable listened as he scribbled notes and then nodded. "I'll have dispatch run the plates. If it turns out to be your ex, we'll pay him a visit. If it doesn't, we'll still flag it for follow-up. Do you have a picture of the man?"

Amy picked up her phone and scrolled through the pictures. Kyle remembered when he first met her at the wharf. She had said the phone was new, so she had nothing before receiving it. He found the tracking app on it and disabled it.

"Sorry, no pictures."

Danvers straightened. "In the meantime, I suggest you all stay together tonight. Keep the doors locked. I'll have another officer cruise by a few times overnight."

"Thank you," Maggie said. "We appreciate it."

Kyle walked the officer to the door and watched him walk to the car. Then, the man turned the other direction and headed towards The Knot Pub. The tension hadn't lifted yet, but something about having the authorities in the know made things more manageable.

He closed the door behind him, glanced at the car outside, then latched the deadbolt and secured the chain.

If it was David, he'd made a mistake. One, they wouldn't let slide.

Maggie stood near the window, one hand on the curtain, as the RCMP officer walked towards the pub. The street looked so calm and ordinary. Peaceful. That damn car still sat like a shadow, and unwanted ghost parked in front of Izzy's house.

Amy's fear, a bone-deep terror, broke her heart. She couldn't bear the thought of anyone disturbing Amy's hard-won peace.

Amy had looked stronger — lighter, braver. Tonight had taken that from her. It reminded Maggie of the time when they had to deal with a similar situation, and it was a painful memory for both of them.

Kyle returned to the living room and gave Maggie a light nod.

Gordon sat on the arm of the couch now, one hand on Amy's shoulder. Maggie and Gordon had been married long enough to understand each other's unspoken words. She saw the guilt from earlier clinging to him. She would talk to him later and reassure him he had failed no one, but her focus was on Amy.

"It's late," she said, moving towards Amy, her hand reaching out to touch her, "but we should bring you to our place for the night. I'd sleep better knowing you're not alone."

Amy raised her head, her eyes glassy but grateful. "Thank you. I-I didn't want to say it, but I don't think I can stay here tonight."

"You don't have to," Maggie said, crouching beside her. "You've got us now."

More tears welled up in Amy's eyes.

"Maggie and I, we'll pack you a bag," Kyle said. "Just a few things to get you through the night."

Maggie stood and turned to follow Kyle upstairs, but not before glancing back at the young woman who'd become like a daughter to her in such a short time. Perhaps it was that Amy or Izzy reminded her a little of herself? Or that Maggie had never ignored someone in need.

She'd promised tea, but she'd do better than that. She'd help Amy find safety again, no matter the cost. And God help the man who tried to take that away from her.

Gordon sat in the armchair near the end of the sofa, one hand on his mug of cool tea, the other clenched around his phone. He hadn't spoken in the last few minutes. Maggie and Kyle had taken Amy upstairs to get a few essentials. That left him down here, alone with his thoughts, and the view of the car parked like a bad omen on the street. The car, a dark sedan, seemed to loom in the darkness, its windows reflecting the dim streetlights like sinister eyes.

He hated that car, everything it represented, and how easily it had upended everything. The phone vibrated in his hand, and he almost spilled his tea. He fumbled, his heart in his throat, and answered before the second ring.

"This is Gordon."

"It's Constable Danvers," came the reply, his voice crackling over the phone. "Checked the pub. No one by the name of David Carter, no one matching Amy's description, was there tonight. Staff have seen no one like that for a couple of days. Said he left in a huff after a young lady showed him up."

Gordon let out a slow breath and mopped his face with his hand. "The car's still here. Out front of the house. No movement."

There was a pause before the constable spoke again in a calm professional voice. "A rental agency owns that car. Plates come back to Halifax. We're tracking down who rented it. Could take a bit of time depending on the paperwork."

"So you're saying it *could* be him."

"It's possible. Or it could be someone unrelated to the case. Someone staying at a nearby rental. We'll canvas the neighbours in the morning."

Frustrated, Gordon cursed as he stood and paced to the window. The car was still there. Still unoccupied. "What do we do in the meantime?"

"Stay put for now. If anything changes, movement occurs, or someone approaches the house, call 9-1-1. Don't hesitate. We'll have a car patrolling the neighbourhood throughout the night."

"The wife and I are taking Amy back to our house. She's afraid to stay here."

"That's fine. We'll still be in the area."

Gordon thanked him and ended the call. A wave of relief washed over him. He stood in that position, staring at the ghost of a reflection in the window. Frustration and worry filled his face, but a glimmer of hope also appeared. He turned and headed towards the stairs. Amy and Maggie needed to know what the officer said. There were still no definitive answers, but he was a step closer.

"That was the RCMP," Gordon called up.

Footsteps rustled above before Kyle appeared on the landing.

"They didn't find David at the pub. Car's a rental. Could still be him … or not. They're going to monitor things tonight."

Kyle nodded. "Thanks, Gordon."

In return, Mr. MacLeod gave a quiet nod and turned back towards the window, watching, waiting, and hoping it was all a mistake.

Forty-Four

Gordon and Maggie MacLeod's House, Falkland Street, Lunenburg, Nova Scotia

July 15, 2019

In the MacLeod's guest room, Amy stood wrapped in the quilt someone had folded at the foot of the bed. The soft scent of lavender, a familiar fragrance from her childhood, calmed her in a way she hadn't expected. Maggie brought tea upstairs to her shortly after getting Amy settled in the room. It sat untouched on the nightstand despite Amy's promise to drink it.

She avoided the window, knowing the temptation to pull the curtain aside would be too strong. She avoided checking whether the car remained parked or had gone. At least if she didn't know, she could pretend that she was safe, if only for this one night.

The gentle murmur of voices downstairs drifted up to her. Kyle, Maggie and Gordon spoke in low tones. They had given her the space she needed while they hadn't left her alone. Her phone vibrated. For a second, her heart stopped. She almost didn't look, but when she did, it was Kyle.

You okay up there? Need anything?

Tears pricked Amy's eyes. She blinked them back and sent a message back to him.

Okay. Just tired. Thanks for being there tonight.

His reply came almost immediately.

Sleep if you can. We're not going anywhere.

Amy sat on the edge of the bed with her legs tucked under her, then opened her phone messages. After hesitating, she tapped on Emma's name, her best friend, who always understood her.

Thought I moved past all this. The fear, the memories, feeling trapped. David showed up, or at least I think he did. I'm okay now. I'm with people who care, but for a minute, I thought I was right back there again. Just needed to tell someone who understands.

Her finger hovered over the screen before hitting send. Amy laid her phone down, climbed into the bed, and pulled the blanket to her chin.

Outside, the town of Lunenburg settled into its own quiet, but Amy knew her mind wouldn't.

Emma might be asleep. Or at work. But sending the message had helped. Amy wasn't hiding anymore.

This house wasn't Izzy's, and she wasn't alone. For tonight, that would have to be enough.

Maggie, her hands trembling, placed the empty mugs into the sink and ran warm water to rinse off the milk and sugar. A thick silence hung in the house. However, Amy's posture, Kyle's jaw, and Gordon's brow revealed their underlying fear and tension.

She dried her hands and walked to the living room. Kyle and Gordon were conversing near the window, behind the closed curtains. Amy went upstairs soon after her arrival, uttering a mumbled thanks and promising she was better now. It was clear to Maggie that she shouldn't take those words at face value.

"Do you think she'll be able to sleep?" she asked, joining the men. Their hushed tones and the gravity in their expressions added to the tension in the room.

"Doubt it," Kyle said, his concern for Amy clear. "She'll try; at least here, she's not alone."

Gordon nodded. "RCMP said they'll follow up in the morning. He wasn't at the pub, so now they're checking if he's staying in town but under a different name."

Maggie folded her arms and stared at the front door, then at the sets of keys on the hallway table. "It shouldn't be like this. Amy shouldn't have to sense being hunted because someone couldn't handle being told no." Her frustration was clear.

No one answered, but the silence was sufficient agreement.

Kyle paused when Maggie entered the room. He and Gordon had been discussing alternate plans should the RCMP not find David. His instincts told him to go check on Amy again to ensure she was okay, but he also understood Amy needed space now. She was safe and that had to be enough.

A strange mix of calm and lingering tension filled the MacLeod's living room. Gordon stood by the window with his arms crossed, staring at the closed curtains as if watching for David to return.

Kyle ran a hand down his face. He'd never hated someone as much, or the way he hated David. Not only for his actions but also the effect his actions had on Amy — making her insignificant, vulnerable, and uncertain about her own judgment.

A soft ping from upstairs jolted him out of his reverie. A phone notification. He glanced up, but the house remained quiet.

"She mentioned sending a message to a friend," Maggie said. "Emma, I think. Perhaps that was her responding."

Kyle nodded, relieved. "Good, she needs people like that. People who remind her who she is."

Gordon turned away from the window. "RCMP promised they'd keep someone on patrol through town overnight. If he's here, they'll find him.

Kyle took a deep breath. "Thanks for being here, both of you. Amy is better because of it, I'm sure."

Maggie smiled. "Of course, she's part of our family now, whether or not she realizes it."

That hit him harder than he expected. Amy was a part of something, like someone who belonged. Kyle wasn't sure when it had happened, but he couldn't picture life without her in it anymore.

He sank into the armchair nearest the couch and leaned forward with his elbows on his knees. "If she wants to stay here a few nights, I'll sleep on the couch. Just until she's ready to go back."

Maggie arched a brow. "You think she'd let you stay downstairs while she took the guest room?"

Despite everything, a smile tugged at his lips. "Good point."

Forty-Five

Gordon and Maggie MacLeod's House, Falkland Street, Lunenburg, Nova Scotia

July 16, 2019

Amy picked up her phone out of habit, and Emma's name was on the screen. Her friend had received the message she sent last night. Three replies waited for her.

Amy, I can only imagine how difficult this is for you. But remember, you did the right thing by reaching out. You're not alone in this. I'm here for you, always.

What you experienced was real. Your current emotional state is justified. But you're not there anymore. You're safe, and you're not alone. Remember, I'm just a text away, day or night. I'm always in your corner, ready to support you.

Amy, you've shown incredible strength in this situation. I'm so proud of you.

Emma had never been a fan of David, and it took a while for Amy to realize he'd played her all along. But now that she had, despite the fear of the previous evening, she wasn't letting that man walk over her again.

She pulled on the fuzzy robe at the back of the door, shoved her phone in the pocket and made her way to the kitchen.

The smell of fresh toast and coffee, mingling with the faint scent of flowers from the garden, greeted Amy as she padded downstairs. The soft morning light, filtered through the kitchen window, cast a warm glow across the table, illuminating the delicate patterns on the tablecloth.

"Good morning, Amy," Maggie said, sliding a mug towards her. "You sleep all right?"

Amy offered a half-nod as she sat, her eyes still heavy with sleep and worry. "So so." She wrapped her hands around the warm mug and inhaled the aromatic steam, a slight comfort amid her turmoil. "Thanks for everything last night. I don't know what I would've done without you."

"You're safe here. That's all that matters."

The house went quiet, except for the rustle of Gordon flipping through the morning paper.

Amy reached for her phone, remembering the police asking about pictures of David. She typed out a message to Emma.

The police asked last night if I had any photos. Never thought to check with you. If you have anything with his face in view, it would help.

She hit send and then looked up and found Maggie watching her.

"I asked Emma if she had pictures of me and David together. The RCMP said it might help."

"Smart girl."

Kyle appeared in the doorway, rumpled from sleep but alert. "Anything from the police yet?"

"No," Gordon said. "But I expect we'll hear something soon."

Amy turned her attention back to the screen, her heart fluttering at the thought of Emma's reply and what it might stir up.

Her phone buzzed again as she took her first sip of coffee.

Found three! Sending them now. Hope they help. Call me if you need to talk. Anytime.

Three images popped up seconds later, and Amy hesitated, her thumb hovering over the first one. The screen went blurry before she realized it wasn't it, but her eyes. She blinked back the tears and opened the first photo.

There she was, smiling and leaning close to David, her boyfriend of a little over a year. His arm was around her shoulders, his expression a mix of charming and smug, which Amy had convinced herself was confidence. This picture was from one of the few trips they took together. Niagara on the Lake, Niagara Falls and a wine tour.

She swiped to the next. A close-up selfie on the boardwalk around Ramsay Lake, their heads tilted together. Someone else took the third. They were at a bonfire at someone's cottage party; she was wrapped in a blanket, his hand on her waist.

Amy exhaled and then saved all three. She handed the phone to Kyle, who'd sat across from her, sipping coffee and watching her.

"These okay to give the police?"

Kyle glanced through the images. "They're clear. Good enough for facial recognition."

"I've got them now if the RCMP still need them."

"You did good," Kyle said, reaching across the table and placing his hand on hers

"I hate I even need to do this."

"Now it's not just your word. There's proof. We'll build on that."

Amy glanced out the living room window just as a white RCMP cruiser pulled up in front of the MacLeod house. Her stomach clenched, and she took a deep breath to steady herself. "He's back."

Kyle stood from his seat at the table. "Danvers?"

"I think so." She stepped towards the door. "I'll get it."

By the time Amy opened the front door, the officer was climbing the porch steps, carrying a clipboard and wearing a professional but friendly expression on his face.

"Morning, Ms. Scott." He tipped his head. "Sorry to disturb you so early."

"It's all right. Come in." She moved away, allowing him entry, and Kyle joined her in the foyer.

Danvers nodded to both of them. "Just wanted to follow up. Still no sign of your ex on foot or around the vehicle, which is still parked across the way. We've put a notice on it and are keeping it under surveillance. If no one returns to claim it in the next twenty-four hours, we'll have it towed."

Amy gripped her phone tighter. "I … I have some photos. My friend Emma had some on her phone and sent them to me this morning."

"That's helpful," Danvers said. "May I see them?"

She unlocked her phone and brought up the images. The officer studied each one, then accepted her offer to forward them. He gave her a number, and she sent them to him.

He checked his device to ensure they'd come through. "We'll add these to the file and circulate them. If he's spotted anywhere around here, we'll know."

"Do you think he'll come back?"

After a pause, Danvers answered her question. "Hard to say. Some people show up just to rattle the cage, then disappear. Others stick around. Either way, you did the right thing by calling it in. And you're not alone in this."

That simple reassurance helped more than Amy expected.

"We're staying with her," Kyle said, his voice firm.

Danvers nodded. "Good. You've got a solid network here, Ms. Scott. That makes all the difference."

Amy managed a small smile. "Thank you."

"If anything changes, or you see him, call immediately." Danvers tipped his head again. "We'll keep in touch."

Amy watched him go, and as the cruiser pulled away, she turned to Kyle. "He doesn't say much, but I can breathe a little easier now.

"Then he's doing his job," Kyle said. "And so are you."

Kyle stayed by the window after Amy left the room and watched the cruiser drive away. The street looked quiet again, peaceful. But beneath the facade, something in him bristled. It wasn't just one thing. It was the combination of them. The car, a familiar yet ominous sight. Amy's fear was an unmistakable emotion that had gripped her since the incident.

He'd never seen her so shaken. And this morning, she was trying to hold it together. He admired that.

Maggie's kettle whistled from the kitchen, and the aroma of

toast and coffee drifted through the house. The MacLeods' place always projected an atmosphere of safety. Kyle was grateful for that, now more than ever.

He raked his fingers through his hair and walked away from the window. He should have recognized the car. But how? He never saw it the day David stormed into the pub to take Amy home with him. Those few words in that message from Amy had slammed into him like a freight train, and his jaw clenched.

She had come to Lunenburg for a break, a fresh start. He hadn't expected the ghosts of her past, the memories that haunted her, to follow her here.

He crossed into the dining room where Maggie was setting the table. "You okay?" she asked.

Kyle nodded. "Just thinking."

Maggie raised her head. "She's stronger than she knows. But it helps that she's not doing this alone."

He responded with a smile and said, "Yeah. That won't change."

Kyle meant it. As long as Amy needed someone, he'd be there for her. Somewhere along the way, this had stopped being about doing the right thing and being about her — her laugh, determination, and stubborn streak. Even the way she looked at him when she thought he wasn't paying attention. He didn't want to see that look turn to fear again.

Footsteps on the stairs pulled his attention in that direction. Amy was coming down holding her phone, but her expression was softer than before, and there was a glimmer of hope in her eyes.

Kyle moved towards her. Whatever came next, they'd face together.

Amy stepped off the bottom step where Kyle waited. After the police left, she went upstairs, showered, and dressed.

"You okay?" he asked her again. He reached out and took her hand.

She nodded. "The pictures rattled me. But that's not all. I remembered something when I was upstairs." Amy paused and then said, "There was a time, about six months before I came here. A few things between David and I niggled at me. I tried to tell one of the other nurses. Emma wasn't around that day, and she'd been trying to point these things out to me all along, but I wouldn't listen. Anyway, I told this other woman a few little things. I hoped she'd pick up on the signs."

Kyle's brow furrowed, but he remained silent and listened.

"She didn't. Or maybe she did and didn't want to get involved. Who knows? But the scariest bit is how quickly David found out. I never figured out how, but he knew. And that night ... he wasn't only angry. He was cold. Like nothing I said mattered." Amy took a deep, shuddering breath. Recalling this upset her more than she expected.

Amy looked up. "I think I buried that. But something that Constable Danvers said struck a chord. That's when I remembered. Not the complete memory, just that snippet. Knowing that trying to say something didn't make a difference."

Kyle's grip on her hand tightened, a silent reassurance of his understanding. "You're saying something now. You're not alone this time." His words were a gentle reminder of his unwavering support.

His statement almost undid her.

"I want to believe that. I do."

He didn't push further or try to give her false promises. Instead, he shifted a little closer, wrapping his arm around her in a comforting embrace. He held her while she breathed through the tears she hadn't meant to shed, a silent testament to his care and reliability.

"I'm not going anywhere," he said. "You don't have to do this alone anymore." His words were a promise, and Amy was relieved, and allowed herself to be vulnerable in his embrace.

Forty-Six

Gordon and Maggie MacLeod's House, Falkland Street, Lunenburg, Nova Scotia

July 17, 2019

Amy sipped her coffee, cradling the warm mug in her hands. Despite the peaceful morning, her nerves were on edge, a lingering anxiety from the past few days. Maggie and Gordon bustled around the kitchen, their voices a soft murmur in her ears, a comforting backdrop to her unease.

A knock on the front door startled her, and she almost dropped her mug.

Gordon crossed the room. Through the window, Amy spotted a familiar RCMP cruiser parked on the street outside the house. She set her mug on the table and stood, her heart thudding.

"Morning," Constable Danvers said when Gordon opened the door. His voice was calm and almost cheerful. "Sorry to bother you folks again, but I wanted to update you as soon as possible."

Gordon ushered him inside. Amy remained rooted to the spot, wringing her hands.

"The car parked outside the house for the past two days,"

Danvers said, checking his notebook, "Peter MacIntyre rented it at the Halifax airport. No connection to David. And not to you at all, Ms. Scott. We verified it this morning."

Amy blinked, and the relief washed over her like a cleansing wave. It was a sudden and unexpected release. Her knees buckled, and she sank back into her chair. "So ... it wasn't David?" she asked, her voice just above a whisper, but filled with a newfound calm.

"No, an unfortunate coincidence — same make, model, and colour. Simple mistake to make." Danvers smiled, his words a balm to her frayed nerves. "Mr. MacIntyre is in town for a few days, staying at The Lunenburg Inn, just around the corner. Their parking lot was full, and he wasn't aware of the off-street parking just beyond it on the left. He apologized for spooking you and has moved the car away from in front of your house. You were never in any danger from him."

"Thank you for letting me know," Amy said as she raised her hand to her chest.

"I figured you'd want to hear it in person," he said. "And if you need anything else while you're here, just call the detachment."

Gordon showed him out while Maggie pushed a plate of scones towards Amy.

"You hear that? You're safe. It's all over," Maggie said.

Amy nodded, and a few tears spilled down her cheeks. Safe. She could go back to Izzy's house and ... breathe.

Even though he had showered at the MacLeods' home, Kyle wore the same clothes as he had the night he and the couple brought Amy back to their house. He hated to leave her, but she was in safe hands. They wouldn't let anything happen to her. He would be gone about half an hour at most, his heart heavy with concern for Amy.

Amy, her hair dishevelled and her eyes still showing signs of fear, sat at the dining room table, cradling a mug. Steam rose from it. Kyle, his face etched with concern, walked into the dining room and placed his hand on her back. "I'm going to nip back to mine for a change of clothes. You be okay?"

She nodded in response, then said, "It wasn't him. It wasn't

David. I frightened myself over nothing."

"It wasn't nothing," Kyle said, his voice filled with empathy as he rubbed her back. "You had genuine fear. The car was identical to David's, and he'd been in town a few days ago."

"I should go back to Izzy's. I only brought enough clothes for one day, and that was yesterday."

"You're welcome here as long as you need, Amy," Maggie said. "It's nice having someone in the house besides Gordon."

"No, I need to do it," Amy said, her voice filled with determination.

"Make you a deal, then I'll walk you to Izzy's, where you do what you must do, then we'll walk down to mine together. That way, you're not alone." Kyle hoped Amy would agree to it.

She must have because she got up from the table, disappeared upstairs, and reappeared with the small bag she'd brought the other night.

Overwhelming gratitude filled Amy as Maggie and Gordon walked her to the front door. She hugged them both, her vision blurred with unshed tears. "Thank you, again … for everything," she managed, her voice choked with emotion.

Kyle opened the door and allowed Amy, carrying her overnight bag over her shoulder, to walk out ahead of him. When they reached the bottom of the porch steps, he slipped his hand around hers. Warm, steady, constant.

The morning sun, casting a dappled glow through the trees, seemed to wash away the events of the past. The quiet street and the gentle breeze conspired to make yesterday and the night before seem more distant, almost unreal.

"Take it easy today," Maggie called after them. "You deserve a little peace."

"We're just across the way if you need anything," Gordon said, his voice a reassuring presence in the quiet morning.

Amy raised her hand and waved, her heart filled with a profound thankfulness that settled in her chest like a warm, comforting blanket.

The short walk across the street seemed to take longer than it should have, but her steps were hesitant. Kyle stayed close, matching her pace without rushing her.

Forty-Seven

Isabelle Morrison's House, Falkland Street, Lunenburg, Nova Scotia

July 17, 2019

When they reached Izzy's front door, Amy paused. Her hand hovered over the doorknob. Kyle remained silent and waited by her side.

A moment later, Amy exhaled, turned the key and pushed the door open. The scent of lemon and wood polish greeted her. Morning light streamed through the windows, illuminating the cozy furniture and colourful throw pillows.

Home, at least for now.

"We'll take it one step at a time," he said softly.

She nodded. "One step at a time."

Amy stood inside the front door before letting the house's stillness envelop her. Kyle stayed by her side, solid and steady.

She wandered through the front room and ran her fingers over the back of the sofa and the edge of the bookcase. Everything was as she'd left it, but it seemed different. Maybe it wasn't the house but her, rattled but determined not to let fear claim this space. She was resolute in her mission to make this house hers again, confirming her strength and resilience.

The tea towel she had folded a couple of days ago still hung on the oven handle in the kitchen. Her half-finished grocery list sat on the table. These were ordinary things, the markers of everyday life. She touched the list with her fingertips, finding comfort in the familiar, grounding herself in the routine, a source of security and stability in her current situation.

Kyle lingered in the doorway.

Amy glanced towards the front of the house. "I should … check upstairs, too," she said in a quiet but steady voice.

"I'll come with you."

They climbed the stairs together, the old treads creaking under their feet, each sound echoing the tension in the air. Amy peeked into the bedrooms and the bathroom, her heart beating faster until she was sure no one had been inside.

When she walked into the main bedroom, her phone vibrated from the back pocket of her jeans. She pulled it out, heart pounding, until she saw Emma's name on the display. Amy exhaled, and a cautious sense of normality returned. She opened the text message.

Hey, just a heads-up, heard through the grapevine that David's back in town. Just in case you hadn't left yet. Stay safe, okay?

Before Amy did anything else, she would take another shower and get into clean clothes.

Kyle left Amy upstairs to shower and dress. He wandered into the living room and paused before the massive bookcase. As he perused the titles and authors on the spines, he realized they were books Izzy used for research. *The True Crime Dictionary: From Alibi to Zodiac: The Ultimate Guide to Cold Cases, Serial Killers and More* by Amanda Lees. *The Crime Writer's Handbook* by Douglas Wynn, *The Real CSI: A Forensics Handbook for Crime Writers* by Kate Bendelow, and the list continued. On another shelf were Izzy's novels.

The woman was a prolific writer. Amongst the gruesome titles were books on nature, birds, and flowers. He supposed that with what she wrote, she needed the calming influence of flora and fauna.

Kyle hated the look he'd seen in Amy's eyes. That blend of fear and weariness. She was strong, he knew that. She had faced so much, yet she was a lot stronger than she gave herself credit for. He wished she could see herself the way he did.

The faint sound of the shower running drifted down the stairs. He sank onto the sofa. The house was too quiet without her puttering about in it. Despite knowing she needed time to herself, he counted the minutes until he saw her again, if only to reassure himself she was okay.

He raked his fingers through his hair and sighed. The weight of his perceived uselessness bore down on him, and he couldn't shake it.

Kyle's instincts kicked in when he and Gordon first spotted the car. He went straight into problem-solving and protection mode, ensuring Amy's safety. With that threat lifted, he could only wait for Amy to open up and see what she needed from him.

And he would. No matter how long it took, Kyle was determined to be there for Amy, to support her through whatever she was facing.

Amy padded down the stairs barefoot, her hair still damp from the shower. The smell of her shampoo lingered in the air, a reminder of the comforting routine she had just completed. Her sense of self returned now that the hot water had washed away the lingering tension.

She paused halfway down, catching sight of Kyle on the sofa with a book open on his lap. The sight brought a lump to her throat, not sadness but relief. It was the comfort of knowing someone cared enough to wait for her washed over her like a warm wave.

When she approached, he looked up, and a warm smile, like a gentle embrace, lit his face. There was no pressure, no questions, just steady, quiet support, a support that enveloped her like a warm blanket.

Amy slipped into the armchair beside the sofa. They sat in a comfortable silence that was not awkward but soothing, for a few moments. "I realized … the message I sent Emma the other night was rather cryptic. She caught on after I asked her to check her phone for pictures. I guess I didn't want to believe it was happening."

Kyle didn't interrupt her, but nodded for her to continue if she wanted.

Amy lifted her gaze to meet his. The fierceness she found there clenched her heart. She didn't have to be brave every second. It was okay to lean on someone else for a while.

She continued. "I thought if I didn't say it out loud it wasn't real. But it doesn't work like that, does it?" Amy let out a shaky breath.

"No," he said. "But you don't have to face any of it alone."

Kyle leaned back on the sofa. "Ready to head down to my place? I need to clean up, too. I promise no privateer costume."

That drew a giggle from Amy. It was good to laugh again. At first, she thought Kyle looked ridiculous in his flamboyant costume when he led the walking tour, but as time passed, she thought he looked rather hot.

Amy glanced around Izzy's house. At first, she was relieved to be back, but now the house seemed too big and quiet. A change of scenery, a smaller lived-in space that wasn't filled with memories for her, sounded good.

"I'd like that," she said then smiled at him.

"Good." Kyle stood, offering his hand. "Grab what you need, and we'll go. Take your time. There's no rush."

Amy slipped her hand into his; a surge of strength came over her.

She ensured she had her phone, bag, and house keys, and they left Izzy's enormous house bound for Kyle's cozy apartment on Lincoln Street.

Forty-Eight

Kyle's apartment, Lincoln Street, Lunenburg, Nova Scotia

July 17, 2019

Kyle unlocked the door, nudged it with his shoulder, then stepped aside to let Amy enter first.

As she entered the apartment, a fresh, unfamiliar scent greeted her. The space was as tidy as ever, but it seemed to hold a distinct energy today. Kyle didn't need to clear the floor of clothes, as he often did. The skylight above cast a warm glow, illuminating the hardwood floors. The apartment, now seemed to exude a sense of calm, as if it had absorbed some of Amy's presence, a stark contrast to its usual state.

As Amy took off her sandals, her gaze fell on the weathered piece of wood with the name of the boat, *Seaworthy*. Her heart ached for Kyle, knowing the painful memories it held. The first time he brought her here, he had shared the tragic story of the accident that took his father's and brother's lives. Today, more pictures were hanging on the wall around the piece of fishing boat. Kyle had mounted framed photographs of a sailboat and a sunset over the wharf on the wall. Amy's deep empathy for Kyle's loss was palpable, making his grief almost tangible.

"These weren't here the other day," Amy said, her eyes wide with surprise as she turned to face Kyle, the sudden change in the apartment catching her off guard.

Kyle wasn't there. The rush of water running in the shower told her where he was. She could almost hear his sigh, a mixture of relief and regret, as he realized she had seen the recent additions to the wall.

She didn't go into the kitchen today. Instead, she opted for the overstuffed couch, but before she sat on it, she removed her jacket and draped it over the sofa's back.

About ten minutes later, the sound of the shower ceased, and Kyle emerged, his hair damp and tousled. "Thirsty? I've got coffee, tea, hot chocolate, and an excessive amount of ginger ale," he offered, his tone light but his concern for Amy's comfort clear.

"Ginger ale sounds great," she said, her shoulders relaxing as she settled into the soft sofa, the day's weight lifting off her.

Kyle headed for the kitchen, the familiar scent of home and safety enveloping him. A quiet sense of relief filled him. Amy was here. She was safe. Today, they might catch their breath. He returned to the living room holding a can with a glass over it bearing a picture of Tweety Bird and handed it to Amy. The one in his other hand was the Tasmanian Devil.

"These are quite the glasses," Amy said as she placed hers on the coffee table and poured ginger ale.

"Throwback to mine and my brother's childhood."

"I tried to ask you earlier about those photos on the wall. They weren't there the first time I came here. I rather like them. Did you buy them in a shop here in town?" She sipped her drink.

"No. Believe it or not, I took them."

"Wow. They're good." Amy stood and walked to where they were on display.

"Nah … you think so?" Kyle joined her where the art hung.

"Yes, I do." She gave his arm a gentle squeeze.

"I was going to offer to cook," he said. "However, my culinary skills mostly involve grilled cheese sandwiches, scrambled eggs, and anything I can microwave without setting off the smoke detector." Kyle's voice carried a warm humour and a touch of humility.

His lips tugged into a smile. "That's pretty much my menu."

She sipped her ginger ale and settled into the couch. They sat in companionable silence for a few moments, as the weight of the past few days slowly slipped away.

Kyle tilted his head towards her. "Later, we could do the world's simplest dinner. Grilled cheese and tomato soup. But, that's only if you're feeling adventurous."

"You make the soup with milk?"

"Is there any other way?"

Amy grinned. "I like the sound of that. A gourmet evening."

"Only the finest five-star service here," Kyle said, teasing, clinking his glass against hers like a toast. "Welcome to Café Kyle."

She laughed again, the sound filling the room with a lightness and relief that hadn't been there before. Some shadows that had clung to her since that terrible night loosened their grip.

When their dinner was ready, Kyle had committed to the fine dining air. He laid a tea towel over his arm like a maître d' and spoke in a horrible French accent. "Mademoiselle, your dining experience awaits."

Amy laughed so hard she almost dropped her glass. "Is Café Kyle always this fancy?"

"Only for our VIP guests," he said, setting a plate in front of her with an exaggerated flourish.

The grilled cheese was a perfect golden brown, and the aroma of the tomato soup filled the air, promising a comforting meal.

He sat across from her and raised his eyebrows. "Bon appétit."

Amy picked up half her sandwich and clinked her glass against his. "Cheers." Her eyes sparkled with amusement, and a smile played on her lips.

They savoured the simple meal, finding comfort in its unpretentiousness. After a few bites, Amy leaned back and smiled. "I always thought if I ever took time off, I'd do something dramatic like fly to Paris or backpack across Scotland."

Kyle grinned at her. "You still can, you know." He leaned his elbow on the table, resting his chin in his hand. "Okay, bucket list question — if you could wake up tomorrow anywhere in the world, where would it be?"

"Right now? Somewhere peaceful. A cozy cottage by the ocean. Maybe here," she said, "but without the drama."

Kyle's gaze warmed. "I think we can arrange that. Minus the drama, of course."

"Your turn. Where would you go?" she asked then laughed.

His expression became thoughtful. "I'm torn between Scotland during the Highland Games season or … Disney World. I'm a kid at heart."

Amy burst out laughing. Between fits of giggles, she said, "I can see you wielding a foam sword, dressed in a kilt, or wearing Mickey Mouse ears."

"You say that like it's a bad thing," he said, mock-offended.

Her smile reflected a lightness she hadn't known for days. Sitting here in Kyle's cozy apartment with him, the outside world didn't seem so frightening anymore.

Kyle gathered their plates and carried them to the sink as they finished their meal, still wearing the towel draped over his arm. Amy stood and started to help, but he waved her off. "No, no, tonight you are an honoured guest."

Amy rolled her eyes but sat and watched him. His presence was a comforting balm, easier to be around than she had expected. When he returned to the table, wiping his hands on the towel, she didn't shy away when he sat a little closer.

Kyle reached for her hand, like it wasn't a big deal, but when his fingers brushed hers, the contact sent a shiver up her arm. She curled her fingers around his, taking in his undeniable strength and unwavering steadiness.

As he gazed at her, the playful facade he often wore vanished. His thumb traced her knuckles in a deliberate, unhurried arc, his touch conveying a tenderness that filled the space between them with unspoken words.

The air shifted, and Amy's breath caught.

For a moment, Kyle leaned in. It wasn't enough to scare her, not enough to assume, just enough that if she wanted to meet him halfway, she could.

Despite her initial hesitation, Amy made a conscious choice. She squeezed his hand and leaned into his shoulder, a silent but clear affirmation of her feelings.

Kyle let out a slow, quiet breath. They stayed like that for a long moment — no rush, no pressure, just a calm understanding blooming between them.

Maybe peace wasn't a place, Amy thought. Perhaps it was a person.

Amy glanced up at him. "Thanks for today. For not pushing. For being ... normal."

He shrugged. Amy's gratitude left him uneasy, something unexpected. "You've had enough crazy for a while. I figured I could at least give you a morning or evening."

She laughed again, a sound that was like a melody to Kyle's ears, and he tried to memorize the way her eyes crinkled at the corners.

"Not boring," she said. "Comfortable."

He could live with that. He needed nothing fancy, and he didn't need to impress her. He wanted to be someone she could lean on when the world spun sideways. That was all that mattered to him.

Kyle reached across the table and brushed the back of her hand with his fingers. "Good. That's what I was going for."

They remained in that moment, their hands not quite touching, sharing a silent understanding that didn't need words.

That evening wasn't about grand gestures or significant moments. It was about the simple things — trust, warmth, and connection. Just the way Kyle preferred it.

Amy stood, pushed back her chair and started to gather the dishes.

Kyle stood right then, too. "Hey, guest privileges," he said, reaching for her plate before she picked it up.

Amy arched her eyebrow at him. "Pretty sure the guest rule expired after dinner was served."

He flashed a playful grin and snatched the plate from her hands, giving her a wink. "All right. But, if you're helping, you're on drying duty. House rules."

He carried the dishes to the sink. Amy followed, grabbing a dish towel from the drawer. The kitchen was small but cozy. Its space made it easy to bump into one another, but neither seemed to mind.

As Kyle washed, he flicked bubbles at her, sparking a playful back-and-forth. She rolled the towel and snapped it at him. After she dried each plate, she stacked them on the counter, adding to the light-hearted atmosphere.

"So," Amy said, "should I be worried you have house rules already worked out? Sounds way too organized."

Kyle chuckled. "When you live alone, you either get organized or live in chaos. I pick my battles."

She smiled and something shifted inside him. He wanted her to be comfortable, not like a guest or someone just visiting.

Had she seen something in his face? If so, she bumped her shoulder against his. "For the record, I think you're doing a pretty good job."

"Yeah?" He handed her another wet dish.

"Yeah." She dried it, stacked it on the others, and said, "Even if you're a terrible server."

"Tough crowd. Remind me to withhold dessert privileges next time."

Amy gasped in mock offence. "There's dessert?"

"There was. I might have to rethink sharing, now."

She shook her head, grinning as she folded the towel over the oven handle. "You're impossible."

Kyle leaned back against the counter, arms folded, watching her. "Maybe. But you're still smiling."

She met his gaze, and for a moment, their playful energy softened into something more tender — an honest moment between two people starting to find something real.

He broke the moment first, nudging her towards the living room. "Go sit down. I'll get the dessert."

Amy hesitated as if she might argue, but in the end, she smiled and obeyed, curling up on the couch and pulling a throw blanket over her lap.

Kyle couldn't quell the quiet, satisfied sensation in his chest. She was here. Safe and smiling. Somehow, despite everything, the night turned into something special.

He grabbed the dessert plates and joined her, ready to stretch the evening out longer.

Amy tucked the blanket around her legs and leaned back into the overstuffed couch cushions. The soft clinking of plates and Kyle's movement around the kitchen reached her ears.

These simple, homey sounds wrapped around her like another layer of comfort. In the wake of the past few days, it was a relief to just be, without tension, or fear's chilling presence. A normal evening.

A few moments later, Kyle appeared carrying two small plates balanced in one hand and forks tucked between the fingers of the other. He made a show of bowing as he presented her plate. "Your dessert, m'lady," he said in an exaggerated formal voice.

Amy laughed and accepted it. "You're determined to keep this bistro vibe going, aren't you?"

Kyle dropped into the armchair across from her. "What can I say? Commitment to character."

She shook her head and turned her attention to the plate. A slice of what looked like homemade apple crisp sat there, the top golden and crumbly. "This looks amazing," she said, her stomach rumbling.

"I cheated," Kyle admitted after he took a bite of his own. "Got it from the bakery down the street."

"Still counts."

Amy dug in, and the first bite melted on her tongue. Sweet, tart, and buttery all at once. She closed her eyes and savoured it.

When she opened them again, Kyle watched her with a soft, somewhat amused expression. Her cheeks warmed. "What?" she asked, brushing a crumb from her lip. Her cheeks warmed.

"Nothing." Then, after a pause, he said, "Just glad you're here."

Those simple words and how he said them — no heavy expectation, no pressure — unravelled something tight inside her chest.

"I'm glad, too."

They ate in silence for a while, the room filled with only the sounds of forks clinking against plates and the occasional contented sigh.

When Amy finished, she set her empty plate on the coffee table and curled back up with the blanket. She felt full, and not just from the food. Something deeper, something like peace.

Kyle leaned forward, elbows resting on his knees. "So what's next for you? Assuming no unexpected surprises show up at your door?"

Amy smiled at the teasing note in his voice then said, "Back to Izzy's house. I think it will be different now. Safer. Thanks to you, Maggie, and Gordon."

Kyle's expression grew serious. "You don't have to rush anything, Amy. If you're not ready, no one will blame you."

"I know." She tightened the blanket around her. "But I want to. I don't want fear deciding what I do anymore."

Kyle's mouth curved into a slow smile. "Good."

Their eyes met, and for a moment, the cozy room, the plates, and the world around them all faded. That was the moment Amy felt it. The pull between them was warm, confident, and full of possibility.

After clearing the dishes and tidying the kitchen together, Amy grabbed her jacket from where she had draped it over the couch earlier.

Kyle met her by the door, shrugging into his zip-front hoodie. "I'll walk you back."

She smiled up at him, touched by how he offered, as if it had never crossed his mind to do anything else. "Thanks."

Outside, the air was crisp and cool. The sidewalks were quiet, the occasional car passing by, and the muted sound of water lapping against the wharf. Amy felt a sense of calm, a rare moment of peace in the chaos of her life.

They walked side by side, their footsteps light against the old streets. For a while, neither spoke, but the silence wasn't awkward. It was a comforting blanket, filled with the soft undercurrent of trust growing between them.

Amy pulled her jacket tighter around her. "Tonight was nice."

Kyle glanced at her with his gentle smile in the dim light.

"Yeah, it was."

She hesitated, then said, "I can breathe again. Like, Lunenburg isn't where everything went wrong."

Kyle's hand brushed against hers in a light, almost accidental touch that made her heart jump. He didn't pull away. Instead, he slowed a little, giving her space if she wanted.

"It's your fresh start, too," he said, his voice carrying a weight of shared understanding. "Not just where it almost ended."

Amy let his words settle inside her, warming her more than her jacket ever could, like a gentle embrace in the chilly night.

Forty-Nine

Isabelle Morrison's House, Falkland Street, Lunenburg, Nova Scotia

July 17, 2019

When they reached Izzy's house, Kyle followed her up the steps but didn't crowd her when she turned at the door. She pulled the keys from her pocket, then paused with her hand on the doorknob. "Thank you. For everything."

"You don't have to thank me." His voice was rougher now. "I'm just glad you let me be here for you."

They stood under the porch light, their hearts beating in sync, and the world shrank into the small space between them. Amy felt a surge of warmth and hope, thinking how easy it would be to lean into him and let the connection between them pull her closer.

But she wasn't ready — not quite. The comfort of Kyle's presence and the fear of letting him in tore at her heart.

Instead, she smiled, genuine and full of hope that the future might be brighter. "Goodnight, Kyle."

"Goodnight, Amy."

She unlocked the door and stepped inside, pausing once to look back at him. He was still there, hands tucked into his hoodie pockets, waiting until she was inside.

Amy closed the door behind her, the sound echoing in the quiet night. Her heart was lighter than it had been in a long time.

Amy leaned against the closed door and took a slow, steadying breath. Tonight had been different. Lighter. Her lingering fears hadn't vanished, but they were no longer heavy.

She slipped off her shoes, the cool floor soothing her tired feet. She hung up her jacket, breathing in the familiar scent of home, then padded quietly upstairs. The familiar creaks underfoot comforted her and reminded her she was back in a place she could claim as her own, at least for now.

She changed into her soft flannel pyjamas in the bedroom and tied her hair in a messy bun. The simple act of getting ready for bed made her more grounded, more herself.

She slid under the covers and reached for her phone on the nightstand. The screen lit up the dim room with a message from Emma, sent soon after Amy had returned.

Glad you're okay. Call me tomorrow if you want to talk. Big hugs!

Amy smiled, her heart swelling with affection for her friend. She typed out a quick reply, her fingers dancing on the screen.

Thanks, Em. I'll call tomorrow. Miss you.

Setting the phone down, Amy turned off the light and snuggled deeper into the bed. She saw a slice of the night sky through the window, the stars faint but steady.

She would see Kyle again tomorrow, although she didn't know what he had planned. He was like that. Filled with surprises. Their relationship was always an adventure, and a flutter of excitement at the thought of what he might have in store for her made her shiver.

As her eyelids grew heavier, Amy held onto that small, precious commodity called hope. It was a beacon of light in the darkness, a promise of better things to come.

Fifty

Lunenburg Farmers' Market, Green Street, Lunenburg, Nova Scotia

July 18, 2019

Kyle stepped aside to allow Amy to enter the market building first. The hum of conversation and laughter wrapped around her as she wandered through, hand in hand with Kyle. They stopped many times so he could chat with the vendors. It was the norm here in this small town. Locals talked with vendors, catching up on their latest news.

The community centre's open doors let in the salty air, mingling with the smells of freshly baked bread, herbs, and smoky fish. Amy inhaled, taking in all the rich aromas. She paused at one table where the vendor had homemade jams and bought a couple of jars. One was for use at Izzy's, the other to take home, and maybe give it to Emma, unless she saw something more in her friend's style.

Amy paused at one table. The sign read *Fresh Lobster Rolls —just like Nan made 'em.'*

"You want one?" Kyle asked, raising his eyebrows.

"I've never had one before. I'm not sure if I'll like it."

"Two lobster rolls, it is then."

"But, what …"

"I'll eat the second one."

"I'll buy us something for dessert."

With a warm smile, the vendor prepared their rolls and wrapped them well to keep them warm. As they continued through the market, Amy spotted several watercolour paintings on display. One, in a prominent position, was of Bluenose II. She bought it to take back to Sudbury to remind her of her time here in Lunenburg.

"Can we stop by Izzy's so I can drop these things off before heading to our picnic?"

"Sure. C'mon. Her place is right along the way." Kyle's tone and familiarity with the route made Amy relax as they left the market building.

Fifty-One

Isabelle Morrison's House, Falkland Street, Lunenburg, Nova Scotia

July 18, 2019

"Don't be too long. I can't vouch for the safety of the lobster rolls. I might get hungry and eat them," Kyle said, teasing.

He leaned against the railing and watched Amy disappear into the house. She had been lucky with the weather. So far, there had been no rain, but the farmers at the market needed it. A warm breeze soughed through the leaves in the trees overhead. Somewhere farther away, the faint hum of someone mowing their lawn mingled with the birdsong in the trees and shrubs on the property. It was a typical Thursday morning in Lunenburg — quiet, familiar — but far from routine.

Kyle glanced towards the bag containing the lobster rolls, still warm from the vendor's oven. He exhaled, letting his gaze wander over the houses on Falkland Street. The MacLeod home across the street. He'd walked this street at least one hundred times, if not more, but today it looked … different. Was it Amy? Perhaps the way she smiled and chatted with the vendors like she'd always known them? Like she was already part of the town.

That scared him a little.

Not since the accident, he wasn't used to wanting things he couldn't name. Not since the years when most conversations with his mother had ended in silence, and the house had grown more quiet than he could bear.

But then, Amy had walked into his life.

Now, he wondered what it would take to ask someone to stay. Not just for the season. Not a summer of leisurely mornings and walks through the town and the market. But for the messy, unremarkable days, too. The real ones.

With a creak of the door, Amy stepped back onto the porch, brushing her hands together.

Kyle straightened, and a soft smile tugged at the corners of his mouth. "Ready?"

She nodded as she fell into step beside him. He had a destination in mind but wanted it to surprise her.

As they strolled, a subtle but unmistakable shift occurred within Kyle. It wasn't fear or doubt that he felt, but a burgeoning sense of hope, like a small flame flickering to life in the darkness.

Fifty-Two

Blockhouse Hill, Lunenburg, Nova Scotia

July 18, 2019

When they reached the top of Blockhouse Hill, Amy couldn't help but marvel at the beauty of the place. She pulled out her phone and snapped pictures before sinking onto the bench with a soft sigh. Kyle handed the paper-wrapped lobster roll to her. It was warm in her hands, and the smell of the sea air hung in the breeze. The view stretched out wide before her. The sky, wavering between sun and cloud, framed Lunenburg's colourful waterfront. It was a breathtaking sight, a peaceful scene that made her chest ache with its beauty.

Amy glanced sideways at Kyle. He was quiet, too, sitting beside her with one leg stretched out and the other bent, elbow resting on his knee. He gazed at the harbour, but his mind seemed miles away.

She looked down at the roll in her hands but didn't take a bite.

This town had settled into her, like morning fog lifting one layer at a time. The days had passed with a rhythm which Amy hadn't realized she needed. Walks. Quiet. The warm, contented sensation of people who saw her without asking her to explain herself. Asking nothing of her at all.

And then there was Kyle.

She turned to him again, noting the faint lines near his eyes when the wind made him squint. The way he hadn't pressed when she needed time alone. The way, like now, he waited for her, not rushing her, and not filling the silence with empty words. His patience and understanding were like a warm blanket, comforting her in the silence.

David would have despised this. The pace, the quiet, the openness. He would have ridiculed the 'quaint little town' and grumbled about the lack of reception for his cellphone. He would have made her feel foolish for lingering too long in a museum or the market or tearing up at a name etched in stone. But Kyle was different. He listened. He watched her with steady attention, making her aware that what she said mattered. Like *she* mattered.

Amy swallowed hard, and her fingers tightened on the edge of the sandwich paper. She wasn't sure what scared her more — that she was falling for Kyle or that she already had. And time was running out.

Beside her, Kyle turned to meet her gaze. He didn't smile, but looked at her with his steady, brown eyes. It was like he knew she had thousands of words behind her eyes and would wait for any of them.

She managed a small smile and said, "Thank you."

He didn't ask what for, just nodded. "Anytime."

For one moment, Amy imagined what it would be like to hear that word daily for good.

"Now, at least try your lobster roll." The lines at the corners of his eyes crinkled when he smiled.

Amy unwrapped the still-warm lobster roll. A burst of flavours filled her mouth when she bit into it for the first time. Each tender, juicy piece folded in the clean, sweet, briny taste reminiscent of the sea. The meat, cool and buttery, was sweet without being overpowering, and melt-in-your-mouth tender. A whisper of lemon and creamy mayonnaise bound the pieces together, enhancing the natural flavour. The bun's toasted texture added a delightful contrast, soft inside, crispy outside. Every bite she took felt like a taste of the coast — fresh, simple and satisfying.

She took another bite, chewed, and then looked at Kyle.

"This is … incredible," she said, wiping the corner of her mouth with a napkin. "The lobster's so sweet and tender — like they just touched it, just enough to let it shine. And the bun? Toasted to perfection. Soft inside, crispy outside. Whoever made this knew what they were doing."

Kyle grinned, watching her enjoy it more than she realized.

"It tastes like the ocean," she said, glancing towards the harbour. "But not in a fishy way. It's fresh. Clean. It's just … like here, you know? It's a familiar and intriguing taste, a unique blend of the sea and the chef's skill."

He nodded, amused and moved by how she took it all in.

"I don't think I've ever eaten something that felt like a place before. But this does. It tastes like Lunenburg."

Kyle leaned back and grinned. "Careful, Amy. You wax lyrical about lobster rolls, and I'm gonna get jealous of a sandwich."

She laughed, almost choking on her bite. "Relax. You've got way better manners than this lobster roll."

"Good," he said with mock relief. "I was worried I'd have to dress in a butter drizzle and call myself lunch. Might have to toast myself to golden perfection and see if I can compete."

She nudged him with her shoulder. "You're ridiculous."

He returned her bump. "Yeah, but I'm *your* kind of ridiculous."

Their conversation paused. Kyle brushed a crumb from his jeans and turned to Amy. "You okay?"

After a brief hesitation, she nodded. "Yeah. Just … trying to hang onto this moment a little longer."

He leaned back, taking in the serene surroundings. "It's a good one. Solid view. Quiet. Few moments like this."

Amy turned towards him. "That's the thing. I didn't realize how much I needed quiet until I found it here."

Kyle looked at her, a hint of sadness in his eyes. "And now you have to go back."

She swallowed. "Soon. I keep checking the house swap app

for messages from Izzy saying she's finished and ready to come home. So far, nothing."

A breeze tugged a strand of her hair loose, and he reached out and brushed it behind her ear, his touch gentle and lingering. "I'm going to miss you, Amy," he said, his voice rougher than usual, his hand still near her face.

Her breath caught. "You're not making this easy."

"Not trying to."

She laughed and blinked fast. "Good."

They looked at each other for a moment, their shared emotions filling the space. Something unspoken stretched between them, delicate and aching.

Kyle stood first and offered his hand to help Amy up. "Come on. I'll walk you back."

Amy took his hand but didn't move right away. Instead, she stepped closer so that their shoulders brushed. "I'll remember this hill. And this view. And you."

He said nothing, but gave her hand a gentle squeeze.

Somehow, that said enough.

Fifty-Three

Trot in Time Carriage Tours, Bluenose Drive, Lunenburg, Nova Scotia

July 20, 2019

The soft clop of hooves on the asphalt was calming and surreal. The carriage, a vintage beauty with plush cushions and intricate carvings, turned from Bluenose Drive onto Montague Street. Amy leaned back, enjoying the warm breeze. The town, viewed from here, resembled a storybook illustration. Colourful houses lined the hills, their paint faded by the sun.

Kyle sat beside her on the narrow seat, one arm draped along the back. She wasn't sure if he realized he was doing it, or if she cared. His warmth enveloped her. The steady rhythm of the horse's gait and the driver's lilting voice, recounting local legends and pointing out old homes, added to the experience. The sea's scent mingled with the sweet aroma of the flowers in the nearby gardens, creating a heady mix that filled her senses.

"I've lived here my whole life," Kyle said, his voice low. "And yet, seeing it like this? It's different."

"More romantic?" she teased.

He smiled at her. "Yeah, a little."

The driver, Terry, sporting a handlebar moustache and a penchant for puns, turned in his seat. "You folks picked a good day. Not too hot. Not too crowded. And you've got the scenic route, past the old Lunenburg Academy next."

Amy nodded, her eyes drawn to the distant white shape of the academy building, standing proud against the blue sky. "It's beautiful."

"Haunted, too," Terry said.

"Everything is haunted in this town, isn't it?"

"You say that like it's a bad thing." Kyle chuckled, then directed his following comment to the driver. "We took part in the Haunted Lunenburg walk."

The carriage turned again, offering a glimpse of the harbour glittering behind the shops and houses. Amy exhaled, her fingers brushing Kyle's on the seat between them. She didn't move them away. She didn't want to.

"I can see why you stayed," she said.

"I can see why I want you to," he said, his voice so soft she wasn't sure if she'd heard him right. But she didn't ask him to repeat it. She let the words settle, like dust in the afternoon light.

The tour ended at the base of King Street, near the wharf, where the salty scent of the ocean mingled with something sweeter. Vanilla and strawberry drifting from the small ice cream shop across the road. Amy just had time to thank Terry and wave goodbye before Kyle tipped his head towards the shop.

"Want one?"

She didn't hesitate. "Only if they have black cherry."

They crossed the street with the ease of people who weren't in a rush. Everything in Lunenburg seemed to move more slowly, more gently. The sound of seagulls, the gentle breeze, the sight of colourful houses, and the smell of salt in the air. There wasn't a push to be anywhere else. No need to perform or pretend. Not with Kyle. Not here.

A few minutes later, Amy balanced a waffle cone while they strolled towards the wharf's edge, the scoop of ice cream softening under the sun. Kyle chose mint chocolate chip, saying it was underrated and under-appreciated, much like he felt.

She rolled her eyes at that.

They sat on the edge of the dock, letting their feet dangle over the water. Boats bobbed, and the creak of ropes and the slap of waves making for a lulling backdrop.

Amy licked her cone, then looked at Kyle. "Do you believe in ghosts?"

He grinned. "You're asking me that after we did the Haunted Lunenburg walk and the carriage tour?"

"Humour me."

He looked out over the water, and his grin softened. "I think some places remember. Some people do, too. Sometimes that remembering is like ... company."

She said nothing right away, but let the breeze brush past her skin, sticky with the heat and the sweetness of her cone. "What do you think Lunenburg remembers about you?" she asked, her voice soft with a hint of vulnerability.

It took a long time for him to answer. "I think it knows I'm trying."

That settled deep in her chest between the ache of wanting to leave and the pull to stay.

Amy bumped his shoulder with hers. "For what it's worth, I think it's working. We're in this together, eh?"

He turned to her with a lopsided smile, and they just watched each other for a few seconds. The moment teetered, on the edge of something new, something not quite ready to be said out loud.

Instead, Amy offered him the last bite of her cone.

And he took it.

Fifty-Four

*Isabelle Morrison's House, Falkland Street,
Lunenburg, Nova Scotia*

August 5, 2019

Amy logged in to the home swap site to see if there was any news from Isabelle. She had finished her novel and submitted it to her editor before the deadline. They could return to their own cities at any time.

With its friendly people and the allure of the colourful houses, this town had woven its way into Amy's heart. She didn't want to leave, but Isabelle seemed ready to return. Amy had an open-ended return-to-work date thanks to her doctor, allowing her to prolong her stay in Lunenburg. But this also meant she had to find another place to stay, a prospect that tugged at her heartstrings.

She needed to speak with Emma and find out what was happening back in Sudbury. Was David still annoying people? Amy didn't believe he had even left Lunenburg. The uncertainty of his whereabouts was a constant source of tension, making her wonder if he was lying low, plotting his next move if he was still in town.

It would take a few days to arrange her bus and train passage for the trip home. The leg from Lunenburg to Halifax was the easiest part. From there, she was at the mercy of VIA Rail and the days that the Ocean returned to Montreal from Halifax.

The most challenging part would be breaking the news to Kyle that their time in Lunenburg was ending. Amy's heart ached at the thought of leaving, but she had a job and an apartment to return to, a reality that weighed on her.

Fifty-Five

Fishermen's Memorial, Bluenose Drive, Lunenburg, Nova Scotia

August 5, 2019

Amy found herself at the Fishermen's Memorial on Bluenose Drive. Somehow, in her wandering, she had never seen it before. The tall, granite pillars, arranged in a circle, stood in solemn dignity above the harbour. Each pillar bore the engraved names of men, whispering of lives lived and lost at sea, and their fishing boats. A breeze tugged at her hair, carrying the odour of salt and something more profound, something older. She stepped closer, a sense of reverence for the beauty of the memorial settling over her.

Were Kyle's father and brother listed on it? She moved from pillar to pillar, tracing the engraved names until she found the surname Ferris. Robert (Bob) Ferris, Logan Ferris. Father listed first, and the son was below him. A lump formed in Amy's throat, thick and unexpected. The simplicity of the names hit her harder than she anticipated. She felt a wave of sorrow wash over her, a deep ache in her chest that seemed to grow with each passing moment.

Did Kyle come here often? Or on the anniversary of the boat's destruction? Or for one of the memorial services they held? She'd overheard people here talking about having attended. She wondered what these visits meant to Kyle, how they helped him cope with the loss of his father and brother, and how they might be affecting him now.

She moved around the pillar, and on the next side, a list of the lost ships' names appeared. She ran her fingers down the smooth, sun-warmed surface until she reached the name of Kyle's father's boat, *Seaworthy*. The irony of the name struck her like a slap. *Seaworthy*, a name that now held a profound sense of irony and reflection.

Amy traced it, her fingertips lingering in the grooves. A gust of wind stirred her jacket, echoing the ache that had settled low in her chest. Her actions, filled with a sense of loss and reflection, echoed the weight of her emotions.

Amy sank onto one of the granite benches at the memorial. It was quiet here, save for the cries of the gulls and the waves slapping against the pier. Kyle hadn't told her how old he was when the accident took place. He mentioned his mother died in the last few years. Would she find her grave in Hillcrest Cemetery?

A single leaf rustled across the pavement and made her glance up. The granite pillars stood steadfast and unyielding against the horizon. It wasn't just a monument to lost lives and the grief left behind. Amy sat a little longer, the silence not offering any answers — only space.

Amy lingered longer at the memorial, her eyes resting on the name *Seaworthy* one final time. Then, as if by instinct, she turned and made her way back towards the heart of the town.

She didn't head straight to the cemetery. Instead, she took a quick detour to the house on Falkland Street. The front garden, Izzy's pride and joy, was alive with a riot of summer colour — deep pink peonies, white ones, too, and daisies. Amy paused by the low wall and gathered a handful of blooms.

Fifty-Six

Hillcrest Cemetery, Gallows Hill, Lunenburg, Nova Scotia

August 5, 2019

It was a peaceful walk to the cemetery from Falkland Street, even though most of it was uphill. The quiet hush of the vast place greeted her as if she were an old friend. Birdsong in the distance, leaves rustled overhead, and the occasional creak of branches shifting in the breeze were the only sounds.

Finding the grave would be like finding the proverbial needle in a haystack. Amy began a methodical walk row-by-row, reading the names on the stones. She started on the Kissing Bridge Road side, where the haunted walk she and Kyle did one night began. At least it was daylight, so any animal, wild or otherwise, wouldn't scare the life out of her when it streaked past. It still might, but at least it would be visible.

It didn't take too long to return to the grave of Sophia McLaughlin. With it being light out, she could read the plaques affixed to the wrought-iron fence surrounding the burial site. Tears pricked her eyes when she recalled the story their guide told them of the circumstances of the young teen's death.

Amy continued her row-by-row prowl. She stopped at some gravestones, not because of the names, but the design. To her surprise, she found that the desired stone listed Kyle's father and brother. She was sure he told her they never recovered their bodies. She wasn't about to press him on that subject. Amy pulled out her phone and took a picture of the headstone. Unlike some others, it was plain. Their surname was at the top in uppercase letters. Mother's name (Eileen) in the middle, father (Robert) on the left, and son (Logan) on the right.

Her throat tightened. She hadn't expected the sight of Kyle's mother's name to hit her quite so hard. There was something so final in stone, so unforgiving. The dates told their own story — Eileen had lived for years after she lost her husband and son. Alone.

How had Kyle endured all this? The weight of it. The silence. The absence.

She knelt, placing Izzy's flowers before the marker. A few graves away, a black cat basked on a sun-warmed headstone. Was it the same animal that shot past her the night of the haunted walk? Amy continued staring at the animal. It opened its eyes and glared at her for interrupting its lounging, then put its head back down and resumed sunbathing.

The sight of the cat unnerved her, but not like it did in the dark, brushing against her leg. Amy returned to the task, her fingers touching the granite's rough surface, and said, "You'd be proud of him." She stayed for a few minutes longer, her hand resting on the base of the stone, the wind threading through her hair.

Amy didn't speak aloud. She had no words that would have made sense, anyway. Only quiet respect for acknowledgement.

The one thing she and Kyle had in common was that their fathers were deceased. Hers died in 2015 from mesothelioma; his from a fishing accident.

David had played on Izzy's sympathies by lying about Amy's mother's health to find out where she was. Not anymore. She would no longer let David walk over her and gaslight her. She still smiled when she recalled his defeat at her hands in The Knot Pub where she had stood up to him and asserted her independence.

After a time, she stood, brushed the grass clippings from her knees, and took one last look at the names carved in granite. She turned and walked back towards the town, the sounds of Lunenburg growing louder with every step, as if pulling her back to the here and now.

Izzy wanted to come home, so Amy had to ensure the house was in the same immaculate condition when she arrived. Amy took pride in maintaining the home, reflecting her care for Izzy and her desire to provide a welcoming environment.

Fifty-Seven

Lunenburg Esso Bus Stop, Falkland Street, Lunenburg, Nova Scotia

August 7, 2019

The air was thick with unspoken words as Amy stood by the packed suitcase outside the Esso station where the bus would arrive. The tension was evident, hanging heavy between them. Staying in Isabelle's mansion had given her a taste of a life she never thought she'd have, and now it felt like an unbearable weight. Kyle stood opposite her, arms crossed, his eyes shadowed with something she couldn't quite decipher.

He spoke after a long awkward silence. "You sure you have to go?" His voice was rough, forced, and casual, but she heard the catch.

Amy swallowed hard, her heart heavy with the weight of her departure. She forced a small smile, trying to mask her emotions. "I've booked the buses and trains. Life is waiting." But her voice cracked on the last word, betraying her inner turmoil.

Kyle took a slow step forward, then another, until he was close enough that she could see the storm in his brown eyes. "And what about this life?" he asked, his voice just above a whisper.

She released a shaky breath, reaching up to touch his cheek with trembling fingers. "This life … wasn't supposed to happen. I wasn't supposed to …"

"Fall for me?" he finished for her, catching her hand, pressing it against his chest. His heartbeat pounded beneath her palm, matching the ache in hers.

She let out a choked laugh. "Yeah. That."

Silence stretched between them, thick with everything they hadn't figured out yet. The unspoken emotions hung in the air, a testament to the depth of their connection. Kyle exhaled and pulled her into his arms. She clung to him, her fingers fisting the back of his shirt, memorizing the way he felt, the way he smelled — salt air and something him.

"I don't want to say goodbye," she whispered into his shoulder.

"Then don't," he said against her hair. "Say 'see you soon.'"

Tears burned as she pulled back just enough to meet his gaze. "See you soon," she promised.

Kyle leaned down and kissed her forehead before stepping back. His hands fell to his sides, reluctant but letting go.

With one last, aching look, Amy turned towards the direction the bus would come from. She gripped the handle on her large bag like it was the only thing keeping her upright. She didn't look back. She couldn't.

Not yet.

Kyle stood in the parking lot, hands stuffed deep into his pockets, clenching his jaw so tight it ached. The low hum of the engine and distant chatter did little to distract him from the sharp weight pressing against his ribs.

Amy stood by the bus, her suitcase beside her, phone in hand. She wasn't looking his way, but the tension in her shoulders was apparent as she fidgeted with her purse strap.

She didn't want to leave. And yet, she was still going.

He placed Amy's large suitcase in the cargo hold under the seating area, then walked her to the door. "See you soon," he said with a catch. Seamus was in Amy's free arm, and he ruffled the top of the stuffed animal's head. "You, too."

An announcement sounded overhead, calling for final

boarding, and that was it. The last chance to say something. The last opportunity to ask her to stay.

But Kyle wasn't that guy. He couldn't ask her to give up her life in Sudbury just because he didn't want her to go.

So he just stood there.

Amy turned, as if she sensed him watching. Their eyes met across the distance, and she gave him a soft, sad smile.

Kyle managed a lopsided, familiar, teasing smirk even when his heart wasn't in it. He raised a hand in a half-wave.

She hesitated, then lifted her own, mirroring him.

Then she turned, picked up her suitcase, and climbed the steps onto the bus.

Kyle breathed out, leaning back, fighting the urge to chase after her. He didn't want another day without her.

The engine rumbled to life and the door hissed shut. The bus pulled away, carrying Amy with it, her hand pressed against the window as if in a wave.

Kyle didn't move.

Didn't leave.

Not until the bus had turned the corner and disappeared down the street, taking a piece of him with it.

Fifty-Eight

VIA Rail Station, 1161 Hollis Street, Halifax, Nova Scotia

August 7, 2019

The first thing Amy did when she arrived at the train station in Halifax was check her large suitcase. She didn't need to drag it around with her, nor did she want to. Whether she stayed in Sudbury after her return remained to be seen. A move back to Lunenburg meant giving notice to her landlord, closing up her apartment, quitting her hospital job, moving her furniture, and finding alternative employment and accommodation. The order wasn't important.

Now, alone in the station, she was nervous. After standing up to David in the pub, she hadn't felt anxious about walking around the town. No sensations of being watched. Had David stayed in Lunenburg and followed her here? He couldn't use the tracking app anymore because Kyle got rid of it. But that wouldn't deter David. He'd follow her and torment her. At least the anonymous texts had stopped, and Emma sent her one saying he was back in Sudbury.

Amy sat on the hard bench inside the Halifax train station,

arms wrapped tightly around herself. The station was busy but not chaotic — travellers moved about, some lost in their own world with headphones, others chatted in hushed voices.

Her train to Montreal wouldn't leave for a few hours, and every minute felt like an eternity.

She'd told herself over and over that she was being paranoid. That David wasn't here. The tracking app was gone and wiped from her phone before she left Lunenburg.

But that didn't mean he hadn't found another way.

Her fingers drummed against her thigh as she glanced toward the entrance. Every time a man walked through, her breath hitched.

She took a deep breath, focussing on other boarding calls to reassure herself of her safety and his unawareness of her presence.

Then her phone pinged.

A number she didn't recognize. No name. Just a message.

Thought you were so smart in The Knot Pub.

Amy's stomach dropped.

I see you're on your way home. Came to your senses.

Her fingers tightened around the phone.

He knew. But how?

A chill crawled up her spine as she scanned the station again, heart hammering against her ribs. Was David here? Watching? Had he followed her from Lunenburg? Her breath came in short, shallow gasps, her body tense with fear.

She swallowed hard, her mouth dry. She could ignore the message, pretend she hadn't seen it, but that wouldn't make the fear disappear. Her mind was a whirlwind of fear and uncertainty, each thought a battle against the rising panic.

What if he wasn't just watching? What if he was waiting?

Her mind raced through options. Stay in a crowd. Find a security guard. Call someone. Emma? Kyle? Would calling Kyle even be fair when she'd just left him behind? Each option seemed fraught with its dangers and uncertainties, leaving her more trapped than ever.

Her thumb hovered over her screen.

What the hell was she supposed to do now?

Amy scrolled through her messages to Emma's last text and

typed.

David's here in Halifax. He had to have followed me from Lunenburg.

While waiting for Emma to respond, Amy picked up her purse and Seamus and moved to another seat with her back to a wall with more people.

Her phone pinged again.

Impossible, Ames. He's back here. I saw him yesterday.

That wasn't possible. If David was back in Sudbury, how would he have known she was in Halifax on her way home? Amy copied and pasted the two texts from David and sent them to Emma with a note.

Explain these.

She should have stayed in Lunenburg, as Kyle wanted her to. Things had gone so well there.

He probably followed the person who swapped homes with you. If he saw her leave, he likely assumed you were coming home.

That could be how it happened, but it didn't make Amy any more relieved about the messages.

You're right, he's trying to get in my head. I'm safe, but I hate he still gets to me.

Fifty-Nine

Montreal Central Station, 895 Rue de la Gauchetière Ouest, Montréal, Quebec

August 8, 2019

Amy, her mind filled with Emma's unsettling messages about David and the house swap partner, found a seat against a half wall. The platform for her next train was just beyond the stairway and the escalator. Spending last night on the train had eased her paranoia, but not her vigilance. She remained alert, watching reflections in the windows and trying to make herself as inconspicuous as possible.

Just as Amy started to relax, a man resembling David approached her area. Amy hid her face, but couldn't resist stealing glances to track his movements. Her heart raced as she feared he might spot her. He disappeared into the Business Lounge or a restaurant, leaving Amy with heightened alertness.

With her phone gripped in her hand, Amy wrestled with the idea of reaching out to Kyle. What could she say? As she waited to board her train to Toronto, she distracted herself by scrolling through the pictures on her phone. She paused at the first one she took of Kyle in his privateer costume. She brought her finger to his lips in the image and whispered a soft 'sorry.' The tears she had been holding back since leaving Lunenburg broke free. She fumbled in her pockets, found a tissue, and dabbed her eyes.

Sixty

Fishermen's Memorial, Bluenose Drive, Lunenburg,
Nova Scotia

August 10, 2019

    Amy left on Wednesday. To him, it already felt like she'd been gone a lifetime, ever since he watched her bus leave from the Esso station. The space beside him had stayed with him ever since. Quiet and unmistakable. Their first meeting on Zwicker Wharf captivated him. She smiled hopefully, yet guardedly, clutching her stuffed Scottie dog as if it were a lucky charm. At first, he had thought it ridiculous, a grown woman with a toy in tow, but he realized how wrong he'd been. It mattered to her. And because it mattered to her, it mattered to him, too. He felt a deep sense of responsibility towards her, a commitment to her well-being that he couldn't shake off.

    In her absence, Lunenburg felt changed somehow. The streets were still colourful, and the harbour was still busy with the usual rhythm of boats, gulls, and wind. But without Amy, it all felt a little less alive. Her absence seemed to cast a shadow over the vibrant town, leaving a void.

Kyle didn't visit the Fishermen's Memorial unless he was leading a walking tour and never mentioned his personal connection to it. It had always felt too close, too exposed. But today felt different. Long overdue. It seemed like the right time. He stepped into the centre to orient himself with the stone that bore his father's and brother's names, as well as the name of their vessel. *Seaworthy*, yeah, right. Talk about an oxymoron. When he determined he had the right one, he ran his index finger down the smooth granite surface until he came to their names. His father first, and his brother below.

He hadn't told Amy why he refused to go out on boats. Not really. Just the condensed version. Once, he had gone out with his father and hadn't passed the harbour before seasickness rendered him useless. His dad had to turn around and bring him back to the pier. He had never forgotten the look on his father's face, the tight-lipped disappointment, and his brother's relentless teasing that followed for years.

Moored just beyond the memorial, two fishing vessels bobbed on the water. The smaller boat reminded him of *Seaworthy*, except his father's boat was painted a bold, unmistakable red.

The memory of the day they got the news hit him like a wave. Kyle sat on the second-highest step, elbows resting on his knees. He couldn't remember who came and broke the news to them — another fisherman? The police? What he remembered was the sound of his mother's cry, guttural, raw and echoing through the house in a way that still made his stomach clench.

She was now buried in Hillcrest Cemetery. Although he never found his father's and brother's bodies, the engraver carved their names, birthdates, and death dates into the granite headstone beside hers. A family monument to lives cut short. The weight of their loss hung heavy in the air, a constant reminder of what could have been.

Kyle hadn't thought to bring flowers. It hadn't occurred to him until he saw a small bouquet of wildflowers lying on the ground before one of the other stones.

He glanced at his empty hands and then the stone path at his feet. A small sun-bleached stone caught his eye. Smooth and flat, the thing Amy would have pocketed for no reason other than it felt nice in her hand. He bent down and picked it up, brushing off the grit.

Kyle didn't speak. There was no one to hear him, anyway. In his mind, he saw their faces — his father's stern, weathered features, and his brother's mischievous smirk, that never faded, even when he was being a pain. He felt their presence, as if they were standing right beside him.

He placed the stone at the memorial's base, just below their names. It wasn't much. It wasn't anything, but it was what he had. "I'm sorry," he whispered, barely aware the words had passed his lips.

For what? Not going out again? Not becoming the man they expected? For surviving when they didn't? He wasn't sure. Maybe it was all of it.

A breeze stirred the air, bringing the aroma of salt and seaweed. The tranquil atmosphere of the memorial site enveloped Kyle, soothing his troubled mind. A gull cried overhead before the quiet returned. Kyle stood there longer, letting the silence settle around him. Then, with a deep breath, he turned towards the road.

He didn't know what came next, but he wasn't walking alone for the first time in a long time.

Kyle hadn't gone far when his phone vibrated in his pocket. Although tempted to ignore it, something nudged him to check. Amy. Her name lit up the screen. No subject. No context. Her message was brief.

Thinking about you today. Hope you're doing okay.

He stopped dead in his tracks. How did she realize where he was or what he'd just done? And yet, she seemed to sense the undercurrents. Her unexpected support was comforting and reassuring, like a warm blanket on a wintry day.

His fingers hovered over the screen before he typed back.

You too. Just left the memorial.

After a moment's hesitation, he added more.

I left something there. Nothing big. But it felt right.

The dots danced on his screen, followed by her reply.

That's everything. That's remembering.

Kyle stared at her words, letting them settle into the space that had felt empty all morning. A quiet warmth bloomed in his chest — not joy, but something else — something like peace.

He put the phone in his pocket and kept walking.

Sixty-One

Amy's apartment, Jean Street, Sudbury, Ontario

August 11, 2019

Amy sat at the kitchen table in her apartment, the late morning sunlight spilling through the window onto the half-folded laundry in front of her. Her mug of coffee had gone cold beside her, a silent testament to her inner turmoil. She hadn't touched it in over an hour, lost in her thoughts and emotions.

Her phone rested facedown on the table, but she continued glancing at it like it might buzz on its own, but it didn't.

It was late when she got home the day before, so she went straight to bed. She'd dreamt about Lunenburg again. The memories, so vivid and real, felt like a bittersweet embrace. The sound of the wharf under her feet, the breeze at Blockhouse Hill, Kyle's laugh when he mispronounced Seamus the first time. Ordinary things that clung to her like the salt air, a reminder of a life she once had.

Since she woke, she couldn't shake the sensation that something was pulling at her. Lunenburg.

Amy rose, crossed the room and picked up the dried sprig of lavender from Izzy's garden. It was a reminder of the peaceful moments she spent there. She hadn't meant to keep it, but it ended up in her carry-on, and she didn't have the heart to dispose of it when she unpacked. Her thumb brushed the fragile petals.

Without thinking, she picked up her phone, opened the thread between her and Kyle, read the messages from the day before, and typed a new one. Kyle, the one person who always understood her, received her message.

Hope Lunenburg is treating you well today.

Amy stared at it for a second, then hit send before she second-guessed herself.

Some things didn't need to be explained.

Amy walked to the living room and opened the curtains. There was no sign of David's vehicle, which brought a sigh of relief. Amy, a nurse at the local hospital, pulled out her phone and texted Emma, her colleague and confidante.

Home. Got here last night. See you tomorrow?

Amy's phone pinged, and she jumped. At first, she was reluctant to open the message in case it was another anonymous one. Thankfully, it was from Emma.

I'm on noon to midnight this week. You coming back to work?

Was Amy ready to return to work? The question loomed over her, casting a shadow of uncertainty. She was still nervous and jumpy, and the thought of running into David somewhere sent shivers down her spine. He was the last person she wanted to see, and the prospect of facing him at work was daunting.

Not ready.

Amy set her phone on the table and retrieved her laptop from her bag. She was determined to find a job as a nurse somewhere else, away from David's reach. She cherished her nursing career, and the thought of giving it up was unbearable. Yet, the fear of David's potential violence loomed over her. She had seen the evidence of his temper on Emma's arm before she left for Nova Scotia. It wasn't unthinkable that he could turn violent.

She typed RN jobs into the search engine and scrolled through the results. The majority that came up were all in her area. Most hospitals, nursing homes, and retirement homes wanted bilingual staff. Her French was atrocious, having not used it since she finished high school. Even Ottawa was a bilingual city. Amy wanted something further afield. And at least the same pay grade. She tried again and added Nova Scotia to her requirements. Nothing promising. A couple of temporary positions in Halifax. A long-term care position up near Cape Breton, but not a single thing in or near Lunenburg. Nothing felt like the right fit.

Amy stared at the screen, the weight of her decision bearing down on her. It was easy to dream when she was walking quiet trails and eating lobster rolls on hillsides. But reality was a different story. That she was even considering a change? That was significant, wasn't it?

Did the town even have a hospital? She googled it and found that Fishermen's Memorial Hospital was located there. It had a website. She could apply online if they accepted applications that way. Amy scoured the site but couldn't find a place to submit a resume. That meant she would have to apply through the province, and there was no guarantee she'd get a position in the town she wanted. Back where she felt safe and loved. Where neighbours were friendly and looked out for one another.

Amy shut down the job board tab and opened a blank document. A fresh resume was required. One that reflected who she was, not just where she'd worked and what she'd done. She needed it to show the nurse she'd become. The kind who knew how to listen. One who had seen how a slower pace, a caring community, and a little breathing space could shift everything.

It took over two hours, longer than she had expected. Amy reread it twice, made changes, then uploaded it to Indeed and sat back. The submission confirmation blinked at her from the screen like a question mark.

Would anyone even see it? Amy didn't know, but it was out there. A small piece of her reaching back towards the place she wasn't quite ready to let go of. It was a beacon of hope, a sign that she was not giving up and was fighting for her right to live and work without fear.

She wouldn't be a prisoner in her own home, so she picked up her phone, keys, and stepped out the door. Every step she took was a step towards freedom, towards a life where she could practice her beloved profession without the constant threat of

David's violence.

Outside the building, Amy shoved her hands deep into the pockets of her hoodie. The pavement remained soaked from the previous night's rain, and the sky was grey. A few cars passed, their tires hissing on the wet asphalt. Down the block, a dog barked.

She took a deep breath, expecting … didn't know what. But what her lungs pulled in wasn't what she wanted. The air wasn't as fresh as it was in Lunenburg. The salty tang, seaweed smell, wood smoke, and sun-warmed scent of the Back Harbour Trail were missing. So were the cries of gulls, and the creaks of boats tugging at the moorings. This smelled like the city. Dust, gasoline, and wet concrete. The absence of these familiar scents and sounds only deepened her longing for Lunenburg.

Her chest tightened — not sharply, but in that quiet way that meant she was somewhere she didn't want to be. Not today.

She stood there a moment longer and listened to Sudbury's hum. Then she turned and let herself back into the building, putting the chain on her door once back inside.

Her apartment felt too quiet. Amy slipped off her shoes, hung her hoodie on the hook, and crossed into the living room, where she picked up the sprig of lavender again. This time, she inhaled the flower's soft scent. Her fingers lingered on the petals, a simple act that evoked the place she longed for.

In Lunenburg, everything had felt clearer, quieter inside her, even when the town buzzed around her. And then there was Kyle. He never pushed. He just *was*. Steady, kind, real. That may have made the difference.

Her phone lit up, and her heart jumped a little.

Hey. Just thinking about you. Passed Zwicker Wharf this morning and caught myself looking for a certain Scottie dog holding court on an Adirondack chair. Lunenburg's quieter without you. Hope Sudbury's treating you well today.

Her lips tugged into a smile, and a warmth, like a gentle embrace, filled her from the inside out. Kyle's message had a way of reaching her, even across the distance.

Amy spent most of the day finishing her laundry. She put the folded clothes from the kitchen table into her dresser. It was drudgery, but it kept her from checking her phone every five minutes to see if she'd received an email from the job search website.

About six o'clock, she put a frozen meal in the microwave. It must have been something Izzy bought when she was at Amy's during the house swap. After cooking, she emptied the rice into a bowl, topping it with the spicy chicken, peppers, cashews, and sauce. It was delicious. Amy savoured every bite.

Around nine o'clock, she made herself a cup of green tea. Once she finished it, she'd head off to bed. One time zone covered Nova Scotia, another New Brunswick, and crossing into Quebec, she was back in her accustomed time zone. It would take her a few days to get her body clock back in rhythm.

Fifteen minutes later, a loud, sharp knock sounded on her door. It was too familiar. Amy's spine stiffened and her stomach turned. Then came the voice.

"Amy, I know you're in there."

David. She froze. For the briefest of moments, she contemplated pretending she wasn't home. But it was too late. His voice was on the other side of her door.

"I saw your lights on. Don't play games."

Heart racing, she unlocked the door but left the chain in place. Amy took a deep breath, then said, "What do you want?"

His face twisted. "What do I want? You're the one who came back. I figured you'd stopped sulking and realized you belonged here."

This was rich, but it was David. "Don't flatter yourself."

"Don't start with me, Amy. You owe me a conversation. Hell, you *owe* me, period. You cost me my job."

Her blood went cold. "I wasn't even in the *province*, David."

"You think that matters?" He shoved the door, stretching the chain to its limit. "You said things to people before you left. Someone must've reported me. They wouldn't say who. But I'm certain it was you. You were always undermining me."

Amy slammed the door shut and released the chain. When she opened it, her voice was steady. "Get out, David. I don't owe you anything."

He blinked. "You — what?"

"I'm not the same woman you used to bully into silence. You don't get to come into my space and make demands. So leave. Now!"

He stared at her with his teeth clenched, then said, "So what, this is you now? Standing on your own? You're nothing without someone to take care of you."

"I was nothing with you. Now, I'm figuring out who I am at last."

David's bravado crumbled a little. He lowered his voice to a growl. "You think this is over?"

Amy didn't flinch. "It's been over for a long time. You're just the last to figure it out."

He stared at her a minute longer, then turned on his heel and stormed off. She locked and bolted the door, leaned against it, and released a shaky breath.

Her hands fumbled as she grabbed her overnight bag and stuffed a few essentials into it — laptop, toothbrush, pyjamas. She grabbed the spare keys to Emma's building, threw on her jacket and slipped out the back door of her building.

The night air was sharp. She walked fast, with purpose, ignoring how her pulse pounded in her ears.

Sixty-Two

Emma's apartment, Ste Anne Road, Sudbury, Ontario

August 11, 2019

It was almost eleven when Amy let herself into Emma's building and took the elevator up. The second the apartment door shut behind her, she allowed herself to breathe. That was only the second time she had ever stood up to David, her courage growing. The first was in Lunenburg, and Kyle wanted to intervene on her behalf, but she didn't let him.

Emma was on duty until midnight, so it would be about twelve-thirty with the bus before she got back to her apartment. Rather than startle her friend when she walked in, Amy sent her a quick text.

At your place. Will explain when I see you.

The quietness of the apartment wrapped around Amy like a balm. Her hands still trembled, and the adrenaline was not out of her system yet.

How did David even think what he did was okay? Showing up as if nothing had happened. In the last few months, there had only been a blip, a moment of misunderstanding and hurt that she thought they had moved past. As if she'd been off sulking and was ready to fall in line again.

Of course, it was her fault he got fired. Her fault that his life was off the rails. It always came back to her. Except this time, she didn't crumble. She hadn't backed down or tried to smooth things over. She stood her ground, and with a steady voice, told him to leave.

Amy glanced around Emma's living room — the comfort, the bright colours, the books on the coffee table. It felt safe, like breathing after she'd held her breath for too long. The familiar surroundings of Emma's apartment wrapped around her like a warm blanket, providing a much-needed sense of relief and comfort.

Her thoughts flicked to Kyle. She missed him more than she wanted to admit, she cared for him deeper than she realized. What was he doing? Was he thinking of her, too? She didn't reach for her phone because she didn't want to worry him.

Sixty-Three

Emma's apartment, Ste Anne Road, Sudbury, Ontario

August 12, 2019

Emma's key turned in the lock. Since she received the text from Amy, she wondered what had happened. It wasn't like her friend to pick up stakes and appear on her doorstep late at night for no good reason. Her brief text message spoke volumes, despite not saying much. Something happened that made Amy fear for her safety in her own apartment.

She tiptoed in so that she didn't wake her friend. Emma found her on the couch covered with the throw kept on the back for that reason. Emma was about to get another blanket when Amy pushed herself into a sitting position.

Emma crossed the room in seconds and pulled her friend into a hug. That's when Amy's tears began to flow. She said nothing. When someone you loved was unravelling in your arms, words were useless.

Instead, she held Amy tighter, letting her cry. All the fear, shock, and frustration simmering beneath the surface — Emma sensed it with how Amy clung to her, fists curled into the back of her sweater.

She rocked them back and forth like that when Amy, stressed from nursing school, couldn't breathe because of the pressure. The stakes were higher this time, and Emma understood something had happened.

Once the tears had subsided into ragged breaths, Emma pulled back and looked Amy in the eyes. Her eyes were red and wet, and her cheeks damp. But a fire, a resilience and determination Emma had never witnessed, sparked within her. This inspired Emma.

"I've got you," she said, brushing a strand of hair from Amy's cheek. "Whatever he did, whatever happened, I've got you."

Amy nodded.

Emma didn't push. Amy would talk when she was ready, not before. Until then, Emma would be her safe place, a beacon of trust and reassurance, because that's what friends did.

The two sat in silence for a long time. The only sounds in Emma's apartment were the hum of the fridge and the ticking of the clock over the kitchen door. Amy wiped her face with the sleeve of her hoodie, then took a steadying breath. When her voice came, it was quiet and flat but laced with steel.

"He was in my apartment."

Emma didn't move, but every nerve stood at attention.

Amy looked down at her hands. "He was *so sure* I'd come back to him. Like the last month never happened."

A chill ran through Emma. "Amy …"

"He blamed me. Said I ruined everything. I got him fired. Messed up his life. And I — I said nothing to anyone. I haven't seen him since that night he turned up in the pub in Lunenburg."

Emma raised her hand to Amy's cheek. "Did he hurt you?"

"No," Amy raised her head and looked into Emma's eyes. "But he scared me."

Emma exhaled, but the tension only eased slightly.

"I didn't know what he would do, so I told him to leave. Told him he had no right to be there. And when he did, I grabbed my stuff and came here."

Emma closed her hand around Amy's. "You did the right thing."

"I just … I couldn't stay there. Not alone."

"You're not alone. You never have to be alone with this again. You can stay here as long as you need."

Amy smiled, and a small laugh escaped her lips. "I keep thinking about Lunenburg. About how good it felt to be seen. To be safe. Then returning here made me remember how unreal that felt. But I don't want it to be unreal anymore."

Emma leaned closer. "Then don't let it be."

Amy blinked. "I've already applied online for a nursing job in Nova Scotia."

"Good for you. Now, let's figure out how to get you there for good." Emma said.

Amy sighed. "I don't want to talk anymore."

"You don't have to."

Amy sat on the couch with her legs curled under her, a soft throw blanket over her lap, and a cup of chamomile tea cooling between her hands. The distant hum of the city outside Emma's apartment felt like a lullaby, soothing her nerves.

"So you're really thinking about it?" Emma asked as she settled onto the couch beside her, with a cup of tea.

Amy nodded. A strange combination of nerves and excitement rippled through her. "Yeah, I mean, nothing's official yet. I haven't even heard. But it felt right when I uploaded my resume to Indeed. A door I wanted to walk through."

Emma smiled. "I'm proud of you, you now. It's brave. Not everyone would consider making a fresh start like that."

A lump rose in Amy's throat. She swallowed it down and managed a small smile. "It's scary. But it's even scarier when I think about returning to my old life — to all the places where I kept trying to force myself to it."

Emma set her cup on the coffee table and leaned towards Amy. "That's because you're growing past it. You're not who you were a year ago. You deserve more than surviving. You deserve to thrive.

Amy blinked back tears. "You're going to make me cry."

Emma chuckled, picked up the tissue box, and handed it to Amy. "That's what I'm here for."

Amy took it and laughed through her tears. "Thanks, Em. I

don't know what I'd do without you."

"You'll never have to find out," Emma said. "No matter where you go, you've got me in your corner."

Amy felt a wave of relief for the first time in what seemed like forever. She believed things could and would get better.

Emma watched Amy dab at her eyes and cradle her tea again. This time, her movements were slower, more at ease. It warmed her heart to see hope return to her friend's face. It was fragile and tentative, but it was there. Emma's unwavering support was a warm blanket, comforting Amy in her time of need.

She took a sip of her own tea, letting the silence stretch before breaking it. "If you get the job, we'll figure this out together. Apartment hunting, moving plans. All the fun, not-overwhelming stuff."

Amy laughed, a shaky one then said, "I haven't even thought that far ahead yet."

"That's okay." Emma smiled. "One step at a time. You don't have to have it all figured out right now."

She meant it, too. After everything Amy had been through, all the self-doubt and second-guessing, Emma would move heaven and earth to help her find her footing again.

"I want you to understand," Emma said, "you're not doing this alone. Whether you need help packing boxes or scouting out cute coffee shops in Nova Scotia, I'm in."

This time, Amy's smile reached her eyes, and Emma felt fierce affection for her friend. She'd seen Amy's heart break piece by piece over the past year. Now, she was gathering those pieces back together and shaping them into something more substantial.

Emma would be there, cheering her on every step of the way, a steady presence in Amy's life.

She grinned and nudged Amy with her elbow. "Although, fair warning, if you end up with a place that has an ocean view, I'm visiting so often you might get sick of me."

Amy laughed again, a real, easy sound this time. "I think I could live with that."

Emma raised her mug in a mock toast. "To new beginnings

and ocean waves."

Amy clinked hers against Emma's, her smile steady now. "To new beginnings."

By now, Amy's tea was stone cold. She rose from the couch and padded to Emma's kitchen to pour it down the sink. Amy leaned against the counter. Was running back to Lunenburg the right thing? It would be a moot point if she didn't secure a job there. There would be no return trip to the quaint village, and the people she had gotten to know and love — one in particular, Kyle.

"Ames, come out here. I think I've found you the perfect place to live down there," Emma said from the living room.

Amy returned and sat beside Emma, watching her scroll through apartment listings like it was the most exciting thing in the world. Bright images of weathered shingles and colourful front doors filled the screen.

Lunenburg was charming, but with every click Emma made, Amy felt the tightness return to her chest.

"What about this one?" She rotated the screen towards Amy. "It's a one-bedroom on Duke Street. You can even see the harbour from there. This is so you," Emma said, gushing with enthusiasm.

"It's nice," Amy said, forcing a smile.

Emma gave her a sidelong glance. "Nice? That's the best you can do?"

"I like the bump. That's what they call it, you know. The Lunenburg bump. The kitchen is in it. I don't like that. I'd rather have my living room there."

"Here's another in the same converted house. This one has a private entrance." Emma slid her computer over to Amy so she could get a good look at the pictures.

"I like this one. And I especially like the rent. It's much less than what I pay for where I am now."

"Email them. Tell them you're interested. You're moving to Lunenburg, and this apartment is the perfect size for you."

Amy wrapped her arms around herself, making herself as small as possible. "I don't know. Perhaps I rushed into this. What if it's the wrong move? What if I'm just running away? Besides,

I don't have the job yet, Em." Amy slid the laptop back over to her friend. "I doubt very much they'd rent an apartment out to someone unemployed."

Emma closed the laptop and turned her full attention to her friend. "You're not running away. You're moving towards something. Towards peace. Towards starting over. You still have your job here at the hospital. What can it hurt to show your interest? If things don't work out, then you email them back and say 'Sorry, I won't be moving.'"

Amy bit her lip. "What if it's too fast? I only uploaded my resume yesterday. I've not had a call for an interview. And should that happen, what if I don't get the job?"

"Then you apply elsewhere in Nova Scotia or wait and try again. You're not locked into anything yet, but don't let fear decide for you.

"I don't know, Em. It's … a lot. I'm worried it won't work out. I'll get back there, and Kyle will have found someone else."

Emma softened. "It's a lot. But so was staying in a relationship that made you question yourself daily. This? It's you taking back control. You're allowed to be scared, but you don't have to let that fear stop you."

Amy swallowed hard. Emma's words were comforting, but the lump in her throat wouldn't budge. She wasn't sure if she was ready, but maybe she didn't have to be. Perhaps the decision came first, and the courage followed. "I'm going to take a shower."

Emma remained on the sofa. Amy was in the shower, likely replaying their conversation and self-doubt creeping in through every crack.

She recognized that look in Amy's eyes. It wasn't fear. It was a sense of being stuck, unable to move forward.

Emma returned to her laptop and opened the bookmarked listing again. Duke Street, one-bedroom, private entrance, brick fireplace. Dreaming was the simple part. But Emma was determined to make it a reality.

Her fingers hovered over the contact form. She wouldn't book it, only ask about the unit's availability. Do the smart thing and get an idea of the process. That wasn't overstepping, was it?

She could almost hear Amy's voice, filled with uncertainty. *You didn't trust me to do it myself?*

Emma took a deep breath and typed.

Hello,

I'm inquiring on behalf of a friend who may be relocating to Lunenburg in the fall for a nursing opportunity. Her name is Amy Scott, and you can reach her at ascott83@gmail.com. She's interested in Apartment 2 on Duke Street and would like to find out if it's still available and what the application process entails.
Many thanks,
Emma Williams

She reread it twice, then hit send. As the email faded, she closed the laptop and leaned back, chewing on her thumbnail. She hadn't decided for Amy, only opened a door. Still, guilt filled her chest. But Emma hoped Amy would understand her intentions were pure.

The aroma of flavoured coffee drifted towards the bathroom where Amy was dressing after her shower. When she returned to the living room, she curled her legs up under her on the couch and accepted the cup Emma offered. She should feel grateful, safe and supported.

Instead, there was a prickle like something had shifted while she was in the shower. Emma had become more chipper, even for her.

Amy took a sip and glanced towards the kitchen where Emma was buttering toast like it was the most normal thing in the world.

"You're quiet," Emma said, glancing over her shoulder.

"Thinking." Amy forced a smile.

Emma unplugged the toaster and walked into the living room with two plates of buttered toast. "There's something I should tell you."

Amy's heart dropped to the pit of her stomach. "What?"

Emma set the plates on the coffee table and slid into the chair opposite. "I might've ... emailed the letting agency in Lunenburg about that Duke Street apartment."

Amy blinked. "You *what?*"

"I didn't commit to anything. I just asked if it was available. I was trying to help," Emma said, her voice soft. "You've been second-guessing yourself, and I thought ... if I could take one tiny step off your plate, it would make things easier."

Amy's sense of personal autonomy was strong, and she felt it was being challenged. The coffee, once a comforting ritual, now tasted bitter. "I know you mean well, but you should've talked to me first. It's *my* move. *My* life."

"I get that," Emma said, shrinking. "I didn't want you to miss out because you got spooked. You've come so far, Ames."

Amy's determination was unwavering. "I'm not saying I won't go. I'm saying I have to do it on my terms. If I let something else retake the reins, what's the point of starting over?"

Remorse filled Emma's eyes, reflecting her regret. "You're right. I'm sorry. I should have trusted you."

The tension lingered for a breath too long before Amy exhaled. "Just no more emails without me, okay?"

"Promise."

Despite everything, Amy managed a faint smile. "Now pass me that toast before you try to rent me a U-Haul, too."

Emma had walked to the nearby Sub Shop to get them sandwiches for their lunch. Amy declined the outing. The thought of an encounter with David paralyzed her with fear. She stayed holed up in Emma's apartment, her anxiety about the condo and the looming deadline gnawing at her.

Her phone pinged on the coffee table. She picked it up and swiped to open the email app.

Subject: *Re: Duke Street Apartment Inquiry*

Her heart thudded, her hands trembling as she read the message, and when she finished, she reread it.

MELANIE ROBERTSON-KING

Dear Ms. Scott,

Thank you for your interest in the Duke Street property. We've noted your name and provisionally held the apartment until September 5th. If another party submits a fully completed application with a deposit and first month's rent before then, we will proceed with the earliest qualified applicant.
Please let us know if you intend to proceed.
Regards,
Bill Cummings
Pine Cove Property Management

Her mouth went dry. September 5th. That gave her just over three weeks to decide, less if someone swooped in with a cheque and a pen. The uncertainty of the situation weighed on her, adding to her anxiety.

Amy sat there for a moment, letting the words sink in. A distant car horn, wind rustling the trees outside Emma's apartment, filtered through the open window.

It was happening. No longer a daydream whispered in Emma's apartment. This was real.

She typed a quick message to Emma.

They emailed back, and will hold it until the 5th. No promises. If someone else signs first, it's gone.

Despite the pressure, Amy was determined to figure this out and decide.

The kettle clicked off, and Amy poured water into the two mismatched mugs Emma had dug out of her cupboard. The one in Amy's hand read, in faded gold script, *This might be wine.*

She handed the other to Emma, then sat at the island with a quiet sigh. The subs, purchased earlier, remained wrapped. This would be a meal and a cup of tea.

The weight of the email hadn't lifted since it landed on her phone. It clung to her like a wet wool sweater.

"So," Emma said, blowing over her tea. "What are we thinking about Duke Street?"

"Like I'm on a moving walkway and can't get off."

Emma looked at her. "But do you want to get off?"

"I'm not sure. Part of me wants to run towards it. Fresh start. New coast. Kyle." Her cheeks warmed when she said his name. "I think about the next few weeks, and it's overwhelming. There's the lease to end, packing, finding movers, quitting my hospital job, and saying all my goodbyes."

Emma set her mug down. "It is a lot, but you don't have to do it alone."

Amy smiled. "I understand. You're already apartment hunting on my behalf."

Emma winced. "Okay, fair enough. That was a little pushy."

"No, it was sweet. It's …" Amy paused and chose her words. "This has to be my decision. I need to be certain I'm going for the right reasons, not because I'm afraid of what staying means."

Emma nodded. "That makes sense."

A pause stretched between them.

"Do you think I'm running away?" Amy asked.

Emma tilted her head. "I think you're running towards something. Towards peace and a place that makes you safe and seen. And away from the mess that came before. But sometimes, that's okay."

Amy blinked fast. "Thanks."

"You've been surviving for a long time, Ames. It's time to live."

That stuck. Amy wrapped her hands around the mug and let the warmth seep into her palms. September 5th was coming fast. Maybe it wasn't about being ready. Perhaps it was about deciding.

Sixty-Four

Amy's apartment, Jean Street, Sudbury, Ontario

August 15, 2019

Amy unlocked her apartment door. When she walked up her street, there had been no signs of David's car. She heaved a sigh of relief over that. Whether she stayed in Sudbury was unknown, a looming uncertainty that added to her emotional burden. She knew she couldn't stay here any longer.

Emma's had been her home. Now, she was packing everything up for storage until she found a new apartment in either Lunenburg or her current location. She hoped for the former but didn't want to get her hopes built up in case things went wrong. And in her life, that's what happened most of the time.

She had ordered boxes from one of the local moving companies, which were scheduled to arrive today. While she waited, she emptied her kitchen cupboards and placed her plates, glasses, and other dishes on her kitchen table.

As she removed the last dishware from the top shelf of the upper cabinet, her elbow hit one item, and it dropped to the floor and shattered. Amy's heart sank when she realized it was a dish from the set her grandparents had given her for her first birthday:

a plate, a bowl, and a mug. The latter sat in broken shards on her kitchen floor, a tangible symbol of her past and her loss.

Amy dropped to the floor amongst the shattered crockery. She couldn't hold back the tears. This had moved with her from Ottawa to Sudbury and survived. Packing her apartment up for whatever eventuality was the end.

The doorbell rang, and Amy froze, feeling trapped in her home. Was it David coming back again to cause trouble? She dragged herself up, walked to the door, and peered through the peephole. It was the guy bringing the boxes. She released the chain and opened the door, a sense of relief mixed with the lingering fear of David's return.

She had at least ten boxes, an enormous roll of bubble wrap, and packing tape to seal them up. The cartons were flat. Amy had to assemble them, which wasn't a problem. How many more pieces would she destroy before she got them packed up?

With her dishevelled hair and tired eyes, Amy tackled the bedroom instead since she'd already broken something dear to her heart in the kitchen. She heaved her large suitcase onto the bed and opened it.

She folded a sweater and placed it into the piece of luggage. Her clothing didn't hold as many memories as the mug she broke. Most of the clothes were ones she bought, although her mother had made a couple of hand-knit sweaters for her. At least Amy couldn't break them.

Her apartment looked like a war zone. Dresser drawers half-open, the roll of bubble wrap trailed off the coffee table, and the stack of boxes leaned against the wall. This was limbo. She wasn't home. She wasn't there. She was just …

Every piece of clothing she packed felt like a question. Was she boxing up her life for a fresh start in Lunenburg, or making space to breathe while she figured out her next move?

Amy paused at the edge of her bed, her fingers lingering on the corner of a photo frame. It held a picture of her, Emma, and two other nurses at a Halloween party, all in scrubs and splattered with fake blood. That had been a good night, silly and full of laughter. But it was also a night that marked the end, before things began to unravel, before David.

Amy shook off the thought and wrapped the frame inside one of her sweaters. Her phone buzzed on the nightstand. Her heart fluttered for a moment. Kyle? The hospital? No, it was Emma.

Any more second thoughts? Want me to bring you more boxes or coffee? xo

Amy smiled, touched and exasperated all at the same time. She hadn't told Emma she was leaning towards the move again. She didn't need to because Emma could always read between the lines.

She typed a response.

Boxes, please. Coffee, yes. And talk me down from my spiral when you get here? I need you.

With the message sent, Amy sat back against the pillows and let her gaze drift towards the window. The sky had a washed-out look. It wasn't quite grey or blue, and it seemed like it couldn't decide either, just like her, torn between her past and an uncertain future.

The knock on the door was a comforting rhythm. Familiar with the sound, Amy didn't need to check the peephole. She opened the door to find Emma balancing a tray with two iced coffees and a shopping bag stuffed with flattened boxes.

"Your fairy godmother has arrived," said Emma. Her presence filled the room with warmth as she breezed in with the aroma of the roasted cold brews and her usual confidence. "I bring caffeine, cardboard, and, as always, unsolicited opinions."

Amy snorted and took the tray from her. "You had me at caffeine."

Emma kicked the door shut with her heel and followed Amy into the living room. "How's it going? You still teetering on the edge of an existential meltdown, or have you committed to the Nova Scotia fantasy yet?"

Amy handed Emma a coffee. "Somewhere in between. I cleaned out most of my kitchen cupboards. I also cried over a broken mug from my first birthday dish set. And even though it doesn't look like it, there is a method to the piles on the table. Keep, maybe, and what was I thinking? So, progress."

Emma arched an eyebrow. "The broken mug did you in?"

"Yes." Amy reminisced, a hint of nostalgia in her voice, "I'd had it since childhood, and I knocked it over while getting other pieces from the cupboard."

Emma's expression changed. She took a long sip of her drink and settled onto the arm of the couch. "It's okay to grieve the life you thought you were building."

Amy nodded and sank into the cushions beside her. "I think I want to go back," she said, her voice almost lost behind the lid of her cup. "To Lunenburg, but I don't want to rush into something and then regret it."

"Don't rush, then," Emma said. "But don't stay here because it's familiar. You don't owe Sudbury anything."

"I owe myself a fresh start."

Emma squeezed her hand. "You do."

The two friends sat in silence for a moment, iced coffee cool in their hands, flat cardboard boxes leaning against the wall.

Emma nudged her. "Do you want me to bubble wrap your candle collection, or are we taking another mug break?"

Emma built a box and taped it across the bottom. She started wrapping Amy's keep pile and loading it from the stack on the table. "Don't want to make these too heavy. I'm not so worried about the movers, but when you get to your new place, you don't need to be lugging these great heavy things around. I'll label the boxes according to the rooms they'll be going into. Hopefully, it will make less work for you when you arrive in your new digs."

She glanced towards the living room, where Amy was under a pile of bubble wrap and framed photos. Amy's determined face, surrounded by the chaos of tape, cardboard, and dust, filled Emma with admiration. The sounds and smells of her work only intensified this feeling. She thought Amy looked smaller, not in stature but in energy.

"Do you want all your towels and bed linens together? It might be easier when you get there. Hard to say what you'll have for closet space," Emma called out, trying to engage Amy. She didn't get a reply from under the packing material in the living room.

Emma folded the last of the dish towels with more care than expected. She set it on top of the stack on the counter. She had taken a risk emailing the letting agent for the Duke Street apartment in Lunenburg. Amy was on the list and had until the fifth of the month before she might lose out on the place. Everything would align, and she would get the apartment, job, and the man she had been pining for.

Amy found her way out from under the bubble wrap. "You think I can do this?" she asked, her voice tinged with uncertainty.

Emma leaned forward with her elbows on her knees. "I think you already are."

Amy was halfway through labelling a box of winter clothes when her phone pinged on the coffee table. She felt a surge of anticipation, then dashed from the bedroom to the living room.

Unknown sender. That sounded ominous. Her heart skipped a beat. She tapped open the notification.

Subject: Employment Application – Fishermen's Memorial Hospital
From: hr@fmhospital.ns.ca
Date: August 15, 2019
Time: 10:14 a.m.
Dear Ms. Scott,

Thank you for your interest in the nursing position at Fishermen's Memorial Hospital. We're pleased to inform you we have shortlisted your application. We'd like to schedule a virtual interview at your earliest convenience to discuss your qualifications and potential fit within our team further.
Please let us know your availability over the next five business days.

Warm regards,
Susan Landry
Human Resources Coordinator
Fishermen's Memorial Hospital

Amy read the message twice, and then a third time, blinking. The apartment, the packing, the long talks with Emma. She was done with the thought that it *might* happen. Now it was real. The job interview, a potential turning point in her life, was within reach.

She set the phone down with care, as if being too abrupt would scare the moment away. She sat there in silence for a full minute, her hands clasped in her lap, and her heartbeat loud in her ears.

Then she stood, returned to the box in the bedroom, scribbled out the previous lettering, and replaced it with a single word.

LUNENBURG.

Amy stared at her phone for another minute before she glanced towards the kitchen. "Emma?" she called, her voice unsteady.

A few seconds later, Emma was beside her. "You okay?"

Amy held out her phone. Emma took it, and her brows knit as she scanned the screen. Her face lit up partway through.

"You got shortlisted," she said, her voice filled with excitement. "Amy, that's incredible!"

Amy managed a smile. "They want to schedule a virtual interview."

Emma handed back the phone, her eyes shining. "And? When do you want to do it?"

"I'm not sure," Amy confessed, sinking onto the couch. "It's … big. Real. I packed that box, and now the future isn't just a maybe anymore. It's a reality I have to face."

Emma sat beside her, her presence a comforting anchor. "Of course, it seems big. It *is* big. But you've come this far for a reason, Amy. You're ready for this."

"I know. I …" Amy looked at her hands. "What if I mess it up? What if I'm not ready?"

Emma reached over and took her hand. "You're more ready than you think. And I'll be right with you while you prepare. Heck, I'll even help you pick out your interview outfit."

Amy laughed, and the tension broke like a bubble. "Something else tells me you already have one in mind."

"Three." Emma grinned. "But I'll narrow it down."

Amy exhaled, leaning into the flicker of excitement rising

beneath the nerves. "Okay," she said. "Let's schedule it."

Sixty-Five

Emma's apartment, Ste Anne Road, Sudbury, Ontario

August 19, 2019

Amy sat on the edge of the dining room chair, her laptop on the table before her. The screen glowed with the now-familiar video platform interface. Her heart thudded a little too fast, and the warmth rose to her cheeks despite the cool air drifting through the open window. This was not just another job interview. It culminated years of hard work, tested her resilience, and was a step towards a new chapter in her life.

"You look fine," Emma said from the kitchen doorway, arms folded and leaning against the frame. "Professional. Approachable. Nervous but in a charming, not unhinged way."

Amy laughed. "Thanks. That's what I was going for," she said.

Emma had picked her navy blouse, paired with simple stud earrings and light makeup. Her hair was down but not unruly. Behind Amy was a framed ocean photo. A leafy plant from Emma's collection was also visible on a side table.

She rechecked the time. Two minutes to go.

Emma moved behind her, rested her hands on Amy's shoulders, and squeezed them. "You've got this."

Amy nodded, not trusting her voice. A notification pinged, and Amy sat up straighter as the screen showed a woman and a man in their forties. The woman had silver-streaked hair in a bun; the man, warm eyes and a clipboard.

"Hello, Amy. I'm Susan Landry from Fishermen's Memorial Hospital, and this is Dr. Trevor Langdon. Thanks for joining us today."

"Thank you for having me," Amy said, relieved her voice didn't tremble.

The questions came but weren't unkind. They asked about Amy's experience in emergency nursing, her thoughts on working in a smaller community-focussed hospital, and her approach to handling conflict or complex patients.

Amy spoke more confidently than expected, drawing from years of moments she'd filed away and forgotten. Patients calmed, crises managed, and teamwork forged under pressure.

Her mind flicked back to Lunenburg and its narrow streets as she answered questions about adapting to unfamiliar environments. How the town had wrapped around her like a blanket, and to Kyle, his steady presence and her unexpected comfort of belonging.

"I've learned that adaptability isn't about skill," she finished, "it's about listening, observing, and being willing to keep learning. I think it fits well with the care your hospital provides."

When the interview ended thirty minutes later, Susan smiled. "Thank you, Amy. We'll be in touch soon. Safe travels, if you end up moving east."

The screen went dark. Amy leaned against the back of the chair, her heart racing, her mind a whirlwind of emotions. She felt relief, excitement, and a tinge of fear. The uncertainty of the future loomed large, but she also felt a sense of accomplishment for facing the challenge head-on.

Emma peeked around the corner. "So? How'd it go?"

Amy exhaled a breath she didn't realize she'd been holding. "I think … I think it went well."

Emma grinned. "I'll chill the sparkling cider."

After the interview, Amy teetered on the edge of cautious optimism and a whirlwind of panic, her heart racing with the weight of uncertainty.

Emma, ever the supportive friend, prepared a platter of cheese and crackers with their cider. But despite her efforts, Amy's stomach fluttered like it hadn't received the memo. The stress-inducing part was over, but she could just manage the glass of sparkling cider.

She wandered around Emma's apartment, her heart pounding with each email check. Susan had said *We'll be in touch soon*, not *We'll email you right away with a yes or a no*.

About an hour and a half later, her phone pinged, and she snatched it up so fast she almost dropped it. It was not the hospital. It was a group text about a birthday dinner for a nurse on her floor.

Emma glanced up from her laptop. "You want me to go into full stalker mode and call the hospital pretending to be you?"

Amy smiled. "Tempting, but it's a bit too soon for that. I just had the interview a couple of hours ago.

Emma set her cider glass down. "Have you told Kyle?"

Amy shook her head. "No. I don't want to until I know something for sure. If I don't get the job, there's nothing to tell. And if I do ..." she trailed off, picking at a loose thread on a buttonhole of her blouse. "I want it to be a surprise."

Emma arched an eyebrow. "A pleasant surprise, or where you turn up on his doorstep and he calls the cops because he thinks you're a ghost?"

"The good kind," Amy said with a laugh. "I think. Oh, I'm unsure. We were just starting to figure things out, and I left. If I bring it up too soon, I'll just jinx it. Or I'm chasing something that might not want me back."

Emma's expression softened. "You're not chasing. You're choosing."

That quiet sentence landed somewhere deep in Amy's chest.

She looked out the window where the trees started wearing their late summer red and gold. "I want it to work. Not only the job, or moving ... everything."

"And it will," Emma said. "But in the meantime, I'm banning you from checking your mail for two hours. Change your top, and let's go for a walk or something. How about down to Memorial Park?"

Amy hesitated, then stood. "A walk sounds good." She retreated to Emma's spare room and changed out of the interview top into a sweatshirt. She cast one last glance towards her phone as she grabbed her jacket. Still no email. Still no word. Still a heart full of maybes.

But … maybe it could be the start of something.

Sixty-Six

Memorial Park, Sudbury, Ontario

August 19, 2019

"It's been ages since I've walked through here. It's so peaceful, most of the time," Amy said, looking up into the canopy overhead. The sunlight filtered through the leaves, casting a dappled pattern on the ground. "It's something that David would never do. Not part of his corporate image, I guess."

Emma snorted, a bitter laugh escaping her lips, then looped her arm through Amy's, a gesture of solidarity and support.

"Now that I think about it, we did nothing here in town that was away from either my apartment or his. More often than not, it was mine. It was like he was ashamed to be seen with me in public," Amy confessed, her voice tinged with sadness and frustration.

"Or … maybe besides gaslighting you, he was also cheating on you. If you two weren't out and about together, the other woman — or man, for that matter — would be none the wiser."

Amy turned and stared at Emma. "You think?"

"Nothing that man does would surprise me. Now, forget about him. We're supposed to be out enjoying this lovely weather."

"Kyle and I did a lot of things together. Walking tours, the farmers' market, the Back Harbour Trail, Sawpit Park, Blockhouse Hill, and a horse-drawn carriage ride. He listened to me. He protected me. I think I fell for him the moment we met on Zwicker Wharf." Amy's voice was full of hope, a sharp contrast to her past relationship.

"And now you're preparing to go back to him." Emma's said, her voice gentle, and her words soothed Amy's troubled thoughts. She guided Amy towards an empty bench where they sat in companionable silence. Birdsong filled the air. It wasn't tangy and salty like Lunenburg, but in a green space.

"You'll be the best candidate for the job. It's yours to accept or refuse," Emma said, her voice filled with admiration for Amy's nursing skills. She believed that. Amy was a skilled nurse; her compassion and care shone through in every patient interaction. She had the gumption to speak up and advocate for patients, whether it was a doctor or a family member she challenged.

Emma took a deep breath and let what she said to Amy sink in. The air, for the city, was fresh, and the late flowers still bloomed. But it would change soon enough, the seasons shifting as they always did. Across the park, city workers were clearing one bed to prepare for the coming winter.

Winter. The thought of it made Emma shiver. What were the winters like in Lunenburg? They were on the ocean. She had looked it up on Google Maps when the house swap was a mere idea rattling around in her head. Before she had convinced Amy to do it. The uncertainty of the coming winter in a new place was a concern that lingered in her mind.

Years of shared experiences and mutual support had forged a bond that was irreplaceable. But they could message each other. Not quite the same. FaceTime? Emma could snag a position in Nova Scotia in a year or two, in Lunenburg.

Sixty-Seven

Emma's apartment, Ste Anne Road, Sudbury, Ontario

August 21, 2019

"I still can't believe I haven't heard from the hospital. It's now two days since the interview," Amy said. "I'm thinking I didn't get the job."

"Did the interviewers say in the interview that they would notify only successful candidates?" Emma asked, peering around the kitchen door frame.

"No."

"Then don't worry. You'll find out soon enough."

Amy dropped onto the sofa with a sigh. This waiting was killing her. She wanted to return to Lunenburg and Kyle with all her heart and soul. She missed the security she felt when she was there. Since returning to Sudbury, relaxing during the home swap had vanished, and she was back to her tense, fearful self. The visit from David hadn't helped in that respect, but she'd stood up to him and made him leave. That counted for something, didn't it?

She picked up her phone from the coffee table. No new emails. No texts. She only had a short time before she had to make a move to secure the apartment. The uncertainty of her living arrangements added to her anxiety. It wouldn't be helpful to her if she landed the job and had nowhere to live. Amy wouldn't impose on Kyle or the MacLeods. She didn't know Izzy well enough to ask if she could stay with her until she found a place.

Why were they taking so long to notify her? The waiting was becoming unbearable.

It had been two days since her interview, and Amy was a mess. She sat on the couch, her arms wrapped around her, her eyes fixed on the screen of her phone. It was as if she was willing an email to appear. Emma watched her from a distance, concern etched on her face.

"They'll call, Ames," Emma said, coming to sit beside her friend on the sofa. "It's only been two days. That's not unusual." She was going to add 'if they had a lot of candidates' but thought better of it. Amy was in enough of a state; Emma didn't need to add to it.

"It seems like two weeks." Amy didn't look up. "Do you think I blew it? Maybe I came off too eager? Or not eager enough? Or too vague when I talked about availability ..."

"Amy." Emma took the phone from her hand and set it face down on the table. "You didn't blow it. You were articulate, warm, professional, and honest. If they don't hire you, that says more about them than you."

"But what if they're second-guessing me?"

Emma laughed and shook her head. "They're not second-guessing you. They're doing what hiring committees do. Talking. Weighing their options. Deciding that doesn't just affect you, but their entire team. It's a big deal for them, too, and they want to ensure they're making the right call."

Amy leaned back and let her head fall against the cushions. "You're right. I just hate the waiting. I go from hopeful to convinced it's a no in about five seconds."

Emma put her arm around her shoulders. "That's because you care, and it matters. That doesn't make you crazy. Quite the opposite. It makes you human."

Amy smiled while she stared at the ceiling. "You're good at this."

Emma nudged her. "Part of my charm. Now come on. Let's go get a bottle of fizz to celebrate. Distract ourselves for a while with something less emotionally charged?"

Amy groaned. As she stood, she said, "Fine. But if I don't get an email by the time we're back …"

"Then we'll open a bottle of wine early," Emma said as she grabbed her coat. "Deal?"

"Deal."

Clinking glass, shared laughter, and the occasional honk from a passing car filled the walk back from the liquor store. Emma's celebratory dance impressed the driver when she declared they were buying only the finest $14 bottle of fizz for a future RN in Lunenburg.

Amy had rolled her eyes, but the short walk had done wonders to dial down her anxiety. The fresh air and Emma's unshakable belief that the job was hers had also helped. She felt a wave of relief wash over her, easing the tension that had built up.

Now, just inside the apartment, the mood shifted.

"I will put one in the fridge and the other in the freezer. Yes, we got them out of the cooler there, but it was warm on our way back here. We want this fizz to be at the perfect temperature. Do we check the inbox now?" Emma asked.

Amy hesitated, then pulled her phone out of her pocket. "Let's just get it over with."

The screen came to life, and her breath hitched. One new email.

Subject: Fishermen's Memorial Hospital - Interview Follow-Up

She stared at it. "It's from them."

Emma dropped her purse onto the couch. "Well, don't just stand there. Open it,"

Amy tapped on the screen while her heart pounded like it had a mind of its own. Her eyes scanned the message once, then again, before her hand flew to her mouth.

"They've offered it to me." Her voice cracked, eyes wide. "They … they want me to join the team."

Emma's scream of joy filled the room, a high-pitched squeal that echoed with the thrill of the moment. She threw her arms around Amy, her excitement clear. "Yes, I knew it! You did it!" Emma pulled back and held her at arm's length. "You're moving to Lunenburg. You are going to be amazing."

Amy blinked, tears threatening but not yet falling. "I can't believe it."

"I can. We'll open that bottle now."

They both burst into giddy laughter, their shared joy filling the room. It was the kind that came when fear yielded to something real, something possible. Amy clutched her phone, rereading the first line of the email as Emma disappeared into the kitchen.

It felt like things were clicking into place for the first time in a long while.

Emma took out the bottle she'd tucked in the freezer. Somehow, she opened it without sending the cork flying. Adrenaline and years of experience helped her manage this feat with only a soft pop. The contents foamed to the neck like it, too, had been waiting for the good news.

She turned, holding the bottle aloft like a beacon of hope. "To new beginnings," she declared, pouring with less finesse than she wanted but enthusiasm more than made up for it. Her words were a call to arms, celebrating the courage to embrace change.

Amy still sat on the edge of the couch, phone in one hand, the other covering her mouth. Emma thought her eyes were glassy, but a quiet light of hope was behind them. Or perhaps relief.

Emma handed over a glass. "You've earned this."

Amy took it, still in that dazed state, like she was afraid to jinx it. Emma raised her own. "To Fishermen's Memorial Hospital's newest, soon-to-be favourite, nurse."

They clinked glasses, and Amy smiled. A real one. Not one of the polite I'm-holding-it-together ones she'd been giving out like party favours since David's reappearance. This one reached her eyes. "I'm unsure how to feel."

"Like you're about to have a new lease on life?" Emma

suggested. "Or maybe just … proud?"

Amy exhaled and took a sip. "A bit, not make that a lot, terrified."

Emma reached over and squeezed her arm. "That's okay. Big changes should scare you. But don't forget, you're not alone. And if you think I'm not coming to visit the second you get settled, you don't know me."

Amy laughed. "You're the best."

Emma shrugged with a grin. "I know."

The two drank for a moment, the city noise muted outside the apartment's windows, Amy's future filled with boundless possibility. Emma pictured Amy walking to work, breathing the sea air. She imagined a bright new apartment, and maybe even a privateer appearing at her door with a smile.

But that was for later.

For now, this moment was enough.

The fizz in Amy's glass had gone flat, but she held onto it, anyway, and let the stem warm her fingers. She had moved from viewing the email on her phone to her laptop. The subject line was bold and life-altering. She had read it at least three times on her mobile, now she read it again, but on a bigger screen. It didn't matter; the words didn't seem real. The job offer seemed to have materialized out of thin air, leaving Amy in disbelief.

A job offer. A new beginning in the place Amy's heart had claimed before her head caught up. Her chest swelled with equal measures of disbelief and gratitude. Emma chatted across the room and flipped through a notebook she had already titled 'Amy's Big Move,' as if she were moving. Amy hadn't heard her.

She was going back—not for a visit or a breather, but for real. She was a nurse in Lunenburg, working at Fishermen's Memorial Hospital, living near the ocean and breathing again.

Amy blinked, and her heart warmed with the emotion she hadn't felt in months, maybe years. Joy, cautious but steady, surged through her. The glimmer of a life rebuilt. Then her stomach dropped. "Oh no." The weight of the sudden changes and decisions ahead filled her with a gripping anxiety.

Emma looked up. "What?"

"I have to …" Amy stood, her glass forgotten on the table. "I have to resign from the hospital. I haven't paid the deposit on the apartment. They're only holding it until someone shows up with the first and last and signs the contract. What if I lose it?"

Emma put her pen down. "Amy …"

"No, I have to email them right now. And I need to check the start date in the offer because I thought it was October 1st, but that's not enough time." Her voice pitched upward as she paced. "I need to give my notice. Pack. Ship furniture or sell it. Transfer mail. Cancel utilities. Tell my landlord, and book the movers. God, what if they're booked solid?"

Emma stood, caught her by the arms. "Breathe."

Amy did, but it was shallow and quick. "I can't. What if this is a mistake?"

Emma squeezed her shoulders. "Then you'll make it work. You don't have to do everything today, but let's write a list, okay?"

Amy nodded, but her heart still galloped. She wanted this. She did, but knowing it was real? Was it happening? It was like stepping off a cliff and hoping the net was there to catch her.

She closed her eyes for a moment and pictured the Lunenburg harbour under a pale blue sky. The smell of salt and coffee, and Kyle's grin as he reached for her hand.

Amy opened them again, steadier. "I can do this."

Emma smiled. "You're already doing it." Her words soothed Amy's frayed nerves, a reminder that she was not alone in this journey.

Amy sat in front of her laptop and opened the email from Pine Cove Property Management, the letting agency.

She hit reply, typed, backspaced, typed again, and found the result satisfactory.

Subject: Re: Duke Street Apartment Hold - Lunenburg Rental (September 1, 2019 start)

Dear Mr. Cummings,

I hope this message finds you well.

Thank you again for holding the apartment for me. Your role in this process is crucial, and I'm writing to confirm that I would like to move forward with the lease beginning September 1st. I realize the arrangement was to hold until the 5th, but my new position at Fishermen's Memorial Hospital starts on the 1st. I'm excited about relocating to Lunenburg and want to secure the unit soon.

Please confirm as soon as possible if I may proceed with the e-transfer for the first and last month's rent to secure the apartment. If so, provide the email address and any details I should include with the transfer.

I await your response and am grateful for your help in making this transition smooth.

Regards,
Amy Scott
705-555-1234

She sat back and took a deep breath, then reread the email. "Emma, can you read this for me, please? I want to make sure it's perfect."

Emma came over to Amy's side. After a few minutes, she said, "Perfect, now hit send."

Amy's finger hovered over the send button for a few seconds before she pressed it.

About an hour later, the reply from the property management company came in. Amy's face lit up with a smile. "It's still available," she exclaimed, "and I can do everything online. It's so convenient!"

She opened her banking app, set up the email address for the e-transfer, and confirmed the total for the first and last month's rent. In the memo section, she included 'Apt 2 Duke Street, Lunenburg.' When prompted to enter the security question and answer, she flipped back to the email app, where she had left the message open and entered those.

Subject: Re: Apartment Hold – Lunenburg Rental

(September 1 Start)

Dear Ms. Scott,

Thank you for your email, and congratulations on your upcoming move to Lunenburg. We're pleased to confirm that the cozy one-bedroom apartment with a view of the harbour is still available. We'd be happy to complete the lease with a September 1st start date.

Please find a PDF copy of the lease agreement attached for your review. If everything looks in order, you can sign it electronically and return it by replying to this email. We will consider the unit secured once we receive the signed lease and your e-transfer for the first and last month's rent.

You can send the e-transfer to:
payments@pinecoveproperty.ca
Security question: What town?
Answer: Lunenburg

If you have questions about the lease or payment process, please reach out.

We look forward to welcoming you to our community!

Bill Cummings
Property Manager
Pine Cove Property Management
(902) 555-2368
www.pinecoveproperty.ca

Next, Amy opened the PDF copy of the lease. Despite the legalese, she had signed a lease like that when moving into her current apartment. After scanning and reviewing the terms, she electronically signed the document. She saved a copy, attached it to her reply email, and added a message confirming the funds transfer. She was familiar with these terms, confident and prepared.

"Well, I'll have a place to live when I get there, so that's one less thing to worry about." Amy sighed with relief, feeling accomplished and ready for the move.

"An item ticked off your to-do list," Emma said as she squeezed Amy's shoulders. "Yes, and I couldn't have done it without your support," Amy said, grateful for Emma's friendship.

Sixty-Eight

Emma's apartment, Ste Anne Road, Sudbury, Ontario

August 21 2019

"Well," Emma said, rubbing Amy's shoulder, "that's one giant leap for Amy-kind."

Amy smiled but remained silent.

Emma nudged her, "You've done it. You've signed a lease on an apartment in Lunenburg. It's happening."

"I know," Amy said, her eyes too shiny.

Emma patted her shoulder, a comforting touch that spoke volumes. "You don't have to be brave every second. But this? This was brave. Skimming over a legal document and blindly signing it? Reckless, but brave."

That earned a laugh.

"I ..." Amy shook her head. "I can't believe I did it."

Emma refilled Amy's glass with cold fizz from the kitchen, a small gesture of unwavering support. She had always seen Amy's potential, and now, as she handed Amy her filled glass, Emma said, "I can. I've always been able to see what you're capable of, and I'm proud of you."

The apartment grew quiet like the calm after a storm, or the breath before the next gigantic wave. Emma was unaware of what lay ahead for Amy in Lunenburg, but right now, her friend had made a significant choice in this tiny moment. For now, that was everything.

Amy remained at the table, her fingers resting on her laptop, as if the email might bounce back and demand more of her courage. She wasn't sure if any remained. It was done. She had signed the lease, and sent the deposit. The job was hers. She was officially moving to Lunenburg. The thought sent a shiver of excitement and panic through her chest.

She picked up her glass and took a bigger gulp than planned, and the bubbles went up her nose. Amy snorted and closed her laptop before she spilled or spewed the sparkling wine all over it. She glanced around Emma's open-plan living room and dining room. It had been her temporary haven filled with cozy throws, mismatched mugs, and the comforting scent of vanilla from whatever candle Emma had lit earlier. This was her in-between. But now, the clock was ticking.

Amy tugged her planner from her computer bag, flipped past the pages she'd once scribbled full of reasons not to return, and opened to a fresh spread. September 1st was less than two weeks away.

A nervous laugh escaped her lips. "Okay. It's only a ticking clock, not a time bomb. I'll make a list," she said, uncapping her pen. The practicality of the list-making process brought a sense of reassurance to Amy.

Resign from the hospital. Amy underlined it twice. That needed to happen tomorrow. She was determined to tie up all loose ends before her departure.

Confirm insurance plus utility setup.

Sort out a moving company.

Forward mail.

Purge closet. Again.

Say goodbye.

Her throat tightened when she wrote the last one.

Emma reappeared. "You making a list?"

"Mais oui," she said and giggled. It was one of the few phrases that stuck in her head from her French classes in high school. "What else when I'm panicking?"

Emma grinned. "Just don't forget the most important one." Her supportive words brought a sense of comfort to Amy.

She raised a brow.

Emma leaned forward and tapped the top of the page. "Breathe."

Amy stared at the sheet, then wrote it right at the top with a laugh and a deep breath. And maybe for the first time in months, she felt ready.

Sixty-Nine

Health Sciences North, Ramsey Lake Road, Sudbury, Ontario

August 22, 2019

The automatic doors opened with a mechanical sigh and welcomed Amy back into the hum of hospital life. The whiff of antiseptic, the polished floors, and the muted conversations behind closed doors felt like a second skin — comfortable, predictable, and safe — maybe too secure.

She strode through the corridors past co-workers who gave her tired smiles and nods. It hadn't been long since the shift change, so the hospital hadn't hit its morning rhythm. Her footsteps echoed in her ears.

She clutched the envelope containing her resignation letter in one hand and her phone in the other. A message from Emma blinked on the screen.

You've got this. One brave step at a time.

Amy smiled and swallowed a lump that appeared in her throat. One brave step.

She took the elevator to her floor and headed straight to her manager's office. Karen's familiar voice chatting on the phone while flipping through files drifted into the hall from her open door. She looked up, saw Amy, and ended the call. "Let me call you back," she said. "Amy, hello. Is everything okay?"

She nodded, stepped inside and closed the door behind her.

"I came to talk to you about something important."

Karen's brows furrowed in concern as Amy handed over the envelope. "Is this …?"

"My resignation," Amy said. "I've accepted a job in Nova Scotia. I thought the start date was October 1st, so I'd be giving you plenty of notice, but it's September 1st. Sorry, I couldn't give you more."

Karen opened the letter and read it with an unreadable expression. Once she finished, she looked up. "I can't say I'm surprised. You've been restless for a while. Man problem? I recall the big show of flowers and a phone at the nurses' station. I'm going to miss you."

"I'm going to miss a lot about this place, too," Amy said. "And you're right about the man problem. He was gaslighting me the entire time we were together, but I was too stupid or blind to see it." Amy dropped into the chair before Karen's desk. A fat tear dripped down her cheek. "I'm sorry. I didn't mean to cry."

Karen came around the desk and placed her hands on Amy's shoulders. "It's all right. I hope this new chapter brings you what you need."

"I think it will," Amy said. She stood and left the office filled with a strange mix of lightness and grief. She'd done it. She was leaving. No more what ifs. No more safety net. But also, no more familiar faces, no more comforting routine.

Only forward now.

Amy didn't return to Emma's apartment. Not right away. Instead, she approached the nurses' station to tell her colleagues her news. The morning crew gathered there, filling out charts, snatching sips of coffee and exchanging weary laughs. When she started working in Lunenburg, Amy hoped she'd feel this much at home.

Marissa looked up first when she saw Amy approach, not wearing scrubs. "You're on sick leave, and you still came in? That's some dedication."

"Not really," Amy said. "Hey, can I talk to all of you for a sec? I promise it won't take long."

That was enough to draw the others — Lynn, Sandy, Priya, and Dana's — attention. They stopped what they were doing and looked at Amy.

"I just handed in my resignation," she said. Her words sounded louder in the quiet that preceded. "My last day on the ward was before I went off on stress leave."

A hush fell over the area. Not even a patient's bell sounded.

"What? You're leaving?" Dana asked wide-eyed. "Where are you going?"

Amy inhaled and smiled. "Lunenburg. It's a little town in Nova Scotia. I spent some time there when I did a house swap with Izzy Morrison, the author. I've accepted a position at the hospital starting September 1st."

Dana let out a low whistle. "Lunenburg. That's … far."

"Yeah, but it's right."

Lynn tilted her head. "Is this about a guy?"

The heat warmed Amy's cheeks. "It's not just about a guy."

They laughed, and she relaxed.

"I didn't plan it. But being on the house swap made me realize I was ready for something different. I need a change. This fresh start will do it for me."

"Well," Sandy said, "we'll miss you like crazy. But you deserve to be happy, Amy."

"You'll love the East Coast," Dana added. "I went to PEI once and didn't want to come back."

Lynn stepped forward and pulled Amy into a hug. "Make sure you keep in touch. We'll have group chat updates. And I expect touristy photos — all of them."

Amy blinked back the unexpected sting of tears. "Deal."

For the first time today, it felt real. Amy was going, and now, with their blessing, it was a little easier to let go.

Seventy

Emma's apartment, Ste Anne Road, Sudbury, Ontario

August 22, 2019

When she entered Emma's apartment, Amy kicked off her shoes and let her purse slide off her shoulder to the floor. Her shoulders slumped from the day's weight, but it wasn't stress. It was a strange lightness that came after a major decision, a decision that had been weighing on her for so long. The type of tired that followed relief, a relief that was palpable in the air.

Emma popped her head out from the kitchen, wearing a tea towel over her shoulder. "Well? How did it go?"

Amy sighed. "It's done. I handed in my notice and told the girls at the nurses' station."

Emma crossed the room and pulled Amy into a tight hug.

When they stepped apart, Amy let out a slow breath. "Their surprise gave way to support. Lynn guessed it was about a guy."

With a raised eyebrow, Emma asked, "Is she wrong?"

Amy rolled her eyes. "This move isn't just about Kyle. It's about … well, me. Choosing something because I want it, not because it's the safe or expected option."

"Good," Emma said, her voice filled with unwavering support. "You deserve a life that lights you up. Even if that life is in a postcard-perfect fishing town three provinces from here, I'll support you every step of the way.

Amy laughed and dropped onto the couch. "I still have so much to do. I haven't told Kyle. I mean, I don't want to tell him. I want him to see me on the wharf and have that movie moment where it's — surprise."

Emma grinned. "He's going to lose it, but in the best way."

Amy leaned back, her head resting on the cushion, and gazed at the ceiling. "I hope so," she said, her palpable anticipation for Kyle's reaction. After a momentary pause, she added, "It's happening, isn't it?"

Emma brought her a mug of tea and sat beside her. "It sure is."

Emma watched Amy from the kitchen doorway as she sat cross-legged on the couch with a notepad on her lap, scribbling notes wearing a furrowed brow. She'd been at it for almost an hour, mumbling, flipping between the list and her phone.

It was by far the most animated she'd looked since her return from Lunenburg, a place that had tested her in ways she never imagined. Emma leaned on the doorframe and studied her friend. It wasn't all that long ago that Amy had been curled up on the same couch, doubting everything from her instincts to her courage and worth. Now, she was glowing with purpose, even if she appeared nervous.

This wasn't just about a move or the job offer. This was Amy choosing herself, revealing the strength of her character.

Emma smiled and padded into the room, sitting in the chair across from Amy. "You've got that look in your eye."

Amy glanced up, smirked and asked, "What look?"

"The one that says you're trying to sort out your entire life in a single sitting."

"I ... there's so much to do. Utilities, insurance, mail forwarding, how will I get my couch out of the apartment when it just fit through the door going in?"

"And yet, you're still doing it," Emma said. "You didn't shut down or talk yourself out of it. That's huge, Ames."

Amy set her pen down and looked at her. "It is, isn't it?"

Emma nodded. "You're rewriting your complete story, and this time you're the only one holding the pen."

Amy remained quiet for a few seconds, then smiled. "Thanks for not letting me back out when I panicked."

Emma waved her off, trying not to get misty-eyed. "You'd have done the same for me." Even as she said it, she understood Amy didn't realize how brave she'd been. To walk away from the safety of the known. To gamble on something that might not work out. On someone who didn't even know she was coming back. Emma's admiration for Amy's courage was perceptible.

She was uncertain what would occur upon Amy's Lunenburg return, yet Emma expected a captivating tale.

Seventy-One

Amy's apartment, Jean Street, Sudbury, Ontario

August 27, 2019

Amy wouldn't have been brave enough to take this step six months ago. As it was, she had to be persuaded to do the house swap in July. But here she was, working her way back east to Lunenburg. A couple of days after her arrival in the town, her new job as a nurse would start at Fishermen's Memorial Hospital. She had a place to live, not too far from Kyle's apartment. She had checked it out on Google Street View, and it was less than a five-minute walk between their places.

Her new apartment, with its private entrance and upper-level location in a historic house, was a physical representation of her new beginning. The move's excitement was evident, but so was the fear. After ten years at Health Sciences North, she was about to start at the bottom of the seniority ladder at Fishermen's Memorial Hospital. This career change affected her.

Emma had helped Amy pack up her apartment. Amy packed some smaller things to take with her on the bus and train. They loaded the rest into a moving truck. Excitement for her new beginning warred with nostalgia for the life she was about to leave behind as she watched the truck, laden with her possessions, drive away. If all went to plan, she and her larger items would arrive the same day.

"It seems like we're always saying goodbye, Ames," Emma said. Her eyes were glassy with unshed tears.

"It feels that way, doesn't it?" Sadness tinged Amy's voice. "I have to do it, Em. I can't be in the same city as David any longer, especially now that he's unemployed." The emotional toll of this decision was clear in her voice, a testament to the complexity of her situation.

Despite her sadness, Emma realized Amy was doing the right thing. It took nerve to pick up and leave everything behind. She'd done it once before when she left Ottawa to come to Sudbury to work. Emma acknowledged the bittersweet reality of their parting. "What time is your bus?" Emma asked.

"Four-thirty."

"Not long now, then. Oh, I'm going to miss you so much." She threw her arms around Amy and hugged her.

"Hey, Em, we can still message each other. FaceTime, Zoom or something. I'll always be just a call away."

"I know, but it won't be the same."

"You can always come and visit. It's such a beautiful town. And it wouldn't be your first time sleeping on my sofa."

"Tell me more about your apartment," Emma said.

"Well, it's less than a five-minute walk to Kyle's. About a half-hour walk to work."

"That's a long one, especially at night. You might have been further ahead to find a place closer to the hospital."

"I had to take what was available. Perhaps once I get established, I can buy a small house."

With Amy mentioning the possibility of buying a house, Emma realized the move was permanent. The weight of this realization settled on her heart, and tears she hadn't shed before spilled down her cheeks.

Seventy-Two

August 27, 2019

"Oh, Em. You're going to get me crying," Amy said as she fished a pocket pack of tissues out of her bag and passed them to her friend.

Emma took one and handed the package back.

Amy had her large suitcase, which would ride under the bus, a backpack, which would ride with her, Seamus, and her purse. As she and Emma stood there, Emma dabbed her eyes, and the bus pulled in. Amy slung her backpack over her shoulder and wheeled her luggage through the door to the awaiting bus.

She hugged Emma again and then boarded. There were quite a few people waiting to board, so Amy couldn't dawdle. She put her backpack in the overhead and took a window seat on the same side of the bus as the station.

Emma waved to her, and Amy returned the gesture. She was afraid the last time she boarded a bus to Lunenburg. Not so much this time, and not for the same reason. She hoped she would meet her house swap friend. They had only ever communicated through the website. And there was Gordon and Maggie across the road from Isabelle's. They were good to her when she was there, and she hoped they would be this time, too, bringing a sense of hope to her journey.

Most of all, Amy longed to see Kyle. They had texted and FaceTime'd when their work schedules allowed, but as Emma said, it wasn't the same as being there. Would Kyle be happy to see her? She hadn't admitted it to herself, but had fallen for him. He was so unlike David, and she couldn't help her deep connection with him.

Seventy-Three

Between Toronto and Montreal

August 28, 2019

Travelling alone wasn't enjoyable. If you needed a bathroom break in the station, you had to drag everything with you, whereas if you were with someone, they could look after it. Seamus was an excellent travelling companion but could not carry out that duty.

Before she boarded her train in Toronto, they weighed her large suitcase again to ensure it wasn't overweight. It hadn't gotten heavier since she left Sudbury, and the sticker from the bus station bearing the bag's weight was in plain sight.

Amy settled back into her seat and the gentle sway of the train as it picked up speed lulled her into a state of Zen. She would be in Montreal in about five and a half hours. She'd check her big bag there. There would be about an hour and a half of layover, then the Ocean to Halifax. She had debated telling Kyle her news, but in the end, she decided she'd rather it be a surprise that she hoped would be pleasant.

She pulled out her phone and opened the website where she found her apartment. There were two available in this building, but this one with its own private entrance was the one she preferred. She loved the fireplace, the large windows, and the renovated bathroom. The other apartment's kitchen had a poor layout in the Lunenburg bump. The bathroom was so tiny you had to back out to change your mind. In her mind, she got the better deal, and the best part was that she didn't have to share it with anyone, giving her a sense of privacy.

Seventy-Four

Lunenburg Bus Station, Lunenburg, Nova Scotia

September 1, 2019

As Amy stepped off the bus, a wave of familiarity washed over her, signalling her return to Lunenburg. With Seamus peeking out of her purse, she gazed at the grand mansion she had once called home. A figure on the porch caught her eye, and she approached it. "Hi, I'm Amy Scott. Are you Isabelle Morrison?"

"Amy from Sudbury?"

"That's me."

Isabelle descended the steps with urgency, her pace matching her excitement. As she reached Amy, she pulled her into a warm embrace. "What brings you back to Lunenburg? We didn't plan another house swap, did we?" She let go of Amy but kept her hands on her arms, a sign of genuine concern.

"No, the place has grown on me, as have the people. So much so that I've left my nursing job in Sudbury and have accepted a job at the hospital here."

"That's wonderful news. I am sorry about giving your boyfriend my address, but when he said they rushed your mother to the hospital, I fell for it."

"He and I are no more."

"Just as well. Long-distance relationships tend not to work

out. Where are you going to live? I have plenty of space here if you'd like until you find your own place. Do you have time for a cup of tea and a visit?"

"No thanks to either offer. I've got an apartment on Duke Street. I should be on my way there now. I'm hoping my furniture has arrived." Amy's independence and self-sufficiency were clear as she hugged Isabelle and headed towards her new home.

Seventy-Five

Amy's new apartment, Duke Street, Lunenburg, Nova Scotia

September 1, 2019

Amy looked up the key code on her phone for the lockbox containing her house key. The letting agency had sent it to her when she completed the deal. The steps leading up to the door weren't the easiest to climb with a bag that weighed almost fifty pounds in tow, but she made it.

She opened the door and walked in. It was even better in person than the photographs, and they had impressed her. She pulled her large suitcase over the threshold and left it by the door, then slung off her backpack and set it beside it. This place was smaller than her one in Sudbury, but it was a cozy apartment.

The movers hadn't arrived yet, but they had promised her it would be today. In the meantime, she made a rough plan of what would go where, her anticipation growing with each passing minute. Hopefully, they would do that much and reassemble anything that had to be taken apart, like her bed.

All the windows had mini-blinds. Some were down but

open, but Amy raised a couple to let in more light. Then, she walked through the apartment and pulled up the sashes to let in fresh air.

The rumble of a diesel engine, a sudden intrusion into the apartment's quiet, grew louder. The movers had arrived.

A couple of hours later, everything was inside and roughly where Amy wanted it. Seamus had pride of place on the sofa in her cozy living room, the soft fabric of the cushions providing a comforting backdrop. Amy had labelled the boxes for the proper rooms.

She had never asked if the fireplace was a working one. Still, it wasn't a deal breaker if it wasn't. To decorate, Amy would either use silk flowers in a vase or battery-operated candles. The latter would cast a warm glow on the room.

Before she put her dishes in the cupboards, she wiped them off with a damp cloth. Everything was new and clean, but she wanted to be sure. None of her plates, bowls, glasses, or mugs got broken in the move. Now, it was a matter of putting everything away where she'd know where it was, so she didn't have to hunt for it later. Glasses and mugs over the sink on the left. Plates and bowls over the sink on the right. She might have to get some puck lights or fix an LED light strip under the upper cabinets because that corner was dark. With her shifts at the hospital, it would be dark when she came home and cooked.

That was enough work for one day. It was time to relax. Amy picked up Seamus and walked out the door towards the water. She paused when she reached the intersection with Lincoln and pondered walking by Kyle's apartment. The draw of the water and the place where they first met was stronger, a sign that she was ready to move forward and embrace her new life.

Seventy-Six

Zwicker Wharf, Lunenburg, Nova Scotia

September 1, 2019

Kyle wandered the wharf from one end to the other. When he wasn't at his job at High Liner, the days and nights were empty without Amy. He understood she had to go back home at the end of the house swap, but it didn't make it any easier for him. After his mother's death, Kyle had never felt so alone. That loneliness returned when Amy drove off on the bus bound for Halifax.

He sat in the Adirondack chair he had used when they first met, but it wasn't the same. Out of the corner of his eye, he glimpsed a woman with long brown hair, the same length as Amy's, walking along the wharf. Wishful thinking on his part that it would be Amy. Kyle turned and focussed on the water and the boats swaying with the tide. Even the soft rhythmic clang of metal against the masts did nothing to soothe Kyle, but irritated him instead. The peaceful harbour, with its salty breeze, and the cry of gulls, were a constant reminder that he was alone.

"Is this seat taken, pirate boy?"

Kyle turned towards the voice, his heart racing. It couldn't be. Amy stood before him and deposited Seamus in the chair, a sight that filled him with joy and disbelief.

"Depends. You staying this time?" Kyle asked, trying to sound nonchalant but failing.

"Guess I'm here to stay, for good this time. Lunenburg's grown on me. And so have a few other things ..." She let the words hang for a moment, her eyes filled with determination and love, waiting for his reaction.

Kyle's heart leapt with joy as he saw her. He couldn't believe it. He sprang from his chair, his heart pounding in his chest, and wrapped his arms around her, spinning her in a joyous circle. All the while, she giggled, her laughter like music to his ears.

"I'll be working at Fishermen's Memorial Hospital."

"Best news I've heard in a long time," he said, his voice filled with overwhelming joy. Then he put her down and kissed her.

<<<O>>>

Also by Melanie Robertson-King

The Consequences Collection
Tim's Magic Christmas
The Secret of Hillcrest House
A Shadow in the Past (second edition)
Shadows From Her Past
YESTERDAY TODAY ALWAYS
Cole's Notes (Revised version)
It Happened on Dufferin Terrace
It Happened in Gastown
It Happened at Percé Rock
All Aboard the Canadian with Buddy and his Four Fantastic
Furry Friends!
It Happened at Lake Louise
It Happened at Niagara Falls
WHISPERS THROUGH TIME
ECHOES THROUGH TIME
(King Park Press)

Cole's Notes (A Short Story)
EFD1: Starship Goodwords – a cross genre anthology
(CARRICK PUBLISHING, 2012)

MELANIE ROBERTSON-KING

https://melanierobertson-king.com

Melanie Robertson-King has always been a fan of the written word. Growing up as an only child, her face was almost always buried in a book from the time she could read. Her father was one of the thousands of Home Children sent to Canada through the auspices of The Orphan Homes of Scotland, and she has been fortunate to be able to visit her father's homeland many times and even met the Princess Royal (Princess Anne) at the orphanage where he was raised.

www.ingramcontent.com/pod-product-compliance
Lightning Source LLC
Chambersburg PA
CBHW060343030726
47497CB00003B/579